STARLITE PULP REVIEW #1

Pulp done right.

FEATURING:

Michael Bracken: Michael Ritt: Jim Towns: Andrew Miller: Brian Townsley: Chris Jones: P Moss: James Whelpley: Timothy J. Spadoni: Eric O' Neal: Eirik Gumeny: Charlie Jones

Starlite
Pulp

For information, contact : editor@starlitepulp.com

www.starlitepulp.com

Instagram : @starlite_pulp

Youtube channel : youtube.com/@starlitepulp

Book and Cover design by Tristan Townsley and BT

ISBN: 979-8-218-10291-3

First Edition: December 2022

"There is only one plot: things are not as they seem."

Jim Thompson

"They all want to be Hank Williams/(but) they don't want to have to die"

Turnpike Troubadours, *Long Drive Home*

"A certain ruthlessness and a sense of alienation from society is as essential to creative writing as it is to armed robbery."

Nelson Algren

STARLITE PULP REVIEW #1

EDITOR'S NOTE

What you've got in your hands here is a collection of twelve stories, in various sub-genre's all falling under the umbrella of 'pulp.' In this day and age, Pulp comes up and people think one of three things: the Tarantino film; a type of paper; or orange juice. Two of things are, at least, close. The reason that Pulp novels and stories were originally titled that particular moniker is because it referred to the type of paper that these 'cheap' novels were printed on—the ones you might find in a gas station or a 5 and dime store. Those 'cheap' novels were in the realm of crime, noir, horror, Science Fiction, adventure, westerns, and any combination of those things. That's what we're doing here at Starlite Pulp.

We originally intended to put these tales into 'categories'—noir section, horror section, etc., and then an interesting thing happened. The story submissions themselves started making that difficult. For example, Michael Bracken's story in here, 'Kissing Cousins' is a pretty clear (and excellent) example of straight noir. The Chris Jones story? Definitely a western. So they fit into a category. But then 'The Book of Life' came in and it was a western. Except when it wasn't. The story 'Bessie Lou's First Dance' reads more like an episode of Twilight Zone than anything else. The story I included in here, 'A Fresh Start,' is very clearly a crime story, but aesthetically it looks and sounds like a western. The story 'One More Time Around,' by Eirik Gumeny, involves a pair of private investigators. Except that one of them is a human of nearly 500 years and his partner is a minotaur. So, we threw the categories out the window. Are these all hybrids, you ask? Not at all. The stories by P Moss, Charlie Jones and James Whelpley are all hard-boiled. The Andrew Miller story is a western. And the Jim Towns story—right up his alley, horror (he makes horror movies). One more note here: 'The Big Gray Spot...', a story I immediately took to on first reading, is the first story published by Timothy J. Spadoni, and I believe falls into a 60s/70s horror genre that was more mystery/wonder and less slasher. Any time you have a 'first', that's always something to be happy about. Collectively, the authors in here have been nominated for, and won, numerous national awards, published novels, and are accomplished in so many varied ways (just read the 'About the Authors' section at the end). But these 12 stories are yours, now, dear reader. Sit back, and enjoy. As always, feel free to contact us at editor@starlitepulp.com with any comments, and do us a favor and leave us some reviews out there!

Until next time, here's to the blank page.

BT, Starlite Pulp, Winter 2022

NAKED WITHOUT A GUN
BY P MOSS

"Put the money in the bag."

The poker players did as the masked man demanded because a few million dollars was not worth losing their lives over. Six fat cats whose blockbuster films had a combined world-wide gross of over fifty billion and counting. Producers, directors and a movie star who often played cards after closing at a Beverly Hills restaurant where the proprietor locked them securely inside, providing a waitress to serve drinks to the men who each anted up half a million in cash.

"Now the jewelry."

"This watch belonged to my father."

A second bandit jammed a forty-five in the man's mouth.

"I'm going to count to three."

He pulled the trigger on two.

"Dammit Purvis!" yelled his partner.

Dave Purvis committed his first armed robbery when he was nine years-old, barely able to see over the counter of the liquor store and needing both hands to hold the heavy revolver he had taken from his stepfather's sock drawer. A surreal scene that made the cashier laugh until the kid shot off his ear.

Fast forward twenty years. Countless crimes of violence to his credit with only one arrest, that didn't stick. The consummate professional. Every job like clockwork. Then in the middle of taking down the score of a lifetime his partner called his name out loud and clear, and one by one the men who could identify Dave Purvis died. But there was an empty chair at the table, and Purvis did not need a map to find player number six as he kicked open the men's room door and saw the world's top box office draw screwing the waitress. He put a bullet in his head.

"You said no one would get killed!" screamed the waitress. "Give me my money so I can get the hell out of here."

"You're going to give me something first."

"I want my share."

He pushed her to her knees and the terrified woman had no choice but to unzip his jeans. Did what he wanted and took it all over her face.

"That's your share."

Then Purvis put a bullet in her head.

The sun beginning to rise at their backs, they drove in silence as Benny McBride guided his dented Toyota toward the Venice apartment where he and Purvis would split the money in the duffle bag. Silence shattered by Benny's hysterical wife the second they pushed open the door.

"It's all over the early news," Yvonne screamed at her husband, who without his ski mask looked like the stoner from Scooby-Doo. "Every cop in L.A. is searching for you. The cleaning crew got to the restaurant early and found seven bodies. Seven bodies! What the hell happened?"

Purvis, broad-shouldered with short dark hair and a leather jacket covering the forty-five in his waistband, glared at Benny to muzzle his wife. "Relax, baby. We wore masks and gloves, so they'll never be able to identify us."

"They have your DNA."

"Bullshit. They're trying to trick us into making a mistake," Purvis told the woman who was way too good looking for her husband. Cursing his own mistake of taking a chance on an amateur like Benny because Yvonne was a friend of the waitress who had unlocked the door and let them in. Yvonne worked two jobs to pay rent on the crappy apartment. And having grown tired of waiting for her wanna-be actor husband to stop dreaming and finally realize that he would never make it in the movies, jumped at the chance to steal enough money to change their lives.

"Make some coffee," Purvis told her, eying long blond hair and curves that filled out a tight sweater.

"Don't order my wife around," snapped Benny, trying to sound tough. "Just take your half of the money and jewelry and get out of here."

"That jewelry is going in the trash."

"Are you crazy? It's worth a fortune."

"And you think it's a good idea to try to fence the hottest swag this town has ever seen? Why not save time and just walk into the nearest police station?"

"We can unload the jewelry without anyone knowing who we are."

"Maybe they already know. Maybe they do have DNA. You were stupid enough to tell the poker players who I am, so maybe you were stupid enough to blow your nose into a bar napkin. I'm not going to stand here and argue with you when the cops could break down this door any second."

"Then take half the money and get out of here, but I'm keeping the jewelry."

Purvis knocked him out with a right to the jaw.

"Things weren't supposed to happen this way," Yvonne muttered bitterly, looking at her husband kayoed on the floor but feeling sorry for herself. "All I wanted was a decent place to live and maybe open a café on the boardwalk."

"You don't pull a heist to buy yourself a job, you pull a heist so that you'll never have to get a job. You're as big a loser as he is."

"You don't know anything about me."

"He told you he was going to be a big movie star. That he'd buy you a mansion in the hills with a cook and a maid and a different car for every day of the week." Purvis looked around at thrift store furniture, unframed movie posters and a window overlooking a gas station. "But instead, you're stuck in this shithole. Trying to make the best of a bad situation, which is impossible without either passion or money."

Yvonne would not give him the satisfaction of admitting he was right.

"That's why you wanted him in on the heist." He checked out her ass, making sure she knew it. "But even if Benny had all the money in the world, that loser could never turn you on."

Purvis kissed her and she slapped him hard. Pushed her against the wall, pressing himself against her. His mouth again on hers and this time she kissed him back, sliding her hands inside his black T-shirt as they fiercely made out, then backed away as she heard her husband starting to come to.

"Why the hell did you hit me?" groaned Benny, rubbing his jaw.

"Shut up and get me a suitcase."

Purvis dumped the contents of the duffle on the couch, then put half the cash inside the roller bag Benny had taken from the closet. Zipped it shut. Plucked a Burger King bag from the trash and filled it with the stolen watches and rings.

"I still say we should hold onto that jewelry until things cool down," pressed Benny.

"This case is so high-profile things will never cool down."

"Because you murdered everyone."

"Because you made it necessary."

"Like hell I did. You killed the guy who wouldn't give up his watch before I said a word."

Purvis picked up a throw pillow from the couch and used it to muffle the shot that dropped Benny McBride to the floor.

"You didn't have to kill him!" Yvonne yelled.

"At least his jaw doesn't hurt anymore."

"He was my husband!"

"Don't act like you all of a sudden give a shit," said Purvis as he put the other half of the money in the suitcase that would be inconspicuous on the road. "Especially because you know damn well that it was only a matter of time before he did something stupid to get us all caught."

"As stupid as shooting him with the same gun that killed the poker players?"

"Eventually they'll discover the ballistics match, but they'll never connect me to the killings." Purvis smiled. "They can't tie me to anything. No cop ever has."

"You said yourself this case is so high profile it will never cool down. You'll never get away with it."

"As long as I have this gun," Purvis said as he tucked the forty-five back into the waistband of his jeans, "I can get away with anything."

"What about me?" she snapped. "The spouse is always the prime suspect, which means they'll think I killed eight people."

"Not the way I've got it figured. But you'll have to trust me, and we'll need to move fast."

"If I run, they'll be sure I did it."

"Suit yourself," he shrugged, wiping down everything he had touched in the room.

Yvonne was backed into a corner, knowing that Purvis was right when he said that without passion or money it was impossible to make the best of a bad situation. She looked at him in a way she had never looked at her husband. Looked at the bag containing three million dollars that was about to roll out the door with or without her.

"I'll pack a few things."

"Leave it all. Your purse. Your wallet and keys. Everything," he told her. "Now go to the bathroom and get some gauze and some tape."

Purvis finished wiping away any evidence that he had ever been inside the apartment, then took a knife from his boot and dragged the blade across the palm of Yvonne's hand. Left a trail of blood drops as he led her to the door and had her smear the knob, making it appear as if she had tried to escape from whoever had killed her husband. The police would search for Yvonne, and eventually stop as she would be presumed dead.

Purvis bandaged her hand and grabbed the suitcase. Careful not to be seen as he led her out of the apartment and around the corner where he stole a white Ford Taurus and aimed it toward the Santa Monica Freeway.

Culver City, downtown L.A., then exited in suburban West Covina. Tossed the Burger King bag into a dumpster, then drove around a shopping mall parking garage until Purvis spotted a similar white Ford Taurus and switched the license plates. Back onto the freeway. Destination Mexico. But neither of them had slept in over twenty-four hours so they made a pit stop at a motel outside Rancho Cucamonga.

Sex with a killer on a sagging mattress in a room reeking of disinfectant had never been on any woman's bucket list, but multiple orgasms turned Yvonne to jelly. Arms wrapped around her outlaw lover she dreamed of the romantic life ahead of them in Mexico as they slept until it was dark. Pizza, whiskey and more orgasms until it was time for the 11:00 news.

Non-stop sensationalism about the Hollywood Seven Massacre. Garishness, hyperbole and continuous speculation about the missing three million dollars. Inevitable comparisons to Charles Manson and the grizzly Tate-LaBianca murders. Nothing but conjecture, making it clear to Purvis that the police were chasing their tails. Then after the first commercial break, Yvonne gasped as over the news anchor's shoulder was a picture of her husband.

> In other news, thirty-one-year-old aspiring actor
> Benny McBride was shot to death this morning
> in his Venice apartment, with a blood trail at
> the scene making police believe that his missing
> wife may also have been the victim of foul play.
> If you have any information about the murder
> or the whereabouts of Yvonne McBride, please
> contact the police immediately.

"They're already looking for me!" gasped Yvonne as she began to panic. "How are we going to get across the border? Don't we need passports? Even if we had passports ..."

"Sneaking into Mexico is a lot easier than sneaking out of Mexico, and I know the perfect spot." Purvis offered her the whiskey bottle, but she shook her head. "In the morning we'll continue east then cut south toward the border, and before you know it all your troubles will be over."

All night Yvonne stared at the ceiling. Wondering if maybe her troubles were just beginning as even if they did make it into Mexico, and even if the police did assume she was dead and stopped looking for her, she would still be listed as missing in every law enforcement data base and never be able to cross back over the border. Too late to second guess the decision to run, even though she knew that in the heat of the moment it had been the only decision she could have made. She turned on the early morning news then yelled for Purvis to wake up.

He grabbed his forty-five from the nightstand, quickly alert as he saw that this time the picture over the anchor's shoulder was of him. A mugshot taken years earlier when he had been picked up and released on a charge they couldn't make stick.

> Police now suspect that the Hollywood Seven
>
> Killer is a man named David Lane Purvis, as
>
> DNA collected from the murdered waitress
>
> suggests that she was forced to perform oral
>
> sex on Purvis just before he killed her and
>
> escaped with the missing three million dollars.

Full blown panic as it became frighteningly clear to Yvonne that the man beside her in bed had killed the waitress because she was a witness to murder, just like she had witnessed the murder of her husband. She threw on her sweater and jeans and ran out the door toward a diner across the street and called to two policemen who were about to go inside.

"What can we do for you, ma'am?" asked one of the officers near a newspaper rack where a photo of Dave Purvis was splashed across the front page of the L.A. Times.

Yvonne was scared. Choked on the words as she pointed to the motel.

"Are you in trouble?" asked the officer as he saw her bandaged hand.

"Help me. He's ..."

"Too stubborn to ask for directions," said Purvis as he walked up beside her, noticed the newspaper and positioned himself to block the officers' view.

"Are you two together?"

"Yes, officer," said Purvis with an embarrassed look. "My wife gives me an earful because I'll never ask for directions, but I have to admit that this time I really am lost. Can you tell us how to get on the freeway going east?"

"My wife and I have that same difference of opinion," smiled one of the officers as he pointed down the street. "Go down to the second stoplight and turn right. You'll see the signs."

As the policemen went inside the diner, Purvis grabbed Yvosnne's arm and muscled her back to the motel. Shoved her in the room where she sat nervously, at the mercy of a vicious killer she now realized destroyed life for no reason other than he liked it. A monster who, while committing mass murder, took time out to defile the waitress then killed her too. Sickened at having allowed herself to be seduced by passion, money and the excitement of life on the run.

"You were never going to take me to Mexico, were you?"

"No."

"What about my half of the money?"

"A dead woman doesn't need money."

She lunged toward the nightstand and grabbed his forty-five. Pointed it at him as she

stepped toward the telephone, no choice now but to roll the dice and lie to the police that she had been kidnapped and in fear for her life every second. An innocent victim at the mercy of the Hollywood Seven Killer.

Purvis sat calmly on the bed. Unafraid, but feeling naked as he did whenever he did not have his gun.

"The cops must know by now that the waitress was a friend of yours," he told her. "And they'll figure that you pulled the job together then killed her so you wouldn't have to split the money. That you killed the poker players because they could identify you and killed your husband because, for years, he made you work two jobs to support him."

"Nice try, Purvis, but they have your DNA."

"Which proves nothing except that I had sex with the waitress," he told her matter-of-factly. "But yours are the only fingerprints on the gun that killed eight people, which will put you on death row while I'm sipping margaritas on a white sand beach."

"This is your gun."

"That I wiped clean when you ran to the diner. You're screwed, baby."

Yvonne aimed at his head and squeezed the trigger.

Click.

"And I emptied the clip," Purvis laughed as the enraged woman continued to shoot him with an empty gun, then kicked it out of her hand and across the floor. Took the knife from his boot and slashed the sharp blade across her throat with so much force it almost took her head off.

Purvis wiped down everything he had touched in the room. Rolled the suitcase full of money out the door, fired up the Ford and put Rancho Cucamonga in the rear-view mirror. Stayed within the speed limit as he passed Redlands and Palm Springs, then angled south toward a place where three million American dollars would allow a man to live like a king forever.

For the next hour Purvis relaxed as there was almost no traffic on the dusty back road. Then nearing the Mexican border, a Highway Patrol car came up fast behind him. Rode his tail. But Purvis wasn't breaking any traffic laws and if the cop ran a check, the plates he had switched matched the make, model and color of a Ford not reported stolen. All good, as long as the cop didn't come up with some other reason to pull him over and ask to see his license and registration.

Lights and siren.

Purvis pulled over and rolled down his window, ready to blow the cop's head off. Reached for his gun then realized he had left the forty-five at the motel to frame Yvonne. At the mercy of a patrolman about to luck his way into a career making arrest as he stepped toward the Ford. A good lawyer might convince a jury that all the DNA proved was that he had had sex with the waitress, but the suitcase in the backseat would be all the evidence needed to put him on the express to death row.

Recognizing Purvis from the news, the patrolman drew his service revolver. But there would be no arrest, as eyeing the suitcase he saw the opportunity to heist three million dollars and get away with it by shooting Purvis trying to escape.

"Get out of the car and keep your hands where I can see them."

Purvis pushed open the door and in a quick fluid motion, grabbed the knife from his boot and drove the blade into the patrolman's chest. Twisted it so there would be no doubt. Grabbed the dead cop's service revolver then burned rubber. Music cranked as he flew past desert scrub toward the white sand beach that awaited him. No longer naked as he gripped the revolver in his hand, smiling with the confidence of a man who could get away with anything.

Editor's Note: this story contains language that, while historically accurate, may be offensive. Consider yourself warned.

BURNLEY AND THE GENERAL
BY ANDREW MILLER

"One of my superstitions had always been when I started to go anywhere, or to do anything, not to turn back, or stop until the thing intended was accomplished."

-Ulysses S. Grant

He'd seen traces of Mescaleros on his ride through New Mexico territory, possible signs of their presence, but that turned out to be all and Burnley Howser now arrived in Silver City atop his horse, a gray Spanish Mustang called Winston.

Most finished buildings in Silver City were constructed of red brick or lumber, not the adobe much more common in these parts. Tents were everywhere. Hispanics and whites lived side-by-side. Burnley passed a line of grime-covered silver miners waiting for a bath outside the barbershop. In an alley, he came upon a drunken Indian clothed like a white man.

"What's your name?"

"Ezra," said the Indian, teetering.

"Know your way around this place? Know the people?"

"I lived here awhile now."

"Anyone exceptional arrive of late?"

"A trio of gentlemen with rotten reputations have been making everyone jumpy. Decent folks have been keeping indoors."

"That make it easier for a drunk Indian to move about?"

"Yes. Usually I just blend in with the Mexicans on Chihuahua Hill."

"Who is this trio?"

"How much money you got?" Ezra said, his mind calculating.

"Answer me."

"They're the DeBlanc gang."

From his haversack, Burnley retrieved a fresh half-dime and tossed it at Ezra's feet. "Where are they now?"

Ezra pointed up the thoroughfare. "They've been held up in the Orleans Club for two days, waiting on someone. Don't know who."

"Why hasn't the sheriff taken action?"

"Because the sheriff's owned by Thad Baxter, the main boss in Silver City. He only arrests the people that Mr. Baxter wants arrested."

Burnley tossed another half-dime. Ezra caught it and then kneeled to pick up the first coin.

"Where's a proper stable for my horse?"

"Club's got one."

Burnley rode that way. He noticed that Ezra wasn't following. "Not coming in to drink up them coins?"

"Gammy Babcock, the hotelier, retails good whisky. He's more tolerant than DeBlanc and his cohorts."

Just outside the stable that adjoined the saloon, Burnley hitched Winston to a post. Inside, he encountered a toothless old man named Sutherland who ran the stable. Sutherland spoke with a Virginia accent and took a long stare at Burnley's new eight-gauge shotgun.

Burnley vacillated.

Across the thoroughfare, a group of teen-aged boys idled. The kid in front, clearly the leader, was both the shortest and thinnest and, at thirteen or fourteen, also looked like the youngest. Burnley waved him over.

"What's your name?"

"Henry Antrim."

Henry Antrim looked Irish but wore a sombrero and moccasins. He had a revolver poorly hidden in his pants.

"Where were you born?"

"New York City. Place called Five Points."

Despite his age, the kid spoke with an uncommon confidence. "Want a job?"

"If it pays."

Burnley pointed at Winston. "That's my horse, carrying my goods. Can you watch them both while I go into the club?"

"What about Sutherland? It's his stable."

"Former Rebs and me don't much get along. When I come out, I'll pay you twenty-five cents if they ain't gone." Burnley patted his haversack. It jingled. He could have offered his customary five cents, but Burnley liked the kid and decided to be generous.

Henry Antrim smiled and pulled up his shirt, revealing the Colt. It was an old model and oil-stained. "Your horse and goods'll be safe."

Burnley smiled and nodded. The kid wanted to be thought of as a grown up shootist. "If there's a problem, find me. If you can't, fire twice in the air."

"Got it."

"Good. That horse means a lot to me."

Burnley led Winston into a stall and gave him water. His Open Top Army .44 Colt was holstered at his side. He left his shotgun on the horse. Burnley paid Sutherland for the use of his stable, and then walked through the batwing front doors of the Orleans Club.

Miners and wild-looking cowboys drank and caroused with whores beneath a rebel flag nailed to the wall beside a buffalo head. Along the sidewall were three Faro tables, all operated by Orleans Club dealers. Many of the men Burnley saw carried pistols, knives, or both. Burnley walked to the bar.

"Give me a French brandy," Burnley ordered. "Also, I'd also like to know where I can find Josiah DeBlanc."

"Josiah!" yelled the bartender. "This man's looking for you."

Burnley turned. He saw a man moving toward him that was shirtless and glistened with sweat. He walked with a limp and his pants were held up with suspenders. It looked like he didn't see enough sun. His mustache was recently trimmed and his long and wild blond hair was thinning on top.

"Do you and I have business, sir?" His accent was Cajun. He wore two Smith and Wesson .44s on hip holsters. His eyes were pale blue.

"We never met. I'm a friend of Cody Evans."

The bartender brought Burnley's brandy.

"I haven't heard from Cody in a nig's age."

"He said to look you up."

Josiah DeBlanc looked Burnley over. "You serve?"

Burnley nodded.

"For the Union?"

"Yes."

Josiah looked perplexed. "I never heard of a patriot like Cody fraternizing with Federals." His eyes were calculating. "What's your name?"

"Burnley Howser. Cody said there was no use in writing, since you've been hiding. Didn't even know if I would catch you."

"Why would Cody send you my way?"

"Said you needed good men. I've got experience. My first post was in the Army of the Tennessee."

Josiah leaned forward. "Were you at Shiloh?"

"Yes."

Josiah's face settled into a look of respect. The eleven-year anniversary of the battle had just passed. "Grant the Butcher's willingness to throw his own men into a meat grinder was too strong an obstacle, even against us. Still, we surprised the hell out of y'all that first morning, didn't we?"

Burnley smiled. "But you didn't get us then and you never did."

"*Yet.* We didn't get you yet. Us Rebels ain't gone."

"Cody's hoping for a finder's fee, for sending me to you," said Burnley.

Josiah smiled and ordered an Old Kentucky.

Burnley looked around, studying faces. He spotted Floral Strange alone at a table eating a bowl of posole.

"Since this is a job interview, tell me: Are you a Radical Republican, Mr. Howser? An agrarian mercenary?"

Burnley shrugged. "I've voted twice, once for Lincoln because he was my Commander In Chief, then for the General, because he was my General and because he was raised in Ohio, like me."

A woman's squeal of delight came from the corner. Burnley looked and saw Carlton Weathers sucking on the open-air tit of an enormous whore.

"Since hostilities ended," Burnley went on. "I haven't made my proper reintegration into society. Despite our differences, I suspect you can relate."

"I can," Josiah said. The bartender brought his drink.

Burnley finished his brandy and ordered another, this time a double. "So can you utilize a good man?"

"I can. I just don't know if that good man is you." Josiah turned. "Floral, my skin is dry now. Along with my shirt, please."

Floral stopped eating and picked up a loose shirt from the chair beside him. He walked it over to Josiah, who delicately put it on.

"I'd imagine one whose face isn't on Federal wanted posters could be useful," said Burnley. "Cody also told me that you're all agents of Thad Baxter. I'm after money and I think you're my path to it. I want to work for you."

"My word, Cody told you a lot," said Josiah, not speaking the name of his notorious and powerful employer, the boss who controlled almost all the industry here in Silver City, including most of the big silver mines. "You know, I've been waiting on a good man presently. Holt Kantor himself is en route to this very saloon. There's a face that's been on wanted posters."

"Holt Kantor," said Burnley and kept his face neutral, as he saw that Josiah was studying his reaction.

"Sit down and buck the tiger. Give me a chance to learn more about you."

They walked to a Faro table. Josiah looked at the dealer and told him that he would take over. He took the dealer's seat.

"I apologize if I seem inhospitable, Mr. Howser," Josiah said, suddenly taking a lighter tone. "But my compatriots and I are wanted men."

"I understand. You've got a reputation in New Orleans. I often heard people talk about your exploits."

Josiah opened the box, covered with the image of a tiger, and removed the cards. "It was my home since boyhood, where I worked as a policeman both before the war and after."

Josiah then called Carlton and Floral over. A large wet stain now glistened on the crotch of Carlton's pants. Both took seats. Josiah told them that

Burnley fought for the Union and had been at Shiloh. "The four of us are going to play a civil game together." Josiah shuffled the cards.

"How long did you live in New Orleans, Josiah?" asked Burnley.

"Until August of '66."

"You were gone after the riot," said Burnley.

"Yes."

Floral drank from a flask. "Tell bluebelly. I'm sure he'd like to hear about that day." A grin formed across Floral's lips.

Josiah watched Burnley.

Carlton then said something in French that Burnley could not understand. Upon hearing it, Josiah nodded.

"Wouldn't bother me to hear a story," said Burnley, calmly.

Now that the shuffling was through, Josiah put the cards into the dealing box. "No point of being a mover of history if you can't recount it now and again."

Carlton said, "Exactly."

Josiah began, "I was mad as hellfire after the surrender. Our new country should have fought on. But I went home. Many others felt like me. Aggrieved. Former Rebs filled most of the police jobs. Mayor Monroe was sympathetic to us. Maybe other states had to bow to Old Abe's vision about what this land was to become but my compatriots and I became determined to see that these hordes of wild, newly freed coloreds would never change our Louisiana." Josiah took another drink. "We heard a convention was convening downtown with the goal of remodeling the state Constitution to give all the free nigs voting rights. We were police officers, sworn to uphold the laws of our state. States' rights are always worth fighting for. They set the date. July 30th, at the Mechanics Institute on Canal. Half the darkies going were Union veterans. It was my idea to confront them armed. We needed to defend ourselves." Josiah finished dealing. "When we arrived, they were so full of rage. The devil was in them. They fired on us, the police. So we fired back."

"Your side didn't fire first?" asked Burnley.

"No, it was them. We killed most of the armed ones quickly. The rest we kicked, stomped and clubbed. They hid in the Mechanics Institute. We broke the windows and shot in. Those niggers came crawling out the doors of the building, coughing, covered in blood. Some waved white flags out the windows. But we weren't in the mood to accept surrenders. A ragged bitch with a baby in her arms came to my feet and screamed for mercy. I took it by the foot, hung it where she could see, and shot it's head off. Made sure she saw. I decided that this lazy bitch wasn't worth a bullet so I bashed her brains in with the handle of my pistol.

"Mayor Monroe wanted it this way. We all did. The killing spread out from just those Republican baboons to anyone in the streets guilty of negritude. In all, we killed thirty-four." Josiah sat quiet for a moment, and then added, "And all in the proud name of states' rights."

Floral and Carlton laughed.

"Then what?" asked Burnley.

Josiah made a face that said he didn't follow.

"How'd you end up here?"

"General Sheridan hurried to New Orleans. When he saw what we had done, he brought the hammer down. Some of us got caught. I lost more friends. Mayor Monroe was a close friend of Baxter. Silver had just been discovered here. The Mayor, happy with how I handled the riot, sent me out here to work for his friend. So, for the past few years I've been doing missions for Baxter. The newspapers and the dime novels give us a lot of attention. It's forced us into hiding. Mostly we live in caves out in Apache country. They're all being forced onto the reservation so it isn't such a bad life for us." Josiah pulled up his pants leg and showed off a gunshot wound on the back of his left calf. It was the wound that caused his limp. "I was shot here on the second day by one of you boys."

An hour passed.

Burnley was drunk. After losing ten dollars at a game he suspected Josiah had rigged, Burnley said that he would cut his losses and turn in. He and Josiah made plans to speak tomorrow.

Outside, Henry Antrim waited, still watching Winston at the stable. "Sutherland poked through your things but didn't take anything."

"Sure?"

Henry nodded. "He's suspicious of you."

"Which way is the hotel operated by Babcock?"

Henry pointed. Up the thoroughfare, Burnley saw a sign that said Gammy's Hotel. He handed Henry his pay. "You see any of the DeBlancs leave that saloon, find me there. I'll pay you again."

Henry Antrim tipped his sombrero.

Burnley got Winston back from Sutherland. They rode down Main Street, passing a saloon called the Red Onion, Tunstall's Bank, the shoe shop, another saloon called the Blue Goose, and the laundry. At the hotel's stable, he secured Winston in a fresh stall. Inside, he rented out a room from Gammy, a portly man with whiskers in the style of General Burnside. Then Burnley stepped out back and bought a bottle of brandy from the man in the tent. The man was suspicious at first but became friendly after Burnley said he was a friend of Ezra the Indian.

Alone in his room, Burnley sat by the open window and sipped brandy. He feared sleep and often needed alcohol to get any. He hoped to not dream for his dreams were often dreadful memories of the war.

*

Gunfire woke him. Burnley took cover. The shots came from the thoroughfare. Burnley looked out the window and saw four hooded men riding away from the Tunstall Bank.

He hurriedly got dressed. Carrying his shotgun, he ran downstairs, past Gammy Babcock and onto the street.

"Robbery!" someone screamed.

He ran to Tunstall's Bank. Inside, there was a bank teller face down on the floor with a gunshot wound in the back of his head. Two old men, both bank tellers, leaned over him.

"Who was it?" Burnley asked.

Both tellers were scared silent.

"I said what happened?" Burnley shouted.

"The DeBlanc gang robbed us," said a teller.

"Killed ol' Moses," said the other. He pointed at the dead body on the floor. "Didn't need to do that. He wasn't fighting. They killed him for nothing."

"Then they took our money and were just... gone," the other teller said.

"How many were there?"

"Four," the first teller said.

"Holt Kantor," Burnley said to himself. He was so quiet that no one heard.

Burnley ran back to Gammy's and gathered provisions. Then he rushed down to the stable, got on Winston, rode back past the bank and kept riding west into open country. Winston moved fast. He always knew when a ride was urgent.

*

Josiah walked across the stones to the edge of the river and relieved himself in the shallow water. The morning sky was a hazy blue. There was much growth behind him coming from the cracks in the rock wall of the canyon. A tangle of sprouts and vines quietly parted. Burnley emerged, holding his shotgun. Josiah turned and saw Burnley and his weapon.

"Undo your belt and toss it toward me," said Burnley.

Josiah did it. Burnley picked up Josiah's pistols and put them on a flat stone out of Josiah's reach.

A silence passed.

Burnley said, "I know about you because I learned from Cody himself."

"He's dead?" asked Josiah.

"He's alive. He never fought it out. Just gave up and cooperated for a pardon. Cody sent some telegrams and found out that you had a job coming for Baxter. I didn't know I was going to get Kantor too. He's another target of ours."

"You ain't got Kantor yet."

Burnley's face was cold and gray. "Neither him nor the other two are making it out of this canyon."

Josiah squinted. "What do you mean ours? You and who else?"

"I'm asking the questions. Where's the money from the bank?"

"Gone."

"Don't lie to me."

"It's no lie. We handed it off to one of Baxter's men."

Burnley remembered that while following the DeBlanc gang tracks he had come upon another set of tracks indicating a second party. "You didn't make any money at all by being Baxter's murdering errand boy?"

"Baxter always makes good eventually. For now he said to hide."

"Why target Tunstall's?"

"Mr. Baxter doesn't like other banks opening up in his city. It was a warning against anyone else who might try it. I would have gladly killed you at the Faro table, but I didn't know if that might compromise our mission. I didn't know who sent you or who might come looking if you disappeared."

"When we get back to Silver City, you're going to hang," Burnley said. "I don't care if Baxter owns the Sheriff. Neither of them can help you now."

"One man won't take all four of us in."

"My job isn't to take them in. Just you."

Burnley hogtied Josiah and left him by the water with a gag in his mouth. Then he walked silently to their camp, which was close to the wide mouth of a cave.

Floral sat by the fire. A thick black cigar was clenched between his teeth. He cooked breakfast in a hanging cast iron skillet. Burnley aimed for his lower neck and squeezed the trigger. The shot went high and hit Floral in the face. Pink viscera misted the air.

Rashers of bacon sizzled over the fire. Holt, a few feet from Floral, drew his pistol. Burnley shot him in the chest. From the ground he sent a confused shot up into the sky. Burnley focused and fired a shot into Holt's head.

Burnley ran for the tent. A scared voice cried out, "I surrender!" Carlton's hand peaked out from the tent, waving a white cloth.

"Please, mercy! I surrender!"

"Show yourself!" Burnley yelled. He realized that the white cloth was Carlton's soiled long johns.

Carlton stepped out, unarmed, with his hands up. Burnley shot him in the stomach. Carlton fell back and began to convulse in hard spasms, screaming. Burnley stepped forward and shot him again, this time in the head. He died clutching his long johns.

Burnley wiped blood from his eyes. He searched everywhere but was unable to find the stolen money. It appeared that Josiah was being truthful.

Back by the river, Josiah was still hogtied. Burnley got Winston, led him back to the riverbank, and slung Josiah over him.

For his return, Burnley was forced to take a long and circuitous route. He wanted to avoid the many properties that were owned by Baxter or places where Baxter's men might be.

Josiah screamed muffled obscenities. When Burnley stopped to let Winston and Josiah drink water, he took out the gag and left it out. They continued on. Josiah, now free to speak, accused Burnley of firing the very shot that hit him in the leg at Shiloh, a wound that still raged with torment all these years later.

After crossing a ridge, Burnley saw a lone Mescalero at the top of the next ridge. He was on foot, standing in a patch of chaparral.

"We're in it now," said Josiah.

From behind them, four more Mescaleros appeared. They each rode fleet ponies. The one in front, a muscular, long-limbed war chief, carried a Cavalry sword and a Colt six-shooter. On his head was a white man's bowler. He was adorned in raiding trophies.

"That's Santana," said Josiah.

Santana rode close and spoke in Apache. His voice was deep. Burnley kept his hands on Winston's reins.

"He wants your new shotgun," said Josiah. "He isn't planning on moving to the reservation, so he needs guns. These heathen monsters can't fix them when they break. Give it to him and he might leave."

Burnley took the shotgun by the end of the barrel and raised it. Santana took the weapon and studied it. Then he looked back at Burnley.

For a sustained moment, there was not a speck of hate, disgust or distrust in Burnley's eyes, only respect. Santana nodded at Burnley.

He fired a loud shot into the sky and smiled. Then he rode off. His men followed. One of them picked up the Mescalero that was on foot and they were gone over the ridge.

"I just saved your life," said Josiah.

"Did nothing of the kind."

"You wouldn't have known what to do if I wasn't here."

They rode on.

Josiah became resigned and morose. "Doing this doesn't make you a good man." They rode on in silence. "Spare me that at least."

"I never said I was a good man. Just better than you is all."

*

A makeshift courtroom was assembled at the Orleans Club. Joe Dire, the club's owner, offered to have the trial in his joint to send the message that he was not supportive of the DeBlanc gang, men with Baxter's ethics, or those who still fought for the lost cause of the vanquished Rebel Army. He didn't want Confederate sympathizers around his business anymore.

Josiah Fontaine DeBlanc was charged with the murder of Moses MacBean the bank teller, his part in the '66 riots, and numerous other crimes. A Mississippi-born attorney named Davis Knight defended him.

Six local businessmen were chosen as jurors. A lawyer named Stephen Stockmaster, a long-time supporter of colored rights, volunteered to represent the prosecution. The public, including all the whores of the Orleans Club, were permitted to watch the trial. A U.S. Marshal from Las Cruces monitored everything for Washington. He and Burnley exchanged familiar glances. They never spoke.

"Did you participate in the mass murder of innocent coloreds on that day in 1866?" Stephen asked Josiah during his cross-examination.

"Damn straight I did!" said Josiah. "I'd do it again if I had the chance!"

Davis Knight had once been a successful attorney but since the war he had declined in ability because of drink. He made numerous bitter outbursts about Reconstruction but did little defending. Josiah was found guilty of all charges.

At the intersection of Main and Broadway, Burnley watched as Josiah, manacled, was led up to the gallows. A crowd had gathered. A steady wind blew. It made the U.S. flag soar.

Burnley saw a parked stagecoach with a man watching from inside, cloaked by shadows. Burnley guessed that Thad Baxter was inside, likely contemplating who was really pulling the strings of this hanging.

"Last words?" asked the hangman.

"The South will rise again."

He dropped and dangled beneath the stars and stripes.

Over time, the crowd dispersed. When things were quiet, Henry Antrim approached Burnley. Henry looked upset.

"I'm sorry, Yank."

"What for?"

"You asked me to watch the gang. I left my post."

"What distracted you?" asked Burnley.

"My mother made me come home."

"Forget it," said Burnley. "I got him anyway."

*

The man handed Burnley a cigar. He always smoked one. To the world, he was Ulysses S. Grant, the 18th U.S. President. To Burnley, he was simply the General.

"It's good to see you, Burnley."

The General also handed Burnley a brandy. "You as well, sir."

"The business of war remains preferable to the business of politics. Or at least I remain confident that war suits me better."

"I recently met a man who proclaimed the South would rise again."

The General drank whisky. His beloved wife Julia was back in Washington. Julia kept him temperate. This had been the job of the dedicated

Rawlins during the war, but for many years now Julia had gone at the work alone.

"I saw the story in the paper. Good work," said the General. "Is there anything I need to know about?"

"I made errors."

The General scratched his beard. "Such as?"

"I shouldn't have waited for Kantor. He wasn't the objective. I should have taken them at the club and left Kantor for later."

"Holt Kantor was just as irredeemably pestilential as the other three and the bank teller is not on your head. You kept moving forward, that was key."

The General paid Burnley the amount they had agreed upon for each life. Their agreement was verbal. Whenever they met, the rest of the General's administration merely thought he was visiting with one of the legions of veterans he had commanded during the Rebellion.

"You'll continue pursuing the rest of the men on that list I gave you," said the General. "You'll move forward."

"Yes sir," said Burnley. "While I do, I plan to teach myself French."

The General was silent.

"Many of these targets seem proficient in it."

What kept the General up at night was America's race problem. His powers to combat it were limited. The General recognized that the root of the ideology behind the problem, one that drove men to such great evil, had spread further than the jurisdiction of any American law. The slew of racist murders committed by former rebels in recent years were meant as political messages intended to discredit the outcome of the war. Many of these racist murderers, the worst of them, were evading justice. They were hiding in the territories.

"Despite the setbacks, I never lost sight of DeBlanc as the main target. All of Silver City saw him hang," said Burnley. "I even think Thad Baxter watched."

"Hopefully this sent a meaningful message."

Burnley waited. "DeBlanc and I spoke about Shiloh. He was there with us."

"Whipped 'em on the second day."

Outside the Presidential train car, Burnley mounted Winston. The General was a great lover of animals, horses most of all. But Burnley knew the General did not want anyone to see him drunk, especially not Winston, so he did not get off his private train car. While riding back towards town, Burnley planned to let Winston relax for as long as their work together would allow.

A FRESH START
BY BRIAN TOWNSLEY

I stepped off the bus, dropped my bag onto the road, and adjusted my hat. The town looked about as small as a postage stamp and as colorful as dirt. Then the bus hurried off, as if it didn't want to be here either, and I couldn't see a damn thing but dust. When it cleared, I was as colorless as the town. If you took away the three trucks parked on the street, all whitened by desert driving, and the telephone poles standing sentinel, it could have been 1880 rather than 1949.

The town consisted of a single road of dirt hardpack. The storefronts were weathered by wind and their signs faded nearly into obscurity. I stretched briefly, joints popping audibly, my arms reaching for the sky. I cracked my neck, and exhaled, heavily. Well, I thought, this is what I asked for. Picking up my bag, I headed to the soda shop. I caught my reflection in a passing window and stopped. I had to be honest: I looked like a hobo. Raggedy sportcoat, full beard, lace-up boots whose better days had seen better days. I did have my Stetson still, so there was that—it was an Open Road style, favored by our president, Harry S. Truman. A beat up and stained Silverbelly with a rancher crown and a short brim, it was the only thing on me that looked like it may have once cost more than three dollars. It probably was.

I rubbed my free hand through my beard and made a face at myself in the window. I saw the barber inside the shop looking out at me with an expression that could only be disapproval so I chortled a short laugh and continued on.

The soda shop was really an everything shop, as they mostly were in towns this small. There was a linoleum counter for a soda pop or a malt, but the rest of the store sold everything from motor oil to bandages to ammunition to breakfast cereal. There was a cash register in the back and a man standing at the soda counter.

"Howdy," the man said, wearing a grin. "Something I can help you find?"

"Yessir," I responded. I looked about the store, there were three aisles I noted, and asked, "How's about some shaving cream and a razor?"

The man walked from behind the counter and into one of the aisles. I met him there. He wore work pants and a work shirt with a threadbare cardigan over it, and a sunblasted fedora pushed so far back on his head it seemed to defy physics simply by staying in place. He was somewhere between 35 and 50, and his face was round, with a kindness to it I wasn't sure I could trust.

"That is quite a bushy chin you got down there," he said, extending a hand with both products. Then added: "plannin' on givin' it a cut, I reckon?"

I smiled and shrugged. "When the time is right," I said, and accepted the products. "How's about some .45 rounds as well?" He pointed to another aisle and said, "Yup. Got them too." We walked together to that area and I grabbed a box off the shelf. The weight felt substantial in my hand. Then I nodded with my head towards the counter and said, "lemme get a vanilla cream soda pop too, while we're at it."

He smiled and extended his hand. "Name's Burl," he said.

"Hank," I said in response, and shook his hand.

Over at the soda counter, Burl set to making the vanilla pop, and I set my hat and bag on the stool next to me as I sat. "Say, I'm looking for a fella," I said.

He peered back over his shoulder and said, "Yeah? I figured you must have. Don't nobody stop in this one-horse town as a destination, if you catch my way of thinking. What's the name?"

"Billy Anderson," I said, before adding, "old Army buddy."

He turned then, eyes wide, and said: "Is that right? Well hell, everybody here knows Billy. He's the local celebrity. I mean, they'd know him 'cause of his daddy—biggest ranch in the area—but Billy bein' a liberator at Dachau?" He exhaled a *pshaw!* noise and shook his head. Then he looked again at me. "Say, you weren't there too, were ya? At Dachau, helpin' them Jewish folks out?" He said *Jew-ish* like it was much longer than its given two syllables.

I looked Burl straight in the eye and nodded. "I was indeed. Me and Billy, we were just about attached at the hip in those days. Ain't seen him in a few years though," I said.

He put the soda down in front of me, and said, "Well, I'll be darned. No charge for that there soda then." Then he stepped back and looked at me wide-eyed and shook his head, mouth agape. I realized I was going to have to drink my soda with an audience.

"Thank you kindly," I said, and took my first sip. I hadn't had one of these in some time—they don't much have soda counters in boxcars—and it did hit the spot. "So hey," I said, "you know how I can get ahold of Billy?"

Two phone calls and two hours later, I was hopping out of the bed of a beat-to-hell yellow pickup and onto the dirt hardpack in front of a gated entrance that read *Double A Ranch.* I tipped the brim of my hat to the driver and he waved and drove on, dust billowing in his wake. I looked the ranch over. It looked like the middle of nowhere, because it was. I was in Southern California, but not the Southern California people think of when they hear it. People don't realize how big Californy is. They think Hollywood, Los Angeles, maybe San Francisco, which is way up the state. But this part of Southern California is all desert—the southern Mojave Desert, to be accurate, and most of it is flat, hours from the coast and hours still from the western border of Arizona or the southern tip of Nevada. Not a damn thing out here but space and things that want to kill you.

The ranch entrance was open, so I just walked right on in.

I saw Billy some ways off, him bumping up and down in his seat on the uneven terrain in a Jeep that looked like it had never left the Army. He turned my way, dust gathering behind him, coming hard on the trespasser, and I saw recognition come over him as he approached and the boyish grin take shape. He pulled the

Jeep up right beside me and kept pace with my walking, pushing his cowboy hat back on his forehead.

"Well, I'll be damned," he said. "That you, Hank? Under all them there bristles? Hell, I couldn't hardly tell—you know what gave it away? Same walk," he nodded in confirmation of this fact. "What they call it, *gait?* You got the same gait as Hank, and here I get up close and if it ain't my ol' Army buddy in the flesh!"

I stopped walking. He stopped the Jeep. I smiled at him and said, "Hell, I figured it was high time I see what you stepped yourself into." I gestured towards the horizon. "I see you're, uhhh, ranching dirt."

He smiled at this and shook his head in mock pity. "Same 'ol Hank. We got a shitload of heffers out yonder," and he pointed then to the open spaces past the ranch house, barn, and the handful of other structures.

I looked that way, and nodded.

"Damn if we ain't got some catchin' up to do!" he said, and banged the steering wheel. Billy looked the same. A shock of blonde hair across his forehead, green eyes, and a buck-toothed smile that could light a room. If you looked up 'All American Boy' in the encyclopedia, they could do worse than have a picture of Billy Anderson next to it.

"Well, hell, hop in," he said. "So what, you get an allergy to razors or something?" he asked, as we drove towards the ranch house.

By the time we sat down for dinner in the main house, Billy had taken me on a tour of the buildings. There was a large barn, housing ten horses, a bunkhouse, housing another six men, two equipment sheds, an outhouse, and some other stuff. I grew up in Los Angeles, my mom was a working girl, my dad was an actor who I met twice, and I lived in little bungalows that were lucky to have a back porch. Everything I knew about ranching or being a cowboy came from the movies, and that wasn't much. I rode a horse about as well as I perform open-heart surgery with a pair of pliers. So most of this stuff went in one ear and out the other.

Billy's dad sat at the head of the table, name of Herm. He didn't seem to like me much, but it may not have been me. He didn't seem to like much of anything. Billy sat at the table, as well as his little brother James, maybe 14, and me. I didn't ask about his mom, but I'm pretty sure he told me during the war that she was gone. Not sure on the story there. There was a lady from the kitchen who kept bringing us food. The steaks and potatoes were sure good though.

"So, Hank, what brings you out this way? Don't get many visitors out in this area," Herm said, between bites of baked potato.

"You know, Mr. Anderson, I just figured I needed a fresh start," I said, and took a bite of the steak.

"So, you figure you can work here?" He asked. I couldn't tell if he was being sarcastic or not. He was like that.

"If you'll have me. I'm a hard worker, not much of a cowhand, I'm afraid, but I learn quick," I said.

He put his fork down and looked at me. Not mean-like, just...appraising. Then he looked at Billy.

"Pa, I'll just have him work the fences for a bit, always work there. Have him do odd jobs here and there, maintenance work, things that need doin'," Billy said.

I stuck out my tongue at James, the little brother. He did the same in response.

"Tell you what though," Billy said, pointing his fork at me and continuing, "this boy right here is hell on wheels with a gun, Pa. I've seen him shoot the eye out a crow at twenty yards with a .45. Them Nazi's over there were scared as all get-out of old Hank right here," he said, and winked at me. There was admiration in his voice. He took a bite and chewed, thinking on it. Then: "the Nazi's gave him a name over there. That's how scared they was."

I shrugged, trying to change the topic. "Ehh," I said. "It was war— anyways, I look forward to takin' whatever work you could give me, sir."

"I'm gonna ask you to shave that thing on your face," he said in a way that didn't sound like asking.

"Okay," I nodded. "Next time I go into town I'll get it done proper," I said.

"We're headed in on Friday, Hank," Billy said. "You'll come with," then he looked at his dad, "heading to the bank 'fore the end of the month pickup," he said by way of explanation.

Herm said nothing to this. Then he looked at me and said, "You can start tomorrow. We get up early here, so be ready when Billy gets you."

I said I would.

Herm nodded, and finished chewing his food. Then he said: "I'll be sure to give you a call whenever I need something shot." I thought he was joking, but he may not have been.

I slept in one of the many extra rooms in the house that Wednesday night. It was my first night in a proper bed in a long time.

Thursday morning came soon enough, and just after first light Billy gave a knock on the door.

I spent the bulk of that first day riding around with Billy in the Jeep. I met the other hands, and a small group of us tended the fence lines throughout the afternoon. The weather was odd for this time of year, at least according to the men I was around, as it was hot and humid and overcast, and you could see the thunderheads far off and smell the wet that was coming. A storm was on its way.

After dinner, Billy grabbed one of the hands I had met earlier, name of Tommy, and the three of us drove to a local bar that was a standalone structure and sat at the crossroads of two dirt streets, if they could be called such. It was named Mel's Public House, and had a red neon sign announcing the same.

It was a spare structure, made of cinder blocks and brick, and had booths in a u-shape on three of the walls and a smattering of tables and chairs in the middle of the room. Besides a few neon beer signs and a big mirror on one wall, the only decoration in the place was a longhorn skull, hung high on the wall above the bar. Its horns must have been two feet in each direction. What a burden, I thought, to have to carry those around on your head every day. It was still impressive to look at, though.

Tommy and I took seats in a booth, and Billy brought over three bottled beers and three shot of rye. "Boys," he said, and raised his shot, "glad Hank made his way out here. After what we been through and seen," he and I made eye contact briefly, "we deserve as much R & R time as the good lord can think up," he nodded to indicate that he was done, and the three of us clinked glasses and shot the rye down. It didn't take long for the two of them to be in their cups. I've always had quite the tolerance for liquor, even in the stretches where I barely tipped any back, so I don't think I was halfway on the trip to where both of them already were. And Billy was telling stories.

"You shoulda seen it, Tom," he said, "we was marchin' these Jews out and every rib bone on 'em was sticking out like on a stray dog." He shook his head and sipped his beer, his eyes glassy.

"What unit was y'all with," Tommy asked, wide eyed.

"45th infantry," I answered, staring at my beer. Tommy nodded, as if that meant something.

"And," Billy added, "they was doin' *experiments* on people there, on them Jews. They had this one scientific-like wing, and, I mean..." his voice trailed off there.

"And," I said, "we found people there, men, women, kids, in cages, some that were twisted into weird shapes on tables, some still suffering." I nodded grimly and tipped my beer back.

"So, Hank here," Billy interjected, looking at Tommy but pointing a finger in the hand that held his beer at me, "he lined 'em all up. All these guards 'n scientists, SS freaks, he lined 'em all up. They had these big pits they had dug for mass graves 'n such..." he nodded at me, "you remember those?"

"Of course," I said.

"So Hank here marched 'em all out there and made 'em get on their knees. Shit, there musta been 20 of 'em. And you just went right on down the line, shootin' each sumbitch in the head with a fuckin' Luger. Their own gun."

Tommy asked, "Your commandin' officer sign off on that?" His face was in genuine wonder.

Billy and I looked at each other. Then Billy shook his head. "Fuckin' Gibson was a softie. He saw just what Hank was figurin' to do, and just straight looked the other way. Pretended like it wasn't even happenin'", he said.

I grinned, sheepishly. "Didn't do nothin' that every one of them didn't deserve," I said.

"He just shot each one in the head, and kicked each body down with his boot into the grave if it didn't fall by itself," he looked at me, his glazed eyes igniting for a moment, "remember you had to reload, twice?" Billy looked at Tommy and explained: "See, Luger's only got 8 shots, so that's how I know it musta been near 20, 'cause Hank here reloaded twice." His voice sounded a mixture of drunk and awe and bitter.

"Still got that Luger," I said.

Both men looked at me then with glazed eyes. I sipped my beer.

"No shit," Tommy said. "Well, I'll be."

"In my bag back at the ranch," I said. "Hell, I still got my M1911 .45 too."

"Well, shit," Billy said. "Let's go shoot some shit then!"

We left Mel's Public House and picked up the guns from the ranch. We were tiptoein' about in our boots because of the late hour and all. We dropped Tommy off, since he had already fallen asleep in the Jeep on the way back.

Billy drove out maybe ten miles from the ranch. It looked like the same nothing that we had left, but there was a short foothill there. It was an outcropping of rocks. We put some bottles out on the stone edges in the moonlight. Billy aimed the headlights on our targets, and we sat on the bumper of the Jeep, clinked two more beers together and drank.

"Y'know, Billy, it's interesting that you tell that story about what I did and don't seem to mention what you did," I said, and sipped.

"Aww, hell, you still sore about that?" He asked.

"Well," I said, "I'm not sure sore is the right word. I always just thought it was kinda uncalled for, what you did."

Tommy finished his beer and hurled it towards the rocks. It smashed loudly in the stillness, pieces of glass clinking their way down through the crevices.

"Hell, man," he said, "I was just blowin' off some steam. I wasn't doin' nothing to her that wasn't already being done."

We looked at each other in the darkness, neither fully seeing the other.

"I mean, look. You took the officers, lined 'em up, and shot 'em. I took one of their Jew whores and screwed her. I mean..." he said, and the words just hung there in the silence. The stars were twinkling between the dark masses of clouds that covered them in their passage.

"I sent a bunch of killers, torturers, and cowards to their maker. Terrible people who had done terrible fucking things. We saw the results of some of those things. You hurt someone who was already being abused. So don't try to act like they're the same damn thing," I said. With that, I stood, set my feet, and knocked four bottles off in five shots with the Luger. The shots were deafening in the silence, and echoed across the dark landscape.

"Well, now you made me feel like shit. Hope you're happy," he said, and stood. "It wasn't even any good, if that makes you feel any better. It was fuckin' cold, and she just laid there all still like. Shit I even kinda felt bad after..." I handed him the Luger and he took aim. "I never was much good that this shit," he said, and fired the last three shots. No bottle fell, just bullets ricocheting off stone. "God damnit," he said.

He handed me the Luger and walked to the Jeep. He grabbed a 12-gauge from the rear section, walked towards the bottles, and fired. All three bottles shattered as the buckshot exploded onto the rocks. "More my style," he said, and smiled. I could see the whiteness of his teeth in the darkness.

Friday morning came and we ate breakfast at the table. Dad Herm, little brother James, Myself, and Billy. The same lady kept bringing out the food. Flapjacks, scrambled eggs, bacon, potatoes. The table was mostly quiet. I stuffed myself, knowing we had a big day ahead.

As Billy and I were headed out to the Jeep, Herm said: "You're getting that thing chopped today, yeah?"

I grinned at him, and nodded. Billy threw two large bags in the back, and I threw mine in as well.

"Look like a goddamn caveman," Herm said, as Billy started the Jeep.

Billy and I were both tired and a bit fuzzy from the night prior. On the road into town, the clouds that had thus far only hinted as to their potential began to spit some rain at us as they grumbled with thunder like an old man in a bad mood. I immediately thought of Herm, as I had yet to see the man in any other kind of mood.

Billy stopped the Jeep and he and I put into place a canvas top on the roof bar to cover the front seat and offer at least a tiny respite from the raindrops. "Hey," Billy said, "no hard feelings about last night, huh?"

I wasn't sure if it was a question or a request or an admission, so I shrugged.

He nodded at that. The sky had begun to open up now, and what had been a patter of drizzle became a full-blown dousing. A bolt of lightning shot across the barren landscape, and the thunder that followed reverberated in my chest.

"Thing about the desert," Billy said, "is that there ain't no middle ground. When it's hot, it's damn hot, and when it storms, which it don't much, it's like something biblical."

By the time we reached town, I understood why everybody out here drove trucks and Jeeps. The hardpack road had become a muddy suggestion, and we bounced in and out of puddles one after another.

We passed the soda shop, and shortly thereafter the barber shop where I was to receive my trim. To become civilized again. I pointed at it, but Billy shook his head. "After," he said. "Bank is gonna be busy, let's get that done first."

I couldn't imagine anything being busy around here but nodded amiably. And Billy was right. The bank was the absolute last structure on the main drag, a building that looked more house than business, and I counted eight trucks parked outside at various angles. Billy came to a stop in the mud and got out. He grabbed both bags he had brought and started towards the entrance.

"I'll meet you in there," I said. "Gotta grab something." He nodded and continued on. I rummaged around my duffel and grabbed my Colt 1911 and tucked it in the small of my back. The rain made pattering noises on my hat brim as I approached the entrance.

The bank had a line of men inside, all farmers or ranchers I presumed. Billy was last in line. There was a single security guard, currently in conversation with a man towards the front of the line, thumbs hooked in his belt. I pulled the Colt from the small of my back and shot Billy in the back of the head, then shot the security guard. The bullet caught the man in the neck and he grabbed at it, eyes wide, blood spurting from between his fingers. He took two steps backwards and slumped against the wall, dead.

The silence that followed was momentary but profound. Nobody moved. It was as if nothing had happened. Then all the men were staring at me, many with mouths agape. "Now here, son, what—" started a man in overalls and I shot him in the forehead. After than nobody spoke.

"Put your bags on the ground," I said, calmly. "Now."

The men who carried bags bent over and put them down. I pointed the gun at the bank teller, a short, round man with spectacles. "Empty your drawers of cash back there and bring it out in a bag. Do it fast," I said. The man began moving quickly. "Everybody else, back away from the bags to the wall."

"You," I pointed the gun at one man, "you have a truck out there?"

The man was tall and thin with an enormous Adam's apple that bobbed as he swallowed and he nodded, slowly.

"Good. It got gas?"

He nodded again. "When the teller comes out here, hand him the keys," I said.

We all waited for the teller. No one spoke. One man in the corner sobbed.

When the teller appeared from a side door, he was carrying a bag. "Turn all the way around," I said. The man stopped, confused, then turned in a circle. I saw no weapon. "Good," I said. "Now get the keys from that man," I pointed with the gun, "pick up all of these bags, and throw them in the truck."

One man stepped forward, arms out in front of him, palms out. "Son," he said, "you hadn't ought to—" until I shot him in the forehead, bits of his brainpan fanned onto the wall behind him, decorating the man next to him.

The teller began to sob then, but had already grabbed the keys and was gathering up the bags. It took him three trips to load the truck, but he worked fast. When he was done, he handed me the keys and stood with the rest of the men.

I looked down at Billy's corpse, slumped at an odd angle, his head in a puddle of his own blood, cowboy hat crown down on the hardwood. "I guess I ain't one for the high moral ground after all, Billy," I said. "I just like makin' you feel bad about it. Not my fault you let the fox into the henhouse." I shrugged at the men then. "You all want to live?" I asked the group. They stood on the wall, some with hands up, but they all nodded. "Okay," I said. "Everybody give their truck keys to the teller."

When they had done that, I had the teller put them in a small cloth bag. "If I see anybody here following me, so help me I'll kill your whole fucking family." With that I walked out of the bank and into the rain, which had not let up. The truck started right up.

I stopped at a gas station an hour away and shaved my beard in the bathroom. I took the California driver's license out that I had purchased and held onto for this specific occasion. On it, I stared out at the camera with the name William Thompson. I'd go by Will, I had decided. I walked over to the small shop and the attendant there. "That your car in back?" I asked him.

He looked at me confused, then said, "Yeah, mister. Why?" I shot him in the chest and found the keys in his pocket once he stopped moving. It didn't take long. I transferred the bags into the trunk of the '46 Ford sedan behind the shop and started that up. I left the bag of keys in the abandoned truck.

I shook the rain off my hat and pointed the Ford west. Towards Los Angeles. I figured I'd give Hollywood a shot. Maybe become a stunt man. Shoot whatever needed shooting on a movie set. Ol' Will Thompson, stunt man to the stars. I liked the ring of it. It was, if nothing else, a fresh start.

54

KISSING COUSINS
BY MICHAEL BRACKEN

Nick Brandt had spent much of his acting career working as an Applebee's waiter while praying for his big break. Then Christine Teufel walked into the restaurant and offered him the role of a lifetime.

That morning Nick had lost a hemorrhoid commercial and a three-line role in yet another off-off-Broadway production. He'd been rude to his customers all evening, and his attitude had not improved by the time he approached the busty brunette's table and asked what she wanted to drink.

"I saw you in *Take the Mahoney and Run*," Christine said, referring to a dark comedy in which he played kidnap victim Patrick Mahoney. "You sold me the moment you crawled onstage."

That someone had seen the off-off-Broadway production during its two-week run and had then recognized him from it provided a bright spot in Nick's otherwise depressing day. "I did?"

Nick did not know it, but Christine was quite the actor herself, though she had no formal training and had never trod the boards. She leaned forward, the better to expose deep cleavage, and wet her crimson lips with the tip of her tongue as she batted her long eyelashes. "Absolutely."

Christine ordered water and a Grilled Chicken Caesar Salad, and each time Nick returned to her table, which he did more often than necessary and at the expense of his other tables, her flirting grew more blatant. She ended her meal with a Hot Fudge Sundae Shooter, and when he brought her check, she dipped her middle finger into a dollop of uneaten whipped cream, brought it to her mouth, and drew her whipped-cream-laden finger between her lips.

Nick caught his breath and didn't exhale until her finger was completely clean.

"What time do you get off?" Christine asked. After Nick told her, she said, "I'll be waiting for you at Martell's. Don't disappoint me."

She paid cash, left a too-large tip, and disappeared.

He found her an hour later, sitting alone in a booth at Martell's, nursing a Lemon Drop Martini. As he slid into the booth with Christine, she placed one hand on his knee beneath the table and said, "You seem surprised to see me."

"I—I didn't know what to expect."

"You're quite a handsome man, and quite a talented actor," she said as her fingers slid up his inseam. "I'm the one who should be surprised. I wasn't certain you'd be interested in me. I was afraid I'd be sitting here all night waiting for you."

"I never would have stood you up."

Her fingers reached the spot where one inseam met the other. "I seem to have stood you up," she said. "Can we go someplace where we can be alone?"

"My apartment's a twenty-minute cab ride away," he suggested.

She leaned closer and whispered in his ear, "My hotel room is two blocks away."

"I'm not in town for long," Christine said when they woke the following morning, beginning a whirlwind affair that had them spending more time in bed than most anywhere else. When they weren't in her hotel suite, she took Nick to expensive restaurants and bought him clothing from stores he could never afford on his Applebee's tips. After an exhausting sexual encounter, the evening before she was to return home to Colorado, Christine rose on one elbow and looked down at Nick. "How would you like a job?"

"I have a job."

"An acting job," she said, "but you'll be working without a script—"

Nick perked up. "Improv? I can do improv."

"—and you'll be required to stay in character twenty-four/seven."

Nick had spent one summer working a Renaissance Faire, remaining in character from the moment he arrived each morning until he left each evening. "How much background information can you provide and how much do I need to develop on my own?"

"I can provide everything you need," Christine said.

"How long is the gig?"

"Six months, give or take."

"And the pay?"

"Room and board," she said, "and walking-around money."

He hesitated.

"The accommodations are top-notch," she said, "and the payoff at the end will be substantial."

"Substantial?"

"But only if you inhabit the role completely. Everyone you meet must be convinced that you are him."

Nick flew into Denver three weeks after Christine returned home and checked into a motel where she had rented him a room. The accommodations were nothing like her suite in New York, but the motel staff was lax about checking I.D. She gave him plenty of cash and insisted he not pay for anything with a credit or debit card. On his third night in town, she brought him several boxes of material to study for his new role. Before he looked at any of it, he asked, "Why me?"

"You remind me of my cousin."

"That's who I'm supposed to be? Your cousin?"

"Thomas McNamara," she said. "My grandmother calls him Tommy."

"What if he comes home?"

"He can't. He's dead."

"What if they find out?"

"They won't," she said. "No one knows he's dead."

"Except you."

She smiled. "Except me."

Nick stared at her for a long moment, unsure if he should ask the question that came to mind. "Did you...?"

She smiled but did not otherwise reply.

For the next several days Nick studied everything in the boxes. He compared his reflection to the photographs he found of young Thomas, seeing a strong resemblance to how he remembered his own appearance as a young man. Then he read every piece of paper, from report cards to yearbooks to handwritten notes Christine had prepared. He learned in the process that Thomas had been orphaned at sixteen months when his parents died in a sailing accident near Santa Barbara, that his father's mother had adopted him, and that she had spirited him off to her Rocky Mountain aerie in Colorado where he spent the rest of his childhood.

Thomas had been an average student, had few friends, and spoke often of hitchhiking around the world. Three months after graduating high school and two months after his eighteenth birthday, the paper trail ended.

Or so Nick thought until Christine arrived with one last box. Inside were seventeen typewritten letters signed with Thomas's name and sent to Grandmother McNamara, as well as the portable typewriter upon which they had been written. As Christine pushed the box into Nick's hands, she said, "This is what Tommy's been doing since he left home. You need to fill in the gaps."

Each time Christine visited Nick at the motel, she called him Tom, Tommy, or Thomas. The first time she called him Tommy in bed, though, he paused.

"You can't hesitate like that," Christine said. "You must be him. You can't ever break character."

She also peppered Nick with questions about Thomas—the name of his first-grade teacher, his best friend through grade school, the girls he had dated in high school, his favorite toys, his favorite rock bands, and so much more.

When he was able to answer every question without hesitation, when he could describe his life after leaving home without contradicting anything in the letters sent in Thomas's name, and when he could duplicate Thomas's signature at the bottom of those letters, Christine took away everything she'd brought except the typewriter. A week later she provided him with a Social Security card, a long-expired driver's license, and several other forms of identification generated in the countries the letters claimed Thomas had visited.

She said, "It's time to meet Grandmother. We'll leave in the morning."

"She's who this charade is for?"

"When Grandmother dies, everything goes to Tommy."

"What about your mother? Isn't she a McNamara?"

Christine explained that her parents had died in a fire several years before she moved in with her grandmother. Then she continued. "If Tommy can't be found, the money goes into a trust and I receive a small monthly stipend until he shows up," she explained. "If he never shows up, or he's declared dead, I'll never be able to touch the real money. Grandmother refuses to change her will, fully believing that Tommy will return."

"So, convincing her that your cousin's still alive came back to bite you in the ass?"

Christine nodded. "I'm stuck between a rock and a hard place," she said. "There's no statute of limitations on what happened to him."

Before Nick could respond, she opened a bottle of twenty-one-year-old single malt whiskey and poured equal amounts into a pair of the motel's water glasses. Before long, he forgot whatever reservations he had, and Christine spent the night in Nick's bed, exhausting him with her insatiable appetite. When he woke the next morning, she was already showered and dressed.

"This," she said, motioning to the disheveled bed, "can't happen again."

"Why?"

"Because, Tommy," she said, "we're cousins."

The drive to McNamara Station, a town built to serve a rail line that connected mining communities during the Colorado Gold Rush, but which had not seen a train in generations, took much of the day. The founding family had not been miners but had operated a dry goods store and made a fortune outfitting miners, a fortune that succeeding generations had invested wisely. During the drive, Christine told Nick about Ethel McNamara, trustee of the family's accumulated wealth.

"Grandmother's near-blind. Except for her eyesight, though, she's in fine health," Christine said, "likely to outlive us both."

"And you're just telling me all this now?"

"You've been away, Tommy," she said. "How would you have known any of this until I picked you up at the airport?"

"I flew in?"

"From Laredo."

"What about—"

"You came in on a private plane, so there's no way to track you through the airlines."

"And where was I before that?"

"Mexico."

"How'd I get across the border?"

She glanced at Nick and smiled. "Let's just say there aren't any walls where you crossed the border."

That story fit with some of the adventures hinted at in the letters, so Nick nodded. "I can make that work. What else do I need to know?"

"Three of us live at the house," Christine continued. "Me, Grandmother, and Grandmother's personal assistant. There's a housekeeper who works five days a week, a cook who prepares dinner most weekdays, and a handyman who comes and goes as needed. A service takes care of the grounds. Other than me and Grandmother, none of them know you."

"What about neighbors?"

"Grandmother's house is twenty miles up the mountain from town. There are no neighbors."

"Friends?"

"Grandmother has no friends, just people who work for her."

"No," Nick said. "My friends."

Christine hesitated. "Your best friend moved away years ago. A couple of other guys still live in the area, but I doubt you'll cross paths," she said, "especially if you stay close to the house."

They blew through McNamara Station without stopping. Nick saw little of it beyond the quaint downtown, where well-maintained historic buildings glorified the town's Gold Rush heritage. Then they headed up the mountain on a twisty two-lane road that clung to the mountainside, and Nick did his best to avoid looking past Christine at the sheer drop to the valley below, a fear of heights he'd never realized he had causing beads of sweat to pepper his forehead.

Christine noticed his discomfort when she took her eyes off the road long enough to glance at her passenger. "You'll get used to it."

Twenty miles up the mountain took almost forty minutes to travel until Christine pulled the car into a private drive marked by two stone columns and blocked by a private gate that someone on foot could pass through, but which prevented the entrance of vehicles. She stopped, keyed in her passcode, and then turned to Nick.

"This is it," she said as she rested her hand on his thigh. "There's no turning back."

Nick nodded, and a few minutes later stepped out of Christine's car and stared up at an imposing stone and log mansion built against the mountainside. His previous life was in storage in Queens, storage fees paid a year in advance, so everything he wore, the duffel bag he removed from the trunk and everything in it, and the portable typewriter in its battered leather case were all things Christine had provided for his performance.

He took a deep breath before he hoisted the duffel bag over one arm, grabbed the typewriter case, and followed Christine up the wide stone steps. A pair of heavy wooden doors half again as tall as Nick opened onto a foyer three stories tall and larger than many of the theaters in which he had performed. Twin staircases swept up the left and right sides of the foyer to the second-floor landing, and a crystal chandelier hung from the ceiling far above him.

As he was taking in the unexpected grandeur, two women entered from a doorway to the right. The younger one, a slender blonde dressed professionally in black slacks and white silk blouse, guided the older woman toward Nick. With steel-gray hair cut into a bob that framed her angular face, the older woman wore a knee-length navy blue sheath dress accented with pearls.

"Grandmother," Christine said, "I found him."

"Tommy?" the older woman asked as the blonde guided her closer. "It that really you?"

"Yes, Grandmother, it's me," Nick said.

She held her hands out. "I don't see so well anymore, Tommy. Let me touch you."

Nick took her wrists and guided her hands to his face.

"You've not shaved," she said.

"I'm sorry, Grandmother. It's been a long day."

"Dinner will be ready soon," she said. "Why don't you go to your room and get cleaned up, Tommy. You can tell us all about your trip over prime rib."

Nick doubted he could pack twenty-two years into one dinner conversation, but said, "I'd be glad to, Grandmother. Did you leave my room the way I'd left it?"

"Heavens, no," she said as if surprised by the question. "I threw away the magazines you'd hidden under the mattress, and I had many of your things put in storage. "

Nick kissed Grandmother's cheek. Then he carried his things up the left staircase and down the hall to the bedroom Christine had identified for him a few days earlier when she'd drawn a rough sketch of the home's layout. He found it furnished with a desk, a four-drawer dresser, and a queen bed with a nightstand on each side. The far end of the room was hidden behind dark drapes.

Little remained to remind Nick of the boy he had never been, but on the dresser were three framed photographs from various stages of his childhood—as a baby, at his thirteenth birthday party, and sitting for his senior portrait—and a trophy he had received the year his baseball team won the championship. Whatever clothing left behind all those years earlier had disappeared, and the closet and dresser drawers were empty. The room had a private bath attached and someone had supplied it with towels and appropriate toiletries.

He removed his things from the duffel bag, filling three of the dresser drawers and half a dozen hangers, and he put the typewriter, still in its case, on the desk. After he showered, shaved, and dressed in fresh clothing, he pulled open the drapes and found himself staring through a plate glass window straight down a mountain.

Nick stepped back. He had viewed New York from the upper floors of a few skyscrapers but had never experienced anything from such a height as the one outside his bedroom window. He closed the drapes, took a deep breath to calm himself, and then headed downstairs to the dining room.

Grandmother already sat at the head of the table, with Christine, who had also freshened up and had changed into a black sheath dress, to her left. He took the seat to Grandmother's right. There were no other place settings.

"Would you pour the wine, Tommy?"

"Of course, Grandmother."

A bottle of Cabernet Sauvignon had been decanted while he was freshening up, and he poured equal amounts into three wide-rimmed wine glasses.

"I hope you don't mind domestic." When Nick said he didn't, Grandmother lifted her glass and toasted his return home. "To family."

"To family," Nick and Christine repeated, and they drank.

Over dinner, Nick told Grandmother and Christine he had spent the years away from home traveling through Central and South America, crossing borders with impunity until 9/11 called into question his long-expired driver's license and lack of a passport. Having read adventure novels and old pulp magazines when he was younger, Nick mixed a little fact with a lot of fiction, always ensuring that nothing he said contradicted what he'd read in the letters sent to Grandmother. Though he never admitted engaging in illegal activities, he implied that he kept company with people who may have.

Grandmother laughed a few times, asked several questions, but mostly let him talk. A few times Christine said something that redirected the conversation, giving Nick a sharp look whenever his stories became too fanciful.

After dinner, they retired to the den, where they drank more wine while Nick attempted to redirect the conversation by asking Christine what she had done while he was away.

"She's been sucking up to me, Tommy," Grandmother said, "trying to convince me to leave your money to her."

"Christine had reason to be concerned. I've been away a long time."

"But I always knew you were coming home," Grandmother said. "You sent all those letters."

"I'm sorry it took so long." Nick took Grandmother's hand in one of his and squeezed gently.

Their conversation continued for a while longer, and then Nick excused himself. He told the women he was tired after his trip and thought it best if he turned in early. Upstairs, he found the blonde exiting his room, a folded sheet of paper in her hand.

"We've not been properly introduced," he said.

"Jennifer." She held out one hand. As he took it, she continued. "Jennifer Johnson."

Nick felt the warmth of her hand and took advantage of the moment to examine her emerald-green eyes and the ever-so-faint splash of freckles across the bridge of her nose. He had not realized it when he'd first encountered her, but

Grandmother's personal assistant was younger than Christine by several years. "I didn't see you at dinner."

"I'm not part of the furnishings, but I'm not part of the family, either," she said. "I eat in the kitchen."

"That's a shame," he said. "You would have been welcome company."

"That's kind of you," Jennifer said, "but I'm certain you had a lot of catching up to do."

"Grandmother had many questions. I answered them as best I could."

"I'm certain you did," she said.

"She sent you up here to check on me, didn't she?"

Jennifer neither confirmed nor denied his accusation. Instead, she said, "I brought more towels."

"Thank you." Nick released her hand and watched Jennifer walk away, admiring the sway of her hips, before he entered his bedroom and went through his things.

There were, indeed, additional towels. He continued checking, could not tell if his clothing had been rummaged through, but did discover that the typewriter case had not been zipped all the way closed.

Over breakfast—scrambled eggs and toast prepared by Christine— Grandmother said, "You should write a book."

"I could never."

"But the letters you sent were always so colorful, and the stories you told last night were so entertaining."

"Maybe I could if Christine helped me," Nick said. "She was always better in English than I ever was."

Tommy's cousin glared at him from across the table.

"Maybe so," Grandmother agreed.

Later, Christine cornered Nick in the den. In a low, angry voice she asked, "What was that all about?"

"Your grandmother had her assistant take a sample from the typewriter," he said.

"The little—"

"Don't take it out on her," Nick said. "She was likely following your grandmother's instructions."

Jennifer stepped into the room and hesitated when she saw the cousins together. They stopped talking when they realized she had joined them.

"I'm sorry," she said. "Mrs. McNamara said she left her reading glasses on the table."

All three of them looked at the table.

"Yes," Jennifer said. "There they are."

She crossed the room, retrieved the glasses, and left them alone again.

"That was too close," Christine whispered harshly. "Be careful what you say."

He was, and each day he felt more comfortable in his role as Ethel McNamara's grandson. Days passed, and then weeks. Nick spent his time learning the household's routine, from when meals were served to the housekeeper's cleaning pattern; exploring the twelve-room mansion, four-car garage, and detached one-bedroom pool house where Grandmother's personal assistant lived; and walking the grounds, uncertain how much of the mountainside belonged to the McNamara family.

He also spent a little time with Grandmother in her office, where she spent much of each day listening to her personal assistant reading her incoming mail and directing the activities of the family trust's attorney, banker, and broker. She never discussed the minutia of managing the family trust with Nick, but neither did she discuss it with Christine, and he learned little about the extent of their investments.

As Mrs. McNamara's personal assistant, Jennifer attended to her wants and needs during working hours, so until dinner time each weekday evening, Nick rarely spent time with Grandmother when Jennifer was not also present. Most evenings she then disappeared into the pool house and was not seen again until the following morning.

Weekends were different. Each Saturday, Christine drove Grandmother down the mountain for a mani pedi and to have her hair attended to. While they were gone, Nick had the house to himself, and he spent some of that time in the company of Grandmother's personal assistant.

In the kitchen one Saturday, over ham and Swiss sandwiches Nick had prepared, he asked Jennifer how she came to work for Grandmother.

"My father owns an auto shop down in McNamara Station," she said, "and with no brothers I spent much of my childhood learning auto mechanics from my father. But I had no desire to go into the family business. I was always looking up."

"Up here?"

She nodded.

"My father always serviced the McNamaras' vehicles—he still does—so I got to know the family."

Feigning surprise, Nick said, "You're little Jenny?"

"I was wondering when you'd remember me."

He hadn't, but he'd guessed Jennifer was someone he should have known and wondered why Christine had failed to provide him with that information. "You're so grown up now."

"I'm not a little girl anymore, Mr. McNamara." Jennifer smiled. "I'm all woman."

"You certainly are," Nick said before he could stop himself.

"Ever since I was a little girl," she said, "I dreamed of living up here. Now I do." She smiled coyly. "And so do you."

When Nick recognized the turn their conversation had taken, he corrected course. "So, how did you climb the mountain?"

"After high school, I earned an associate's degree in office administration. I returned home to work for the bank, and when Mrs. McNamara's previous assistant retired, she hired me."

Until that conversation, Nick had been confident of his ongoing portrayal of Thomas McNamara, but he knew then that little things could still trip him up. Late that evening, after everyone else was asleep, he caught Christine in the kitchen, thoughts of Jennifer's subtle flirting and memories of their own carnal encounters in New York and Denver rushing back. He untied the sash of Christine's robe, backed her against the counter, and pressed himself against her.

She pushed hard against his chest, forcing Nick away. "We can't," she insisted between gritted teeth. "You know that."

"So, you don't want to be kissing cousins?"

"When we're finished with this," she said. "You can wait that long, can't you?"

"We might be finished," Nick said. He told Christine how her grandmother's assistant had almost tripped him up earlier in the day. "Who else have you failed to mention? What other information have you failed to provide?"

"Jennifer was just a little kid when you left. I didn't think she would remember anything about you."

"She remembers enough," Nick said.

But whatever Jennifer remembered she kept to herself, and two weeks later Grandmother had Nick drive her down the mountain to McNamara Station Bank & Trust. There, he established a checking account and received a debit card. Then she arranged for the family trust to deposit a monthly stipend directly into his account. The walking-around money Christine had promised exceeded his expectations, and he thanked Grandmother.

"Now you can take me to dinner," she said with a smile, and he took her to the local upscale steak house. After dinner, as he walked her to the car, she said, "I'm so glad you returned home, Tommy. I've missed you."

Having already introduced Nick to the family trust's banker while establishing his account, Grandmother later introduced Nick to the trust's attorney and broker. None of the three men had known Tommy as a child and had no reason to doubt Mrs. McNamara's belief that Nick was her grandson returned from a multi-year trip south of the border.

Nick's confidence in his portrayal of Thomas McNamara increased and the moment of doubt when he'd learned that Jennifer had known him when she was a child was all but forgotten.

The doubt disappeared entirely as the weather grew warmer, and he caught glimpses of grown-up Jennifer sunbathing poolside while Mrs. McNamara was in town being pampered.

One particularly warm Saturday he decided to join her. He didn't own a bathing suit, but he did have a pair of shorts Christine had purchased for him before they left New York. He put them on, grabbed a towel from his bathroom, and went outside.

Jennifer lay facedown on the chaise, her bikini top unfastened. When Nick sat in the chair next to her, she sat up. The top fell away, and she let him marvel at her attributes for a moment before she said, "A girl gets lonely up here, Mr. McNamara."

"Tom." Nick swallowed hard. There was no hiding the surge in his interest. "Call me Tom."

"I'm certain you must be lonely, too," she said. "Mrs. McNamara and your cousin can't attend to your every need, can they?"

Nick did not have a chance to wonder if Jennifer's question had any deeper meaning because she stood, took his hand, and led him into the pool house.

He did not leave it until shortly before Christine and Grandmother returned from town. He had showered and changed clothes by then, and he was sitting in the den watching an old John Wayne western when the two women joined him.

He complimented Grandmother's hair, even though he saw no noticeable change from her appearance prior to leaving the house that morning. After a brief conversation about their trip to town, Grandmother said she wanted to sit by the pool and enjoy the unseasonably warm weather.

Christine led her outside and returned a few minutes later, Jennifer's bikini top wadded up in one fist. "Where's Jennifer?"

"You check the pool house?"

"Of course, I checked the pool house. She isn't there. Where did she go?"

Nick shrugged. "How would I know? It's her day off."

Christine threw the bikini top in Nick's face. "You be careful," Christine said. "I don't trust her."

Nick and Jennifer were careful. They did their best to avoid one another during the week, saving all their pent-up desire for the hours they spent together in the pool house each Saturday.

Several weeks later, when Nick felt he had thoroughly woven himself into the warp and woof of the McNamara family and their business associates, he learned differently.

He was in Jennifer's bed and had just rolled to the side when she rose onto one elbow and said, "You're not Thomas McNamara."

Nick's eyes snapped open. "Why would you say that?"

"Mrs. McNamara might be near-blind," Jennifer said, "but I'm not. I've known all along that you weren't who you said you were, and I think this is something Christine cooked up because you carried in the typewriter she used to type all those letters sent to her grandmother. I know. I checked it the night you arrived, and it has a problem with the letter e not aligning properly. The e is misaligned on every one of those letters."

Nick stared at her for a moment before asking, "What makes you think I didn't have the typewriter with me the entire time I was away?"

"Because I found the rough draft of your last letter—the one letting Mrs. McNamara know you were on your way home."

Jennifer rolled over, removed two pieces of paper from her nightstand, and handed them to Nick. One was the test she'd typed the night Nick arrived and the other was a rough draft of Tommy's last letter home, corrections and additions noted in Christine's handwriting. "I found this in the trash a few weeks before your last letter arrived, and I recognized the misaligned e because I'm the one who reads your letters to Mrs. McNamara. I kept it because I also recognized Christine's handwriting."

"If what you suspect is true, what do you want?"

"I want to know why you two have gone through this elaborate ruse."

"Christine wants her grandmother's money. How exactly she plans to get it, I'm not quite certain," Nick explained. "I only know that convincing Grandmother that I'm her long-missing grandson is an important part of the plan."

"How did she get you involved?"

Nick told her about the trajectory of his acting career, never using the word failure but letting Jennifer know he had no belief that his big break would ever come. He never mentioned that Christine had seduced him before involving him in her plan. "At first I thought I was being hired for the ultimate acting gig, and the idea that I might inhabit a role so thoroughly that everyone believes I am who I say I am was quite a challenge."

"And now?"

"Now? Now what?"

"I don't know who you are," Jennifer said, "but I know you aren't Tommy McNamara."

"What do you plan to do with that knowledge?"

"I'm not planning to say anything to Mrs. McNamara, and I certainly won't turn you in, but I do expect something for my silence. I want to know everything that's going on."

Nick's situation only became more complicated a few days later when he finally learned exactly what Christine had in mind. They drove down the mountain, through McNamara Station to a small town several miles further on, where she checked them into a cheap motel and then spent the next hour doing exactly what she'd repeatedly told him they shouldn't do as cousins.

"We have to hurry things along," she said.

"What do you mean?"

"Grandmother's a tough old bird," Christine said. "We're going to have to kill her. *You're* going to have to kill her."

"Me? Why me?"

"If you don't, I'll tell Grandmother you're a fraud and you'll lose everything."

"And if I tell her first?"

"Tell her what, exactly?"

"I'll tell her what really happened to Tommy."

Christine snorted with derision. "You have no clue what really happened, and no one will ever find his body."

"I'll tell her that you've put on this elaborate charade—"

"More likely that you have," Christine said. "I can convince her that you even had me fooled, that you must have killed Tommy in order to take his place."

Nick knew that Jennifer had proof to the contrary, but he didn't mention it.

"It has to be an accident, and it has to be soon."

The following Saturday, Nick told Jennifer everything.

"She wants me to kill the old lady," Nick said. "I can't do it."

"What happens if you don't?"

"Christine will reveal what I've done," Nick explained, "and she'll try to convince Grandmother that I killed Tommy so that I could take his place. But you can prove that isn't true. You have that letter with Christine's handwriting all over it."

"You stand to lose everything, no matter what you do."

"Well, I'm not killing anyone."

"Put Christine off. Tell her you need time to figure out how to do it."

"But I'm not going to do it."

"Just put her off."

Nick did his best, but Christine was impatient. Wednesday night, she slipped into his bedroom and woke him. "What's the delay?"

"Soon," he lied. "Soon."

"It had better be. I won't wait much longer."

The following Saturday afternoon, several hours after Christine and Mrs. McNamara headed down the mountain for their weekly day of pampering, the county sheriff's car rolled up to the gate and the sheriff pressed the intercom button. Nick and Jennifer didn't hear it in the pool house, so he left the car parked at the entrance and walked in. He rang the doorbell and, when he still had no response to his presence, circumnavigated the house, peering in windows.

As he stepped out of the pool house, on his way inside to shower and change clothes, Nick saw the sheriff. He hesitated and his heart began to race, certain that Christine had made good on her threat to reveal his part in her charade. He took a deep breath. He called across the pool, "May I help you?"

The sheriff turned. "Do you live here?"

"I do."

"And you are?"

"Thomas McNamara," Nick said as he walked around the pool to stand before the older man. "What can I do for you?"

"There's no easy way to break this news," the sheriff said. "There's been an accident."

Earlier that morning Christine's car had gone through a guardrail and plunged into the valley below, killing both occupants. There had been a witness, but it had taken all morning to get to the wrecked vehicle and make a preliminary identification of the car's occupants. "They were—"

"My grandmother and my cousin." Nick felt a tear roll down his cheek, and he'd not had to force it. While he felt no sorrow over Christine's death, he had grown to like the old woman.

"I'm sorry for your loss, but I'll need you to identify the bodies."

The sheriff let him know when and where, and then Nick walked him to his vehicle, still parked outside the gate.

After watching the sheriff drive away, Nick returned to the pool house and told Jennifer what he'd just learned.

"I didn't do it," he said. "I didn't. I swear."

"I believe you." Jennifer gathered him into his arms and comforted him. "You never would have harmed Mrs. McNamara. So, it's better this way, isn't it?"

A thorough investigation ruled the deaths an accident, the result of a failure of the automobile's brakes. Through it all, Nick remained in character.

If anyone had bothered to request a DNA test, the jig would have been up, but everyone—the McNamara family trust's attorney, banker, and broker foremost among them—was convinced that Nick was Thomas McNamara because Ethel McNamara had told them he was. To prove otherwise meant the loss of a significant portion of their annual revenue as Mrs. McNamara's last will and testament left everything to a wildlife charity in the event that neither of her grandchildren survived her and because Nick was quite amenable to maintaining the status quo. In addition to gaining control of the family trust, Nick received a significant payout from both Grandmother's and Christine's life insurance polices.

Nick made few changes. He kept the cook, the housekeeper, the handyman, and the service that maintained the grounds. He threw away the key to the storage locker in Queens that contained his previous life and did not renew the annual contract when the year ended. He purchased a new Lexus, and he learned to drive up and down the mountain without breaking into a sweat each time he did.

Jennifer remained at his side throughout, acting not only as the dutiful employee who knew near as much about the McNamara finances as the trust's attorney, banker, and broker, but also as an ever more trustworthy conspirator who moved from the pool house to the main house.

They married in a private ceremony the next year, following an appropriate period of mourning.

Nick Brandt slowly forgot who he had once been as he and his new wife took to their new life. They hired a new personal assistant, an older woman Jennifer vetted, and left much of the day-to-day responsibilities of running the house to her, just as they left money management to the trust's attorney, banker, and broker.

With few responsibilities, the couple spent a great deal of time together, sometimes even slipping out to the pool house on Saturday afternoons to relive those stolen moments they'd had before the deaths of Christine and Mrs. McNamara.

One late fall afternoon, more than a year after their marriage, Nick and Jennifer had a meeting scheduled at McNamara Station Bank & Trust. At the last minute, when Nick found her already in the garage next to his car, Jennifer told him she wasn't feeling well and begged off.

"Are you certain? I thought we could stop for dinner at the steak house tonight."

"No, I—" Jennifer covered her hand with her mouth as if she'd become queasy at the thought.

"That's okay," Nick said. "I can handle this alone."

As he leaned forward to kiss her, Jennifer moved her hand away. Nick reached up and used his thumb to wipe a spot of grease from his wife's cheek, a spot that had not been there a moment earlier, before planting his lips on her cheek.

As he climbed into the car, he said, "I'll see you soon."

"Good-bye, Tommy."

He backed the car out of the garage, waved once, and then headed down the drive, out through the gate, and down the mountain.

Nick was halfway to McNamara Station when he lost control of the Lexus, and his last thought, as he drove over the side of the mountain and the final curtain dropped on his performance as Tommy McNamara, was the realization that his wife's father had trained her as an auto mechanic and that she had always dreamed of life at the top of the mountain.

DERRINGER DEATHSHOT

BY CHRIS JONES

North Dakota

Winter 1876

The train rattled violently beneath my feet, hellbent on throwin' me off. I stood wide and tried to roll with the railroad's twists and turns, but it was mighty hard considerin' I was movin' backwards.

Snow whipped around my ears at near-thirty miles an hour, sharp as metal shards and colder than hell. The moon shone down through the night and turned the snow an eerie silver.

The backstabbin' old rat Kilgore faced me on a separate traincart some fifteen yards away, doing the same full-body wobble I was, his hand hovering over his holstered six-shooter.

He could see where the train was going, but I could only see where it had been...

"Draw, you double-crossin' son-of-a-bitch!" I yelled into the wind.

There wasn't a chance he could hear me.

He yelled something back. There wasn't a chance I could hear him.

The train lurched around a bend and knocked me over. My Stetson flew off, which was a damn shame because I loved that trusty old hat and my head was right cold.

Kilgore stayed on his feet and took the chance to draw his revolver.

Bang! Bang!

Bullets pinged off the traintop around me. I yanked out my Colt and fired some shots in his general direction, tryin' like mad to keep my aim steady and not fall off the train.

I counted five shots from Kilgore, then thought he must be empty and rose to my feet.

Bang!

A bullet sliced through my arm. The crazy bastard had six bullets loaded...

It hurt like hell but it was no time to gripe about it.

Kilgore started reloading his revolver frantically. I stood up and aimed real careful.

I emptied my Colt at him but couldn't tell through the darkness and whipping snow if I hit him or not. Then he raised his reloaded revolver and started slingin' lead back at me.

A bullet screamed past my face, then another one hit the traintop right next to my foot. I shifted my weight, and right then the train hit another bend and I went hurtling through the air.

Before I even knew what was happening I slammed into the snowbank on the side of the railroad and sank deep into the snow.

I took a second to breathe and check if I was injured, but besides the bullet in my arm I couldn't feel anything, so I got my feet under me and rose.

The hard earth was inches from where I had sunk to. I thanked God and the goddamn stars for the good six feet of piled snow to cushion my fall.

Better six feet under snow than six feet under ground...

Then I looked around at the brutal darkness as the train faded into the distance and began cursing the goddamn blizzard, North Dakota, that rotten worm Kilgore, my own damn clumsiness.

Over ten years of bounty huntin' and scalp collectin' and I'd never been in a jam like this...

Marooned by my lonesome out in the northern wilderness during a blizzard with no food or supplies.

Worse, I had a bullet in my arm and I was bleedin' bad.

Even worse than that, I had lost my hat.

I calmed down a little when I spotted my Colt revolver in the snow not far away and picked it up with frozen fingers.

Then I rubbed the silver dollar that always hung around my neck. My boy's silver dollar.

I had to get it to the Pacific, to the salt water. I'd made a promise to his dead mother, years back when I was still young and had something to live for besides this Godforsaken coin around my neck.

I grunted. *It's not just a coin and you know it.*

I couldn't die until my boy had taken a swim in the ocean.

I dusted off my Colt, reloaded it, lowered the hammer into the empty chamber, slid it into my holster, and took out my makings pouch. I managed to roll a crooked quirley and ducked down into the big hole I had made in the snowbank to light it. I inhaled deep and let the smoke calm me as the blizzard roared over my head.

Then I heard screaming. A man screaming. Kilgore, sounded like. I stood up and squinted into the howling wind. I saw footprints on the railroad tracks.

That godless lout fell off the train too. I hope he broke a few bones. I nearly laughed out loud.

I pulled a red handkerchief out of my coat pocket and tied it around my head to try to keep some warmth in. It was no Stetson, but it would have to do. Then I climbed through the snowbank onto the cleared railroad tracks.

Kilgore's footprints were wild, scattered every which way, like he had been running from an angry mob of hornets.

They led to a strange cleared path through the snowbank and into the forest, not cleared flat by shovels but all jagged as if by some giant animal.

What the hell is this old scuzzball doing...

I drew my Colt and began walking down the path. Kilgore's footprints became even wilder, sideways and backwards and all over the damn place.

My heart thumped in my chest, but I had no choice but to follow Kilgore and fill him with lead.

The bastard had tried to backshoot me in the train for the measly $100 bounty on my head. Luckily I had smelled him sneakin' up behind me...

I had been heading back to Wyoming to escape this blasted cold, shake the sheets a bit with my favorite painted lady Claire in my favorite little spot in Burnstown, drink some of ol' Roy's homemade whiskey, and save up some money to finally make a big push west in the spring.

Now I was likely going to freeze to death in the wilderness, a hundred miles from the nearest town.

I'd be damned if I didn't see Kilgore to the afterlife first.

I heard screaming again. I picked up my pace and jogged into the trees. They seemed to close in around me as I ran, like a door slamming shut and latching behind me.

The running kept me warm and the wind lessened as I got deeper into the forest, following the strange cleared path through the knee-high snow.

I followed Kilgore's frantic tracks until they suddenly stopped. I leaped to the side and cocked the hammer on my Colt, ready for Kilgore to come jumping out from behind a tree, but nothing happened.

My muscles were coiled and tense, my breath shallow, my blood pumping...

But everything was silent.

Then a movement caught my eye and I slung my gun around to shoot. I popped off two shots before I realized it was just a puff of some sort of smoke or gas, rising from the frozen earth.

My gunsmoke blew away in the wind and I narrowed my eyes at the strange geyser.

Then more movement caught my eye, and I saw another geyser, then another.

They were all around.

What in the hell...

"Aaaaahhhgghh!!!"

Kilgore's scream pierced the night again. It seemed to come from all around, or above.

Suddenly he sprang out in front of me with empty hands and wide eyes, mouth open in a silent scream, eyes red with terror like he'd seen the Devil himself.

His voice returned and he yelled "They're everywhere!" before I ventilated him with my last three .45 bullets.

He crashed to the ground in a twisted heap and as I walked toward him to make sure the job was done, the smokey gas from the geysers blew through me and I couldn't help but inhale it.

It was sickly sweet, putrid like rotten honey. It burned my nose and eyes worse than rotgut moonshine.

I pulled the handkerchief off my head to cover my nose but saw shadows flash in the corners of my eyes. I tried again to put the handkerchief over my nose but it was gone. I looked for it but it was gone.

"Lou" a voice called. "We see you, Lou!"

I waved my Colt around and pulled the trigger again and again as the hammer fell on spent shells.

The trees began moving, coming alive.

"Looooouuuuuuu" the voice echoed. "We see everything, Lou!"

I tried to pull the trigger again but the gun wasn't in my hand any more.

I drew the Bowie from my left hip and slashed at the frozen air.

"Looouuuu... We know how Colton died, Lou. We know you let him die, Lou."

I roared then and hacked at the air with my knife. The trees were spinning and I felt like I was looking straight up, but I tried my best to look forward and find where this voice was coming from.

"I didn't let him die!" I roared.

"You might as well have killed him yourself, Lou..."

"No! The Injuns paid for it! I killed 'em all!"

"Too late, Lou... Too late, Lou!"

"There was nothin' I could have..."

"They call you Mean Lou Green..." the voice shimmered all around me. "You're not so mean. You're slow and a drunk... That's why Colton died, Lou!" The voice began cackling. "Your son's blood is on your hands, Lou! Lou Greene the Unclean! You'll never wash it away! Not with blood, not with tears, not even with salt water! Hahaha!"

"Come say that to my..."

My Bowie was gone. *Where the hell did it go?* My mind raced. Then I remembered the two-shot Derringer in my boot and reached for it.

"Two bullets in your Derringer, Lou, but only one way to make up for your son's death! Salt water won't make it right... Only your own blood will! Blood for blood!"

I aimed the Derringer at the voice and fired. A searing pain shot across the top of my head and I flinched and dropped the gun.

The voice faded as my ears began ringing. I tried to look around but everything was white.

White snow, white trees, white sky.

Then I looked down. My hands were red, covered in blood, shaking fiercely. Then blood began streaming down my face, into my eyes, onto the white snow at my feet.

Red and white. Red and white.

My ears rang.

Red and white. Red or white?

They blended together into a cruel pulpy pink that swept over me and flooded my senses.

My eyes flashed open and I saw treetops, stars, and falling snow.

I sprang up but every joint in my body screamed and I fell back down.

I had a few inches of snow on top of me that I brushed off as I stared up at the moon through the bare tree branches and watched my breath rise into the frozen air.

Everything was brutally clear. The air, the sky, the trees, the snow.

I rose to my feet slowly this time and shook off the snow, tried to shake off the memories.

The geysers were gone, but the voice still rang in my head.

Blood for blood, Lou!

I picked up my Derringer from the ground and dusted it off. Still one shot left.

I gritted my teeth to stop them from chattering. If I didn't start moving soon I would freeze solid.

I tried to roll a quirley but my fingers were too cold, so I rummaged through my coat and pulled out my half-full flask of whiskey, took a long pull.

It burned through my guts as I looked around the empty wilderness and clutched my boy's silver dollar around my neck, then looked back at the Derringer in my hand.

My body felt weak from blood loss and nauseous from adrenaline and my head pounded like a fresh hangover.

It would almost be a mercy.

An owl screeched and I looked up to the branch it was perched on, staring at me with big yellow eyes, accusin' me of something or other.

"Yeah, you're right..." I mumbled out loud. "I couldn't have done it anyway. I'm too damn stubborn to die."

Then I tucked the Derringer into my boot with a grunt, took another pull of whiskey, and started walking West.

94

THE BIG GRAY SPOT IN THE KERNUGGLE CLOSET

BY TIMOTHY J. SPADONI

Mildred Kernuggle felt a gentle shaking of her townhouse. Like when the waste management trucks came to empty the garbage and recycling bins every Tuesday morning. But it wasn't Tuesday morning.

Mildred looked around her home which rested in the middle of the maple tree-shaded street of Hampton Lane in the little town of Sandy Shore. She searched for things out of order, because Leo would not be happy about things being out of order.

As she walked through the house, she thought about her marriage to Leo, and the best six months along with the worst six and a half years of her life. The six best months were the ones right after their wedding when Leo was a warehouse manager with a blossoming career, working for the Sandy Shore Container Manufacturing Plant. But then the company automated. To their credit, the company offered him the opportunity to learn to program the new equipment. Unfortunately for Leo, designing multiple simultaneous robotic movements, and the mastery of the equations needed to fully utilize robotic devices were far beyond his capability. When Leo's clumsy attempt at programming the equipment resulted in a complete order fulfillment disaster, upper management wasted no time in replacing him with a young IT graduate. The company reassigned Leo to the packing line.

Leo decided the reason he couldn't understand the programming procedures was due to Mildred not keeping their house "in order." And it was up to him to correct this shortcoming. He based his "correction" on a story that Mildred wished she never told him. It was the story of the worst night of her life.

When Mildred was eight, she lost her way in the Shawnee National Forest during one of her family's nature walks. She searched and called but was hopelessly turned around. The closer she thought she was to finding her parents, the farther away she wandered. She spent the night in the woods and imagined the worst from the sounds in the dark. The rustlings in the trees—a bear creeping up to maul her. The whispers of the wind—an owl about to swoop down to tear at her face. The flutterings in the sky—bats gathering to dive at her head and tangle themselves in her hair. She wouldn't lay down for fear of whatever crawled on the ground and she wouldn't lean against a tree because of what clung to its trunk. In the morning, her parents and a park ranger found her standing and shivering, and still wide eyed with fright. Since then, the dark terrified her. She installed nightlights in every room and kept flashlights with fresh batteries always within easy reach.

Once Leo found out about Mildred's greatest fear, his usual method of correction consisted of forcing her into their bathroom without any lights on. He adjusted the door knob so that it locked from the outside and even rewired the light switches to turn off and on from the outside wall. He removed the nightlight and sealed the door to stop light from seeping in. Locked in the darkened room, Mildred's childhood trauma came rushing back. Despite her cries of terror, Leo kept her in there until he felt she "learned her lesson."

Mildred thought of Leo's corrections as she continued to search for the source of the shaking. He considered himself an expert on all things, especially Mildred. But she learned long ago, that contrary to his own inflated self-opinion, he really knew very little about most things, especially about her. He didn't know that she eventually learned to embrace the darkness which terrified her at eight and during her first correction. During her second correction, she listened for the sounds of the bear, owl, bats, and all the other things that frightened her in the woods. She realized none of those things was in the dark of the bathroom, and instead of fearing the darkness, she learned to love it.

Alone in the dark bathroom, and with time to herself, she imagined a life without Leo, or a life with a different Leo—a Leo that cared instead of bullied, was hopeful instead of bitter, and was filled with laughter instead of complaints. She knew he would never change and wondered if she'd ever have the courage to leave him. But she doubted it would ever happen; she held sacred the "for better or worse" vows she made on their wedding day. She hoped that one day her sacrifice would be rewarded.

She also learned that for all Leo's bellowing about being in charge, what he really wanted was for someone to be in charge of him. Once Mildred conquered her terrors, she felt that in some ways, she also conquered Leo.

Mildred stopped ruminating about Leo when she reached the guest bedroom on the second floor. There she found something very much out of order. An extremely odd, gray, blurry, five-foot circle of...nothing. It hovered in the place where the closet used to be. The door and doorframe, the ceiling, back and side walls, and everything that used to be in the closet were simply gone. Gone were the old coats and clothes that were too worn and out of fashion to wear but that Leo would never dream of donating to the Goodwill because nobody was going to get "something for nothing" from him. Also gone were Leo's overflow of bowling trophies that he stored in the closet because they would no longer fit in the trophy cabinet in the living room.

"Ha!" Mildred laughed out loud seeing his precious trophies gone. Then she quickly covered her mouth just in case he came home early, but laughed out loud again knowing it would be worth it even if he blamed her for their disappearance.

"Oh no, not my candlesticks!" she cried when she realized they were also gone. The crystal candlesticks were her only reminders of her mother, who passed away ten years ago. Perfect for formal dinners but never used because Leo did not believe in anything more formal than a backyard beer fest with Milwaukee's Finest. She would miss the candlesticks most of all.

Something told her not to, but she couldn't help herself from reaching into the area of gray nothing to see if she could find her candlesticks in the murky ball.

"Help me!" she yelled to the empty townhouse when the ball snatched her hand and instantly pulled the rest of her into its center and to a place blacker than any forest or locked bathroom could ever be. Her startled shout was the last sound Mildred Kernuggle made in the townhouse in the middle of the maple tree-shaded street of Hampton Lane in the little town of Sandy Shore.

*

Leo Kernuggle didn't know much about science, math, or history. He knew little about the world outside of the bars and bowling alleys in and around Sandy Shore. But he did know when to grab onto a good thing when it came along and when to duck from a bad one. He was also particularly adept at identifying the things he didn't like, and what he mostly didn't like was his house being out of order. When he opened the front door, the hairs rising on his arms told him his house was not in order.

"Mildred, I'm home. The idiots at work were even stupider than usual and I'm hot, and I'm tired, and I want a beer."

Mildred never left the house without Leo and he couldn't imagine where she might have gone. "Mildred! Where the hell are you?" he called again. "If you're playing games, I'm not in the mood. You know I don't like games." He swiveled his head around, looking for her in the kitchen, living room, and dining room before going upstairs. "Mildred!" he called again.

Leo opened the guest bedroom door and popped his head in. "Mildred, I'm not going to ask you again. What the hell is going on? What the..." He stopped when he saw the gray spot in the closet. "What is this? Where the hell are my trophies? What the hell did you do with them?" He reached out to the strange gray circle to investigate, but the hairs on his arms raised and he backed away just before touching the circle's edge. Leo's sixth sense about danger kicked in, and though he didn't know it at the time, it saved him from Mildred's fate.

Leo left the guest bedroom and looked for his wife in their main bedroom and bathroom, but couldn't find her there, nor anywhere. "What the hell, Mildred, where are you and what's going on?" he called out to the empty house. He went back to the guest bedroom and stared at the fuzzy gray ball in the closet. "Goddammit, this isn't right. Where are my things? And where is Mildred?" Leo said to the empty closet. Leo backed away from it and thought very hard about what to do next. Thinking wasn't one of Leo's strengths, but for once, his connections were all firing at the same time and he had one of his rare bright ideas. He picked up the phone and called the police.

"Sandy Shore Police Department, what can we do for you?" answered Cyndi Baker, the dispatcher on duty that day.

"This is Leo Kernuggle at 1539 Hampton Lane and I'm reporting that there's a fuzzy gray ball floating in my closet. I think it took all of my bowling trophies and I want them back. Oh yeah, and my wife is missing too. If I don't get her back, I'll have to get someone else to clean the house."

"Sir, if this is a joke, I have to tell you that you could be in serious trouble. We don't look kindly on prank calls." The dispatcher warned.

"Listen, honey," Leo said, "this is no joke. There's this empty spot in my closet where my trophies used to be. And some other stuff that I know we had in there is gone too. So is my wife. Now, there's no way she'd go on her own. So, you just get someone over here and have them take a look. I want that thing out of my closet. I want my stuff back. I want Mildred back too 'cause I'm startin' to get hungry and there's no dinner on the table."

"Okay sir, you sit tight and I'll send a car over to investigate. But if this is not a legitimate complaint, I will warn you again that..."

"You just get them over here quick, sweetheart. I don't pay taxes just to wait all day for you people to show up. I've got things to do and..."

The phone went dead in Leo's hand. "Feisty. I like 'em like that," Leo said when he put down the phone.

Twenty minutes later, Officers Judy Grady and Connie Bartino, two of Sandy Shore's best, rang Leo's doorbell. "Took you long enough," said Leo when he opened the door. "Oh, and look at this, they sent two chick cops, a lot of good that'll do me. Well, come on in, the day's wasting away."

The two officers stopped in the doorway. They looked at each other for a second, and then Officer Grady deadpanned to Leo. "Sir, we're responding to a call you made regarding your wife being missing and about some sort of a disturbance in one of your closets. We're here to help, but we have no problem getting back in our car if you'd rather two male officers respond. After we leave, two other officers will be sent to your house...when they become available," she said.

Like most humor, other than slapstick, the officer's intent was lost on Leo. "Yeah yeah sure, and when will that be, next week? My tax dollars, hard at work. No, you two will do. Just come in and I'll show you this disturbance I called about," said Leo, ushering the two officers to the guest bedroom on the second floor.

"Sir, don't you think we should talk about your wife first?" asked Bartino.

"Listen, you just figure out what's going on in my closet. Fix that and then we can talk about getting that wife of mine back."

"All right, sir, we'll take a quick look at your closet, but then we're going to talk about your wife. That's our number one priority," she said.

"Sure, sure. Just come in and take a look," said Leo when they got to the bedroom door.

Bartino and Grady stepped in and saw the odd gray circle of emptiness in the space just beyond the closet door. "What the...what is this?" asked Grady, reaching for the circle.

"Don't touch it, Judy!" warned Bartino. Grady moved her hand back from the edge of the circle just before she touched its edge. Then she took out her baton and instead of her hand, she used that to touch the gray spot.

Something in the gray circle snatched the baton out of her hand and it instantly disappeared.

"Smart lady," said Leo. "I wasn't gonna touch it with my hand either. I think something's not right about that spot, but I wanted to see what'd happen if one of you put your hand on it."

Officer Bartino looked a little sick at what might have happened to her partner if she had put her hand into the gray spot. "Sir, we're going to ask you to step out of the room while we assess the danger of whatever it is that's in your closet," she said, pushing Leo not too gently out of the room.

"Ha! Yeah, you go ahead and assess. I'll be right here when you come out and then you can tell me what you're going to do about my stuff. My trophies were in there and I want 'em back. No one or no damned spot's got a right to take my things. Yeah, and I wanna hear what you're gonna do about my wife too," Leo said, as he lumbered away from the officers.

*

"Connie, this is way beyond our pay grade. I don't even think it's a police matter," said Grady when the door was closed. "You know what? I'm going to call the SSFD and dump it in their laps. You call headquarters and let them know our situation. Then keep an eye on Mr. Kernuggle while I call the fire department."

Bartino started walking out of the bedroom, phone in hand. "Okay, it's a plan. We can talk to Mr. Kernuggle about his missing wife all night, but we'd be crazy not to think it had something to do with that thing in the closet."

"Sandy Shore Fire Department, how can I help you?" answered Rebecca Tonnes, the Sandy Shore Fire Department dispatcher on duty that day.

"Hey Rebecca, this is Judy Grady," said Office Grady.

"Hi Judy, I was going to call you about the local bands for the anniversary dance. We've got to go see them to figure out which one we should pick." Judy Grady and Rebecca Tonnes were both members of the Women's Club of St. Andrew's Parish, and were on the music and entertainment committee for the parish's upcoming 60th anniversary party.

"That's great Rebecca, but this is a police call. If I get a chance tomorrow, we can get together for the party."

"Oh sorry, what's up?"

"Well, Connie and I are at a townhouse on 1539 Hampton Lane. We've got a situation going on in one of their closets that we don't know how to handle, and we're hoping you can send over some guys to check it out for us?"

"Is there a fire?"

"No, we think it's, well sort of more of a possible potential for a problem, maybe? I really can't explain it, which is why I'm calling you. We don't think it's something for the police, and I don't know if it's even for the SSFD, but maybe you guys can check it out and figure out what to do."

"Okay, let me put you over to Delaney. She'll send a team out."

"Thanks, Rebecca," said Officer Grady to the "on-hold" music that had already started playing before she could say goodbye.

"Chief Delaney, how can I help you?" answered the chief.

"Hey Chief, it's Judy Grady."

"Judy, what's going on? You guys need any help with the anniversary party?" Chief Delaney's wife, Susan, was also in the Women's Club of St. Andrew's Parish and also on the planning committee for the anniversary party.

"No, Suzy and I are good. This is more of an official call, Chief. Connie and I are over at a townhouse at 1539 Hampton Lane. This guy's got something weird going on with his closet. It's pretty hard to explain, but I don't think it's a police issue and I'm figuring you guys would be better at handling it."

"Is it a fire, someone hurt, a cat up a tree?"

Judy sighed. "Well, like I was telling Rebecca, we're thinking it might be more of a potential problem rather than an actual one. But we really can't explain it. I think it's something you guys have to see for yourself."

"That sounds pretty mysterious. Are you okay?"

"Oh yeah, we're fine. Just send some guys over and we can show them the situation."

"Okay, Judy," Chief Delaney said, "they'll be there in a couple of minutes. You and Connie sit tight."

"Thanks, Chief." Judy ended the call and started wondering about Mildred Kernuggle and the gray ball in the closet. When she thought of what might have happened to her...

She closed the bedroom door behind her and went down to the living room. She joined her partner to find out all Leo knew about the closet and his wife. It didn't amount to much more than his lamentations about his missing dinner and his complaints about his trophies.

*

Fire engine number six pulled up in front of the Kernuggle townhouse on 1539 Hampton Lane in response to the call from Officer Grady about a situation in the townhouse's closet. Fireman Lieutenant Steven Jeffries rang the doorbell with three other firefighters trailing behind him.

"Hey Steve, guys," said Judy when she let them in.

"Hey, Judy," said Steve. "What seems to be the trouble here?"

"Come on in and I'll show you," Grady said as she led the four men into the upstairs bedroom. She kept them away from the closet and started to explain. "This is the weirdest thing I've ever seen. Be very careful around it and whatever you do, do...not...touch it. I put my baton in there and it sucked the stick right out of my hand. I was lucky I hadn't put the strap on my wrist. If I had, I think I might have been sucked in too. I don't know what it is, but I don't think there's anything the police can do about it."

Steve and the other firemen stared at the gray spot. "What the heck is that thing?" Steve said. He picked up a paperback book from one of the shelves and moved towards the spot.

"Really, Steve, be careful," Judy warned.

He moved the end of the book closer to the gray area and then into it. Nothing happened for a half a second and then it was snapped out of his hand

and winked out of sight into the gray space. "Whoa...what the hell is that? Is that what happened to your baton?"

"Yep, same thing. Any ideas what it might be?"

"I've never seen anything like it either. You guys have any ideas?" he asked his team. The other three firemen shook their heads, and stepped back a little further from the closet. One of them picked up another paperback and handed it to Steve. "Here, Boss, toss this at it and see if it happens again."

He took the book, moved back a couple of steps and lobbed it into the circle of gray. The instant the book touched the edge, it was sucked in and out of sight, just like the other book and what Judy Grady described happened to her baton. "Jeez, said Steve. I have no idea what that is. There's no electric cord going into it or heat coming out of it or anything."

"That's not the worst of it, Steve," Office Grady said. "Mr. Kernuggle reported that his wife is missing. Listening to him go on about their relationship, I'm not thinking she was the type to leave on her own."

"Oh man, you don't think...".

"Yeah, that maybe she got a little too close and Twilight Zoned out of here to where the other stuff went? That's what I think, and Connie and I aren't volunteering to go in after her."

"No, that wouldn't be a good idea," he said. "Listen, I'll tell you what, let's get out of here. I'm not seeing that it's doing anything dangerous on its own, only when something touches it, so I think we can leave it alone while we figure this out. Why don't you get some of that police tape and put it across the door to keep Mr. Kernuggle out of here. I'm going to call the Chief to see what she wants to do."

"Okay," she said, "that's a plan. We'll keep the missing Mrs. Kernuggle in our sights and you guys deal with this closet thing."

Everyone moved out of the bedroom. Office Grady went to get the police barricade tape while Steve sent the rest of his team to the truck to keep them out of danger and then thought about what he should say to the Fire Chief.

He went back into his truck to make the call. Silly, he supposed. He could just as easily have made the call from inside the townhouse, but he felt more in control sitting in engine number six. He punched in the direct number for Chief Delaney.

The Chief answered her phone on the first ring. "Talk to me, Steve."

"Hey Chief, I'm over at the Kernuggle townhouse on Hampton Lane," he said.

"Whatcha got?"

"Well, there's something pretty crazy going on over here and I'm not sure there's anything we can do about it. This is way out of our league."

"What do you mean, out of your league? What's going on?"

"This is kind of nuts, but there's this gray circular disturbance about five feet in diameter or so of something I don't know what, just hanging there in this guy's closet. None of us has ever seen anything like it. It doesn't seem to be dangerous outside of its area, but anything that gets past its edge gets sucked right in and then just disappears. I touched it with the end of a book and snap, that book was gone. The same thing happened to another book I tossed at it. The guys and Judy Grady saw it happen too."

"Steve," said the Chief, "let me get this straight. You're telling me that in a closet in a townhouse on Hampton Lane here in Sandy Shore, there's a gray ball that sucks up anything that gets close to it?"

"Anything we tried, Chief. Yeah, I know how it sounds. Judy said she touched the edge of it with her baton and it sucked that right in too. Oh, get this, Judy says the owner's wife is missing and she thinks she might have gotten too close and ended up where the other stuff went."

"Jesus, Steve, what're we dealing with there?"

"That's what I'm saying, Chief. I don't know what this is. But I pulled my guys out and put them back in the truck. I don't want them anywhere near it. And I don't want the press over here either until we can get a handle on it."

"Okay, okay, Steve. It's your call, but this better not be some sort of bet to see how much of a crazy story I'd buy over the phone," she said.

"Chief, you know me. I wouldn't do anything like that and I would never joke about pulling my guys out of a situation," he said.

"All right, I'll come on over and take a look. Should I bring anything or anyone else?"

"Yeah, I had a thought about that. Why don't you stop over at Doctor Nathan Adamson's house and ask him to join us? I've got a feeling he might be the only one in town that can figure out what's going on."

"The guy that teaches at the college?"

"Yeah, I think he teaches physics and this is more in his area than ours. You tell him what I said and that we need his opinion. We're going to hang tight until you two get here."

"Okay, Steve. We'll be there as soon as possible."

And it wasn't long before the Chief showed up in a SSFD cruiser with Doctor Adamson in tow. Steve jumped out of his truck to greet them. "Chief, thanks for getting here so fast."

"I wanted to beat the press. Once word gets out about strange stuff in this town, the reporters show up like sharks in bloody water. Doctor Adamson was kind enough to come along after I explained to him what you saw. Steve, Doctor Nathan Adamson. Doctor, this is Fire Lieutenant Steve Jeffries. He's the fellow who requested we bring you over to take a look at what they found in that house," she said.

"Lieutenant Jeffries, it's a pleasure to meet you," Nathan said, shaking Steve's hand.

"You too, Doctor," Steve said, walking the Doctor and the Chief over to the house. "And thank you for coming along so quickly. I'd like to get your opinion on what we need to do with it. I'm afraid none of us has any experience with something like this."

"Oh, it's no problem. This is the most exciting thing I've done all week. Contrary to popular opinion, sometimes it gets a little dull teaching the same course every year. I must say, I'm intrigued by what the Chief described."

Doctor Adamson, Steve, and Chief Delaney walked into the townhouse and started to go up to the bedroom so that Nathan could begin his investigation. Leo saw more people coming in and stood in their way. "Now, who are you people and why is it that anyone can just walk in here without so much as a never-mind to me? I still got rights, ain't I?" Leo said, blocking the group.

"Mr. Kernuggle," said Steve, "this is Doctor Nathan Adamson from the college. He's going to have a look at what's in your bedroom. If anyone can figure it out, he can. And this is our Fire Chief, Bonnie Delaney. She'll be running the Fire Department's operation."

"Ah Jeez, another broad. That's just what we need," said Leo to the Fire Chief. "Ain't you got a husband to stay home with and take care of?"

"For your information, Mr. Kernuggle, I have a wife," said the Chief, "and she's perfectly capable of taking care of herself. Now please, move aside so that we can do our jobs."

Leo smirked at the revelation. "Oh, you're one of those, are you? Well, that's all we need," said Leo to the Chief. "This whole operation is just one big boneheaded move after another. I oughta just kick the whole lot of you out of here."

"Excuse me? What did you just say?"

Leo raised his voice and puffed his chest out as much as he could. "You heard me, lady, if that's what you are. You with your fancy title, pretending you can run things like a man. You give me two cents and I'll tell you what I think about..."

"All right, that's enough, Mr. Kernuggle," Officer Bartino said, putting herself between Leo and Chief. "You get back over there and sit down. I don't think we need to hear any more of your opinions about anything."

"Hey, you listen to me," Leo said, getting louder. "This is still my house and ain't no bitches gonna be running around here telling me who I can let in and who I can't. I got my rights, you know."

The officer pulled her night stick out and poked it into Leo's chest which immediately deflated. "You say one more word and you're going to be spending the night thinking about your rights in our house. Do you understand me?" Bartino said, pushing Leo back from the group by the door. "Now, you sit down. I don't want to hear another word out of you, or Officer Grady and I are going to drag your ass right over to headquarters and charge you with interfering with a police investigation. You got that?"

Leo sat down in one of the living room chairs and glared at the two officers.

"Sorry about that, Chief," Bartino called back to Chief Delaney. "We'll keep it quiet down here while you all work in the bedroom."

"That's okay, Connie," she called back. "We get our share too."

"Okay, Doctor, sorry about that," said Steve, leading the Chief and Doctor Adamson upstairs. "Well, here it is," he said, showing them the gray ball hovering in the closet.

They stopped and stared at the weird gray circle of...nothing. "Oh, my," said Nathan. "I've never seen anything like this. You say it just appeared?"

Steve rubbed his neck. "Well, that's what Judy and Connie said that Mr. Kernuggle said, but I've got other thoughts. The guys and I went up and took a look at the top of the house while we were waiting for you to get here. There's a perfectly round hole right through the roof, the rafters, and the ceiling above the ball. We're thinking it must have fallen from somewhere and stopped right here."

"Oh, my God. I can't believe I'm seeing this," the doctor said. "We've always talked about something like this being possible, but no one ever thought we'd really see it."

"What do you mean, Doctor?" Delaney asked.

"I'm sorry, one minute Chief. Lieutenant Jeffries, you say the gray area pulled in a number of items and they disappeared?"

"That's right, Doctor."

"Could you show me?"

"Sure," Steve said. "Here, let me take another one of these paper backs. Now, the first time I held it close to the gray area. Once it passed through the edge, it was pulled right out of my hand and disappeared. I'm not sure I want to do that again; it feels too dangerous. But watch as I throw this one into the ball."

Steve tossed the book at the gray circle from a few feet back, and as soon as it crossed the edge, it snapped out of sight.

"Oh, my," Nathan said. "Please, do that again, maybe from the other side?"

"Sure," Steve said. He picked up another book and tossed it into the gray ball from a different angle. The book disappeared just like the other one as soon as it passed its edge. "So, what do you think, Doctor? The guys and I put down bets that it might be one of those black holes all you physicists keep talking about."

"Steve!"

"Sorry, Chief. It won't happen again."

"Any thoughts Doctor?" Steve asked.

"Well, you might be on the right track with the black hole theory," started Nathan. "But a black hole is huge, far bigger than this. Some of them can be half the size of the whole solar system. My guess is that it might be something we call a micro black hole, something molecular size."

"So, it's still a black hole, right? Then I win my bet," Steve said.

"Steve!"

"Sorry, Chief. It won't happen again."

"Well, yes and no," Nathan continued. "If it were one micro black hole, we wouldn't be seeing a gray area, it would be black dot, if we saw it at all. I'm thinking maybe it's a lot of super micro black holes in a stable orbiting pattern around each other. It's wildly unbelievable, but they somehow found a sort of gravitational equilibrium, right here, right in this closet."

Doctor Adamson sat down in one of the chairs in the bedroom and put his head in his hands. "Oh, I think I'm dizzy. You don't know what this means. No physicist would ever think we could run into something like this. We've got to get someone in here who knows more than me. I'm just a community college teacher, for God's sake."

"All right, Doctor, just take it easy for a minute. Who do you suggest we contact?" Chief Delaney said.

"Okay, let me think...there's an expert at the University of Chicago. Her name is Doctor Anita Hensel. I'm sure she'd drop whatever she's working on to examine this phenomenon. Could you see about getting her here as soon as possible?"

"I'll get right on it," Chief Delaney said, pulling her phone out to call the mayor and start things moving.

"In the meantime," Nathan continued, "we've got to get this room secure. We don't know if this is putting out any radiation, and we could all be in danger. This whole house could be deadly for all we know."

"What do you need, Doctor?" asked Steve, stepping back from the closet as far as he could.

Adamson started ticking items off on his fingers, "We need lead shielding. Contact as many dentists as you can and get whatever lead smocks they have and get them over here. Tell them it's an emergency. There's a couple more in the Physics Department we can commandeer. We also need communications equipment, at least a couple of computers and monitors. Let's get all the furniture out of here and set up desks at the end of the room as far away from the ball as possible. We need all of this done yesterday."

*

Leo Kernuggle simmered over the things being out of order in his house and gave his opinion to any stray ear within shouting distance. And he stewed about how everyone moved in and just took over. Not only had the Fire Department with that bitch of a Fire Chief set up permanent residence, but now the Police Chief was here too. And then there were those two cops who thought they could run him around any way they pleased. At first, everyone wanted him to go to a hotel for his own safety, but he was having none of that. Who knows what they might have taken from his house? He reminded them about his rights and how he was the one to call the police in the first place and then he threatened to call his lawyer. They let him stay if he agreed to stay out of the way. He figured he'd won even if the cops only did it to keep tabs on him.

*

Good news travels fast. Bad news travels faster. Sensational news travels the fastest, and an odd gray ball that sucked up anything that came in contact with it hovering in a closet in Leo Kernuggle's townhouse in the middle of the maple tree shaded street of Hampton Lane was the most sensational news to ever happen in the little town of Sandy Shore. The police tried their best to keep any word of the strange occurrence from leaking out, but they couldn't keep the neighbors from seeing the police cars and fire equipment parked in the driveway and street. This led to a number of them calling the newspapers and television stations, trying to get credit for being the first to alert them of a story.

This security failure led to a phalanx of film crews and reporters flanking the area and reporting on the growing number of cops, headed by Police Chief Kaminski, trying to keep the chaos in order. They also reported on the number of firemen bringing in serious-looking equipment. They yelled out questions to anyone looking important enough to have any information, but so far, all they had were far more questions than answers.

This scene greeted Doctor Anita Hensel as she made her way through the throng and into the townhouse. "Good God," she said, coming through the front door. "Who's in charge here? Aren't you people able to control that zoo?"

"Doctor Hensel," Chief Kaminski said. "Come on in, please. I'm Chief of Police Greg Kaminski. Sorry about the circus out there, but freedom of the press and all that. Reporters, you can't live with them and you can't shoo them away, if you know what I mean."

"Chief Kaminski, I'd like to get right down to business if you don't mind. If Doctor Adamson is right, we don't have much time to lose. Please show me the anomaly," insisted Doctor Hensel.

"Sure, Doctor Hensel, it's upstairs," Kaminski said, leading the physicist up to the guest bedroom. "We need to get you shielded before you go in," the police chief said, offering a lead-lined smock, gloves and head covering for the physicist. "Doctor Adamson doesn't think there's any danger from short-term exposure, but he felt it was better to be safe than sorry. The rest of us are staying pretty far away.

"Thank you, Chief. I don't really think we have anything to worry about. This has to be some sort of a very localized atmospheric disturbance, but I suppose until we know what we're dealing with, it's better to be careful," Doctor Hensel said as she slipped on the coverings.

The bedroom had been cleaned out of all its furniture and work lights were brought in along with a couple of cameras on tripods to document any changes in the ball. A conference table faced the closet and on it were several laptops, a couple of digital recorders, more cameras, testing equipment, pens, and pads of paper. Several chairs were also set up behind and around the table. Lead sheets had been brought in and held up by quickly constructed rods and supports positioned around the room and in front of the table. The fuzzy gray spot hadn't changed position since Leo discovered it the day before.

A smock-protected Doctor Adamson sat working at one of the computers. He rose to greet the physicist when she entered the bedroom. "Doctor Hensel, thank you so much for coming on such short notice, and thank you for taking my request so seriously."

Doctor Hensel stared at the fantastic gray ball hanging in the closet of the bedroom. She looked at the object from each side as much as she could and stepped back. She finally turned to Nathan and responded to his greeting.

"Doctor Adamson, thank you for contacting me. I'd normally dismiss a report like this as preposterous and would've told the cops who came to pick me up that I had more important things to do. But I was impressed by your presentation at last year's Midwest Physics Conference. Your lecture on the mathematical proof that black hole singularities are portals to alternate universes was innovative. When they told me you were involved, I was intrigued.

"However, I was sure what you had here must be some atmospheric disturbance or localized ball lighting. But now that I see it, I almost can't believe it. We'll have to do more tests, of course, but from what you said about what happens when something touches it, I'm inclined to agree with your assessment."

She turned back to the ball wide-eyed. "Can I see its interaction with an object?"

"Sure, Doctor. But I take precautions when I do this." Nathan picked up one of the metal bars that had been brought for testing and inserted it into the end of a five-foot piece of hollow pvc brought in as a makeshift holder. He approached the gray ball and slowly moved the end of the metal bar towards its edge. The tip of the bar pierced the ball and was immediately snatched from the pipe and disappeared from sight.

"Oh Lord," Doctor Hensel said. "I never thought I'd actually see that happen. I think you're right, Doctor. As unbelievable as it might be, I think what we've got here is a case of an honest-to-goodness micro black hole. Stephen Hawking would've loved this."

"Right?" Echoed the doctor. "But it can't be just one black hole, that'd be solid black, not gray. Plus, it would still be headed to the middle of the Earth and not stuck in whatever equilibrium this thing managed. I think what we have is many micro black holes in a stabilized orbit. That would account for the gray color. Photons of visible light go in and are lost when they hit a micro blackhole.

But enough of them must be shooting through the spaces between and coming back out."

"Yes, that would explain the gray," she agreed. "But to really be sure about your hypothesis, we'd have to devise a way to verify it."

"And obviously, we only have a limited ability to study the object here..." Nathan started.

"Yes, we need to get it back to a lab at the university or possibly over at Fermilab," Doctor Hensel finished.

"But how would we move it?" Nathan wondered.

"I believe if we surround the whole thing with industrial magnets, we'd be able to move it without touching it. We could get the police to escort it back to the lab. Then we'd analyze its properties and figure out its uses," Doctor Hensel said. "And I think we can drop the doctors, don't you? From now on, I'm Anita. After all, we'll be working side by side on all the testing and analysis, and of course, the papers we'll be submitting for review."

"That's very generous of you, Anita."

She shook her head. "Not at all, Nathan. After all, your name's going to be the first one said during the presentation of the Nobel Prize in Physics."

Nathan laughed, "That's getting a little ahead of the game, don't you think?"

"I can dream, can't I?" she said. "Besides, I think you're not seeing all the possibilities. If we learn to harness the amount of Hawking radiation that the number of micro black holes might be generating, we could tap into an almost unlimited source of power. And it would be eons before any of these singularities dissipate, if ever. We'd be able to produce the largest amount of clean energy on the planet. It might be possible to supply this entire region with free energy."

"All right, that's enough," Leo yelled, entering the bedroom unprotected and unaccompanied by any of the police who were on the lower level. "I've been listening to you two going on about what you're gonna do, but no one's said one word to me about moving anything out of my closet. This is my house and what's in it is mine no matter how it got here. I've got rights and all this talk about getting free energy is stopping right now. No one's getting anything free from me. I'm still out a bunch of trophies, not to mention a wife too, and you're not moving one thing out of my house without me getting what's coming to me."

"Get out of here!" Nathan shouted. "You don't have any protection on and we don't know what this thing can do."

"You keep your yap shut, Adamson," Leo said, taking another step closer to the pair of physicists. "I wasn't too happy about them bringing you on board. No pencil neck's telling me what I can and can't do in my own house. Now, I'm telling you what you're gonna do. You two get out of here right now."

"Mr. Kernuggle, you need to get out of this room," Doctor Hensel said. "It's not safe for you in here."

"No smart ass, Chicago bitch of a doctor is pulling one over on me," Leo said as he grabbed Hensel's lead smock and started shaking her. This is my house, and you're leaving, right now!"

"Mr. Kernuggle, get your hands off of her!" shouted Nathan.

Officers Bartino and Grady burst into the room, followed by Lieutenant Jeffries, and Chiefs Kaminski and Delaney. "Let her go!" shouted Bartino as she and Grady grabbed at Leo Kernuggle's arms.

Get off me, you bitches!" Leo roared and tried to push the two officers away. Bartino tore Leo's fingers from Doctor Hensel's smock and Grady pulled him back from the physicist. Leo struggled to keep hold, flailing his arms around trying to grab the doctor once more.

"Let go of me!" yelled Doctor Hensel, pushing Leo's chest, sending him stumbling into the two officers. Bartino started to fall back, pulling Leo to the left while Grady pushed him sideways. Leo's left foot caught onto the right one and he tripped to the side, towards the fuzzy gray spot in his closet.

No!" he cried, putting his arms out to stop from falling into the ball. But nothing could stop both of his hands from going past the edge of the gray area. Leo wailed and was instantly pulled into the abyss. His startled yell was the last sound Leo Kernuggle made in the townhouse in the middle of the maple tree-shaded street of Hampton Lane in the little town of Sandy Shore.

Everyone in the room stood in horror at what had just happened to Leo Kernuggle.

"Nobody moves!" Chief Kaminski ordered.

"No," Doctor Hensel said. "Everyone, back away from the anomaly and get out of this room. We've got to contain this thing as quickly as we can and get it to a secure facility. It's far too dangerous to be around people who don't understand it."

"But what about Mr. Kernuggle?" the Police Chief asked. "What are we going to do about him?"

"I'm afraid all that's left of Mr. Kernuggle is your report, Chief Kaminski," Nathan said. "The laws of the universe dictate that nothing comes back from falling into a black hole. Doctor Hensel's right. The best thing to do now is get this away from Sandy Shore and into the proper facility."

The police left the room and retreated to their station in the townhouse to discuss how they'd report on the demise of Leo Kernuggle. Lieutenant Jeffries and Fire Chief Delaney also left, but figured since Leo's disappearance was a police matter, they didn't need to mention it in their report. Doctors Adamson and Hensel continued their discussion regarding the steps needed to move the object and the plans for its study and use for power generation.

The reporters waiting outside wondered when they'd get further news of the object.

Many of the neighbors who lived on Hampton Lane would miss Mildred Kernuggle.

No one thought twice about Leo.

*

Leo Kernuggle woke up in the middle of the guest bedroom in his townhouse on Hampton Lane. He had a terrific headache, and wore nothing but a thin shirt and some sort of cloth wrapped around his nether regions–and he had a metal collar around his neck.

"What the hell's this thing?" he asked, to no one in particular, tugging on the collar but not loosening it. "Hey, what's going on here?" he asked again looking down at what he was wearing.

"That's what I've been trying to figure out," said a woman seated in a chair at the end of the room. She looked surprisingly like Leo's wife, Mildred, but more well-dressed, slimmer, more muscular, and exuding far more confidence than Mildred ever attempted.

"You just sort of popped out of nowhere into my den," she said. "That was eighteen hours ago and you've been asleep the whole time. I thought you might never wake up. You weren't wearing your collar, which normally would have been bad for you, but after I put a spare one on, I figured a correction would be a waste of time since you weren't conscious. I also threw away the strange clothes you were wearing and dressed you more appropriately."

"What? What do you mean you dressed me? And what's this collar thing anyway? Who the hell are you? You look a lot like my waste of a wife Mildred, but you ain't her, I can tell that right away. But sister, let's get a couple of things straight. If there's any correcting to be done, it's gonna be by me to you. Now, you get this thing off me and give me my clothes. Then we'll see about you getting me some dinner and..."

Pain shot through Leo's body, starting at his neck, radiating down his spine, into his groin and down his legs. He arched his back in a spasm and opened his mouth to a silent scream as the pain rolled up and down and all around till it finally came back to his shoulders and neck.

"What, what was that?" he groaned, panting from the torment when it subsided.

"You're a strange man," the Mildred double said. "I've heard there might be tribes of men hiding in the jungles who don't wear collars and have never been corrected, but I always thought those were just rumors. I mean how would they survive? Men are so incapable of independent thought, they'd just starve if women weren't there to tell them it was time to eat. I don't know how you got here or where you're from, but now that you're here, you're mine and you'll do well to follow the rules. You just get up and go on to the shed in the back of the house and Leo will fill you in on your duties."

"Duties? What duties? And what the hell do you mean, I'm yours? Lady, I don't know who the hell you think you are, but there ain't no rules except for the rules I make," Leo snarled. "Let's get this straight: No bitch is going to be telling me what to wear, what to do, and definitely not when to eat."

Agony once again shot through Leo's body. This time, it was much worse than before. His whole body arched as a torturous red flare of pain radiated through each muscle. His heels and shoulders dug into the floor pushing his body up while spasms raced through his arms, legs, and torso. His breathing stopped, his eyes bulged out of their sockets, and the world blurred while Leo existed in a universe with pain as the only reality. When it finally receded, Leo lay panting on the floor with a small trickle of blood dripping from his mouth from where he bit his tongue.

"Maybe you really don't know your place," marveled the woman. "Well, I'll explain things just once to you, but only because it amuses me to do so.

"Let's see, we'll start with the basics. First, all men are the property of women, and in my house, you're mine. Second, the collar around your neck is called a Correction Collar, but you've probably already figured that out. Any attempt to remove it results in a correction, any failure to do your duties, tasks, and assignments results in a correction. Any disrespect to any woman, especially me, results in a correction. Any attempt to escape or leave the property without permission results in a correction. Any woman can correct any man for any reason. And don't even think about destroying your collar.

The Mildred woman continued her explanation. "As far as the controlling devices, they're implanted in each female at birth and wired to our brain. We can correct any male with a thought. Corrections become more painful each time they're applied, but they only cause pain with no actual damage. You will never die from a correction, only pray you will.

"You may stand up," the woman ordered.

Leo slowly rose to a standing position and averted his eyes away from the weird Mildred in front of him.

"Now, go out of the house and around the back to the shed. You'll find Leo there. Tell him you're a new acquisition and he'll give you your duties. By the way, what is your name?"

"I'm Leo too," he whispered.

"Ah, Leo One and Leo Two. That'll make things easier," Leo's new owner said. "Now you may go."

Leo Kernuggle shuffled out of the house and to the shed in the back. His fogged brain couldn't comprehend how he left his townhouse on Hampton Lane and ended up in this hell. He only knew if doing exactly what the new Mildred ordered him to do kept him from another correction, that's what he'd do...to the end of his days.

*

Mildred Kernuggle woke up in the middle of her guest bedroom in her townhouse on Hampton Lane. The sun streamed through the windows, and birds chirped in the yard. The air was clean and crisp and full of life, and she felt more rested than she had in years. She stretched out her arms and greeted the beautiful day, but stopped when she saw her mother's candle sticks and Leo's bowling trophies stacked up on top of an entertainment center she didn't recognize.

She looked around and saw her old clothes from the closet neatly folded and stacked in a corner. She didn't recognize anything else, and was startled to see a man sitting in a chair at the back of the bedroom. He looked at her with a most unusual, bemused smile. This man was almost a twin of her Leo, but tanned and slimmer, with a lovely V-shape to his shoulders, chest, and torso.

"Well good morning, or more appropriately, good afternoon, my sleeping beauty," the man said with a slight East Coast accent. "How are you feeling? You've had quite a long nap."

"What? Who are you and what are you doing in my house? I don't understand. What's going on?" Mildred asked. "Why are my candlesticks and Leo's trophies up there? Where are all my other things and what've you done to this room? Where's Leo?"

"Those are a lot of questions," the man said and then laughed. "I'll try to answer them in order. First, my name is Leo, which answers both your first and last question. But I don't think I'm the Leo you're asking about. Second, this is my house so the question really is, 'What are you doing in my house?' Third, I found the candlesticks, trophies, and clothes lying in the middle of the floor where you are now, but about thirty minutes before you showed up. I just thought it'd be better if they weren't laying all over the place. As far as everything else in here, they're mine because this is my house.

Mildred looked completely confused and frightened. "What do you mean this is your house?"

"I think we've got a lot to talk about, but maybe we should start with me helping you up from the floor?" Leo said, offering a hand to Mildred. He guided her onto a second chair in the room.

"May I first ask a couple of questions of my own? What's your name? What's the last thing you remember, and most importantly, is there anything I can get for you? Are you cold, hungry, or thirsty?"

"My name is Mildred, Mildred Kernuggle," she said. "The last thing I remember is looking in this room and seeing a strange gray ball floating in my closet. I reached out to it and the next thing I know I'm lying on my, or your floor. How did I get here?"

"I don't really know," Leo said, "but I do know that you have a striking resemblance to my Mildred, who I lost to a skiing accident four years ago—God rest her soul. And you say you're looking for a different Leo?"

"Yes, my husband's name is Leo, and you look very much like him, but you're in much better shape," Mildred said, trying to hold back a blush.

"We have a mystery on our hands, Mildred," Leo said with another laugh. "You and your things just popped out of nowhere, and I've been racking my brain as to how that's even possible. There's no doorway or entrance or anything that shows where you came from or how to go back. But you know what? Mysteries are much better solved after a few drinks and a good dinner. Why don't we go into the kitchen? I'll pour us a drink and then rustle up something to eat. I'm sure you're starved. You know, you've been asleep for most of the day. You must be very hungry."

"Yes, I am, thank you very much. But wait a minute, you'll pour me a drink? And you're going to make dinner?" asked Mildred, completely bewildered.

"Yes, why not? When my Mildred was with me, I cooked all the time. I loved surprising her with new recipes. Sometimes I'd even set out candles and flowers. I'd put on my tux and we'd pretend we were on a yacht. Of course, later on we dined on the real thing and had our own chef, but we'd often remember how wonderful those first days were. Sometimes I'd even put the tux on again, just for fun."

"I'm sorry," Mildred said as she walked out of the bedroom. "You have a yacht? But you still live here, in this house?"

"Well, my company did very well, so we don't really live here anymore. We've got our place in the Hamptons and the villa in Cinque Terre, and of course the condo in Manhattan, and the one in Hawaii. But we still have lots of friends and family in Sandy Shore, so we keep the townhouse to have a place to stay when we visit. Look at me, I still say we. I...I guess I mean I."

Mildred looked around at the townhouse which was the exact same layout as her own, with some of the same cabinetry and fixtures but with far more expensive floor coverings and artwork.

She looked down to the floor and whispered, "Oh, how beautiful this place is. I guess I'm really not in my home?"

"No, Mildred, I don't think so. And I don't think there's any way for you to get back there, wherever there is."

Mildred looked around, mystified. "And no way for anyone from there to take me back, I suppose?"

"No, I don't think so, but you know what? You're perfectly welcome to stay here. I don't use the place very much, like I said. You could make it your own again. But of course, if you wanted to go with me when I go back to Manhattan that'd be delightful. I'd love the company and I'd love to get to know you better."

"And the place in the Hamptons... and Hawaii, and...and wherever Cinque Terre is?"

"Of course," Leo said and then laughed once more. "And the yacht too. I don't have anyone to share my life with anymore and I've been ever so lonely.

It may be silly of me, but when I was watching you sleep, I had the strangest feeling that God might have sent you to me. And who am I to argue with God?"

"Oh my," Mildred said. "No one's ever spoken to me like that. And you really wouldn't mind if I came along with you? I'd be ever so good and you'd never need to correct me," she said, wiping away a tear.

Leo grew very serious. "I'm not exactly sure what correcting means, Mildred, but it doesn't sound very nice. I'm going to make a promise to you. No one's going to be correcting you anywhere we go. Not me and not anyone else. That's a promise I make to you on the memory of my Mildred, and that's the most sacred promise I can make."

Mildred stood stunned and put her head down again. "And we can go anytime we like?"

"Anytime," Leo said. "We'll just pack up those candlesticks and trophies and be on our way."

"Oh yes, I'm so glad the candle sticks came with me. I'd miss them very much. But we can throw the trophies away, if that's okay with you, Leo."

"Yes, Mildred," Leo smiled. "We can take the candlesticks and anything else you want. I'll go get the trash and we can throw the trophies out right now."

"Right now would be perfect," Mildred said.

And afterwards she never once thought of the trophies again.

BESSIE LOU'S FIRST DANCE
BY ERIC O' NEAL

Finally! It's here!

The crowing the of rooster brought Bessie Lou back to consciousness, and to the lovely, spectacular, rootin'-tootin' realization that the dance was happening that night. Her first dance! Her heart was already on the dance floor, doing spins, kicks, and flips. It was just a shame that she'd have to get through the day, first. *What a rotten thing, to schedule a big hoedown at the end of the day. Why not put it in the morning? What's so wrong with dancing before breakfast?* Bessie Lou wasn't sure she could contain her anticipation for a whole, dadgum day. She'd hardly gotten out of bed, and it was already as big and intense as a housefire. If having too much anticipation was as severe a condition as Granmammy Josephine's goiter, Bessie Lou was sure Doc Callgoon would put her on bedrest for a month.

Sweet, little Bessie Lou, hardly turned fourteen, hustled downstairs to meet the smells of flapjacks and bacon, which were soon to fuel her dancing daydreams for a terribly long day under Miss Gretta's tutelage. As she reached the kitchen, she heard her Momma having a right giggle with a visitor. Now who would be turned up at such an hour to see Momma?

"Oh, you say too much, Mrs. Duquesne!"

"I declare, it's the truth, my dear tartlet!"

Bessie Lou's Momma was doubled over, one hand on the counter, one hand in the air, pleading for respite from the riotous onslaught of Mrs. Duquesne, the town matriarch. She hardly noticed the bacon start to burn. Thankfully, Bessie Lou took the pan off the heat, and slid the over-crisped fatty meat strips onto the dish with the rest of them.

"Now who is this scrumptious thing?" Mrs. Duquesne asked, turning her attention to Bessie Lou. "I don't recall meeting you."

Momma still hadn't regained her composure, so Bessie Lou spoke up for herself.

"Bessie Lou. I don't reckon we've spoke before, but Momma says you were at my baptizing."

Mrs. Duquesne swatted the idea out of the air. "Oh, I attend so many, as co-chair of the church club. I can't recall every one I visit. But you are a delightful treat. I'm so glad we've met. Officially, that is. You will be coming to our dance, won't you?"

"Of course I will!"

"Like bluegrass to my ears, and one of your Momma's fine pies to my tongue." Mrs. Duquesne turned to go, neglecting to check on the laughing woman, who was still red in the face and tearing up, but then she stopped. "Do wear something delicious tonight ... for the boys, of course."

The town matriarch departed before Bessie Lou could spill the details of all her outfit ideas. Once the dressy woman's cloud of expensive perfume had cleared the air, Momma righted herself and looked at Bessie Lou.

"Breakfast?"

"Mrs. Duquesne visited us today," Bessie Lou gushed to Fannie, whose birthday differed from Bessie Lou's by only a week.

"*The* Mrs. Duquesne? The co-chair of the church club? The head judge of the annual chili competition?"

"The very same mayor's wife!"

Fannie's eyes were as wide as dinner plates, full moons, and Mrs. Duquesne's gaudy hats. "Gosh. I don't think we've ever met. Not since my baptizing."

"The word is 'baptism,' girls," chimed in Miss Gretta, "and that'll be enough chatter. It's time to learn. Now, who can recall the town's motto?"

Reneé Gallifort raised her awful, know-it-all hand. "The town's motto is 'Come for the pie; stay for the friendship'."

"And the official town bird?"

"The cacking longdigger," recited Gary Johnsport.

"The sect of the church?"

"The Order of Saint Duquesne, a subset of the Church of Good Graces," called out Fannie.

"The town curfew?"

"Eight o'dial, save for the night of the Duquesne Dance," said Davy Mammost, who never broke curfew to spy on Rebecca Jaffen, not even once. The class rippled with excitement at the mention of the dance, but Miss Gretta plowed ahead with her traditional reviewing of the town's statistical data. How would the children appreciate their homes if they couldn't regurgitate facts about it at the drop of a dainty white glove?

"The town's greatest attraction?"

More murmuring.

"Save for the dance," Miss Gretta grumbled.

"The inconsistent halting of the moon's trajectory, due to the elevation of town and slight twist in axis, every autumnal solstice," again spoke Reneé.

Bessie Lou felt it necessary to tack on a colloquial addendum to that fact, however accurate it may be. "Often called 'the man in the moon's two-step'."

"Although that is the case," cut Miss Gretta, "you will not be tested on vernaculars in my classroom. Stick to the books, please, Bessie Lou."

Fannie squeezed Bessie Lou's hand, hoping she didn't feel too bad about being called out in front of the class.

"And the town's founding date?"

"Well, now, that depends on who you ask," called a voice at the door.

Miss Gretta looked like she could hardly fit in her high collar and long skirt, suddenly gasping at the warmth Mr. Duquesne brought into the classroom.

"Mr. Duquesne! I – well, I – never did – what could – how may I – we – ?"

While the schoolmarm drowned in her own sweat, the town patriarch surveyed the classroom. His words were long and drawn out, like fresh honey being poured over flapjacks.

"Well, now. Ain't this a savory sight? One o' y'all tell me, now: this here's a bunch o' meat pies done circumnavigated the stars roundabout fourteen years apiece, is that right?"

"Yes, sir!" cried Loretta Y. Wojniak.

"And what, pray tell, did I declare as the minimum age for our once-a-year hootenanny?"

"Fourteen, sir," whimpered Garfield Quinton.

Mr. Duquesne let out a raucous celebratory holler, sending Miss Gretta spiraling back into her chair, and deeper under her ocean of sweat. "Then that means we got a fresh batch o' dancers tonight, don't it?!"

The class broke into cheers and whoops. Only Reneé sat in her seat, redder than a sunburnt red-backed whashwaller.

"I like your enthusiasm! Now, I wanna remind y'all o' the most 'portant part of the dance. Y'all know what that is?"

Their voices fell quiet. This was not something Miss Gretta ever brought up before.

"Oh, don't tell me yer mommas and daddies didn't say nothin' to y'all about this!"

More silence. They leaned forward in their seats. Except for Reneé, who fell farther back in her seat, as if ashamed to receive her first kiss.

"Ok, then. What I want you to remember is this." He lowered his voice, expressing to them a secret all the adults in town already knew. "Y'all dance your little heinies off. Have a grand ol' time. But the first dancers to stop dancin' get a little ... well, you might call it a gentle ribbing. A bit o' time in the spotlight, at their own expense. It's all in fun, now, but it ain't the kind o' thing y'all need on your first dance. So y'all tuck that into your shoes and dance like your social graces depend on it!" Mr. Duquesne kept his eyes on the kids as he threw a hand vaguely in Miss Gretta's direction. She stared blankly at the ceiling, apparently submitted to her stupor. "Awright, then. We can save the learnin' for another day. Class 'smissed, I think."

The kids rushed for their bags, exclaiming their intents to eat big meals before the Duquesne Dance, so they could last longer.

"Hold on a second there," spoke one outstretched finger, pointed directly at Bessie Lou as she flew down the aisle of desks towards freedom.

"Yes, Mr. Duquesne?"

"Mrs. Duquesne done said she visited you and your momma this morning. Why's'at?"

Bessie Lou couldn't think of a reason. "Maybe Momma called her?"

"Unlikely. What's your name again, cupcake?"

"Bessie Lou."

Mr. Duquesne closed his eyes. "Mm, right. Bessie Lou. I like that." He opened his eyes. "Like butter on cornbread. Sweet name for a sweet girl. Well, I'll let you git goin'. My wife does like to check up on people. 'S not like she tells me about every little thing she does, huh?" He chuckled jovially as

Bessie Lou took her leave. Reneé darted out behind her. Had Bessie Lou paid Reneé any mind, she would have seen the girl running straight to Reverend Ihoe's church.

"See you at the dance, Miss Gretta," Mr. Duquesne said over his shoulder.

"Bessie Lou, the crackers go on the third shelf from the top!"

Auntie Bernice hadn't bothered to count the number of times she had to correct her niece's work at Paul and Bernice's One-Stop General Store, but if she had, it would have been more times than Uncle Paul had been kicked by Jaime Heinegal's prize-winning spotted twist-horn. Such big hooves on that beast, too.

"Sorry, Auntie Bernice," Bessie Lou mumbled. She really hadn't meant to put them on the wrong shelf, this time. Sure, there were times before this when she just wanted to put a bee in Auntie's bonnet, but this was pure accident. Whenever her mind tried to shift away from Mr. Duquesne's visit, it ended up doing that celestial two-step, shuddering back into place. What were the odds that both Duquesnes, the mayor and co-chair of the church club, who orchestrate the Duquesne Dance each and every year, without fail, would stop to talk to little, plain Bessie Lou? Miss Gretta did not put much emphasis on arithmetic, so Bessie Lou was not able to accurately calculate such a statistic, but not for lack of trying.

Auntie Bernice hobbled over, leaning heavily on her fully functioning leg. She snatched the crackers out of Bessie Lou's limp hand and shoved them forcefully onto the third shelf from the top, crunching the back quarter of the package. "Third from the top, girl! You've been off your rocker since you first came in here. What's got your gristle-chewer?" She poked her face leeringly into Bessie Lou's. Her sister may have made this dull girl work here, but she never demanded the girl be treated any differently than the old help. That boy knew how to stock a shelf. Split for greener pastures after he got the short end of the stick at the dance, though.

"I talked to both Mrs. and Mr. Duquesne, today." Bessie Lou saw no reason to fudge the truth. Not that she was any good at lying.

"What did the co-chair of the church club and the mayor want to do with you?"

"I can't say. It's not like I spread manure on Mr. Lattaway's lawn."

Auntie Bernice squinted at her niece. "Well ... they're not here, now. So put it from your mind." She began to totter back behind the counter. "Probably something my sister's got up to ...."

The bell above the entrance rang, politely clobbered as the door swung through it. Into the store came a cloud of expensive perfume, upon which Mrs. and Mr. Duquesne rode. Auntie Bernice turned briefly, recognizing the town leaders, before continuing her path behind the counter.

"Afternoon, ma'am," started Mr. Duquesne. "Does your niece work here?"

The lopsided woman casually gestured into the aisle containing Bessie Lou. Mrs. Duquesne leaned to and fro, peering over the tops of the shelves, finally spotting the braided hair she was looking for.

"Oh, *there's* the cinnamon roll I was looking for! I told you we'd find her, darling."

"Didn't doubt'cha for a second, darlin'."

Mrs. Duquesne hurriedly approached Bessie Lou, traveling as fast as her skirt would allow. Mr. Duquesne, however, rested back on his heels, sliding up slowly. He looked over at Auntie Bernice and Uncle Paul, the latter of which was staring, mouth agape, at tiny winged insects zipping about the window above the fruit. The hoof impression on the poor old man's forehead never did heal.

"I simply had to see you again. You were such a reward for the senses, like the first taste of Sunday gravy after a trip abroad."

Bessie Lou couldn't think of a higher compliment from such an esteemed member of the community! Fannie would keel right over if she could hear this.

"I couldn't agree more, Mrs. Mayor," Mr. Duquesne commented, diverting his attention from Uncle Paul back to Bessie Lou. "She's a ripe peach, she is."

Bessie Lou blushed. "It's mighty kind of you to say so. But I don't know what I've done to deserve such niceties."

"W'you just been yourself, little lady! That's deserving enough, ain't it?"

"I think we may be piling the sweet potatoes a little too high, Mr. Duquesne. I think we're obscuring the reason for this sensational rendez-vous." Mrs. Duquesne reached her gloved hand into her purse and pulled out a slip of stiff paper, presenting it to Bessie Lou. "We'd like to invite you, on behalf of the church club who, as I'm sure you know, decorate and cook for the yearly Duquesne Dance, to be one of our featured dancers."

Bessie Lou's heart threatened to slip through her ribcage and snatch the invitation, itself. But the girl, instead, turned an intense shade of red, and could only stare at it.

"It's a high honor, now, young'un," Mr. Duquesne explained. "Like the choice cuts on a spotted twist-horn, some folks are just superior. Mrs. Duquesne and I understand that, and we think it's right for you to be princess of the dance floor."

"As a featured dancer," Mrs. Duquesne continued, "you'll be among the first to start the dance. Then, everyone else joins – as I'm sure you know ...."

Bessie Lou was well aware that the tradition dictated a sort of bell curve of dancers on the floor, starting and ending with the same people, when only the middle of the dance contained the largest number of dancers. It was therefore unnecessary to hear Mrs. Duquesne explain the process. Bessie Lou couldn't hear her, anyway, since she was too busy, cutting a rug on the dance floor in her mind.

"Do you accept?"

She looked up at Mrs. Duquesne, then at Mr. Duquesne, then back at the co-chair of the church club. All she could think to do was to slowly reach up a single hand, close two fingers on the card, and pull it from the white glove in front of her.

"How absolutely tantalizing! This is a great day, Mr. Mayor!"

"I reckon so, Mrs. Mayor!" Mr. Duquesne followed his confirmation with another celebratory holler.

"Wonderful, wonderful," piped up Auntie Bernice. "Now, has my niece finished bothering you, or do I have to send her outside to scrub the windows?"

Mr. Duquesne put his hands up. "Not at all, ma'am. We've achieved what we came to do, and I think we best be goin'." He put his arm around Mrs. Duquesne and guided her to the door, again clocking the bell with the front door. Just before the pair slipped out, though, he leaned back, carefully avoiding knocking off his well-endowed hat. "I didn't mean to be rude, ma'am. Will we be seein' you, too, on the dance floor, tonight?"

Auntie Bernice slapped her leg. "Not with this disappointment. But I'll be in the wings. Wouldn't miss it!"

Bessie Lou was humming with excitement in her new dress. Momma had just finished sewing it while she'd completed her time with Auntie Bernice and helped Uncle Paul back upstairs to his happy room, above the store. Fannie had absolutely melted when she saw the invitation.

"*Featured dancer?* Bessie Lou, you lucky thing, do you know what this means? You'll be getting the most time on the dance floor out of *any of us!*"

The newly minted featured dancer – her very first year, no less! – pressed anxiously at wrinkles that weren't there, trying to improve upon an already perfect night. The sun was just setting, and the cacking longdiggers in the trees were living up to their names. As such, a few men and women from the town stepped out with their guns to give the dance some respect. But Bessie

Lou paid the ear-piercing riot of cacking and cracks of lit gunpowder no mind, as the band had just started playing. Folks in the crowd smiled at each other, happily discussing the events of the day, while they waited for – and then he appeared.

"Good evenin', y'all!" shouted Mr. Duquesne, after belting a hearty holler.

"*Good evenin'!*" replied the crowd.

"It's another fine night in the town of Duquesne, is it not? And tonight, with the peak elevation of the moon, we do declare another twelve hours of celebration for the safety of our little home, carved outta the harsh, unforgiving landscape!"

The crowd cheered wildly. The gunshots stopped. There was a dearth of cacking.

"So why don't we kick off this Duquesne Dance right? Please welcome to the floor, your Mrs. Mayor, Mrs. Duquesne!"

Mrs. Duquesne was lifted to the dance floor by the whooping and clapping of her people. "Thank you, thank you. I am delighted to commence this year's dance with the announcement of the featured dancers. Will the following people please step up ... "

Willie Yarheart stepped up.

Ida Torbrux stepped up.

Doc Callgoon stepped up.

Loretta Y. Wojniak stepped up.

Bessie Lou stepped up.

Clint Uur stepped up.

P.J.C. stepped up.

Reneé Gallifort stepped up.

And Lishteb Seiqqbe stepped up. Purely to monitor, of course.

"Now, all you tasty folks do your best," said Mrs. Duquesne. "Dance as hard as you can."

Mr. Duquesne leaned in. "Work up a nice sweat. Marinade them muscles."

"And you don't stop until you just can't stand, anymore."

The moment Mrs. Duquesne finished, the moon froze in the sky, the band restarted their song, and the dancers began to dance. Each and every one of them danced like they'd been trained to do so. They danced like they didn't know where they were. They danced like they didn't know what was coming. They danced like they'd never seen what happened to those who fell on the dance floor.

After an hour, more dancers stepped up on stage. Miss Gretta was among their numbers. For a dour schoolteacher, she certainly held her own, occasionally trading off partners. With every passing hour, she weaved her way through the crowd, swapping with more and more people. Men danced with women. Women danced with men. Women danced with women. Men danced with men. And the Duquesnes watched.

"It's a good dance, this year," commented Granmammy Josephine, gazing up at the commotion from a chair in the dirt. On the other side of the dance floor, Auntie Bernice tapped her cane on the floor with the beat. "See, Paul? I told you this was a good time. I'm glad you came this year." Uncle Paul sat in his happy room, above the store, across town, clapping intermittently to the thumping vibrations through the floorboards. Crystal Blagnacht sipped punch at the food table while she held Baby Xalmo to her breast. "Sure wish I could have danced, this year," she said to Xalmo.

At the six-hour mark, some of the townsfolk heard their cue in the music to retreat from the dance floor and partake in the now cold foodstuffs. Seven hours passed. Then eight. Then nine. Just before ten hours had gone by, Mrs. Duquesne pulled Mr. Duquesne aside, out of the monitor's earshot.

"I'm rather surprised. I thought someone would have fallen, by now. They're proving to be more resilient, this time."

Mr. Duquesne nodded. "By golly, you're right. Maybe time is comin' we shake things up a bit."

"But I do so love the dance. And it makes them ever so happy."

"Maybe we make it more often."

"They need time to reproduce. And until they're fourteen ... "

"I know, I know," Mr. Duquesne said with a wave of his hand. "But I think, maybe ... "

Mr. Duquesne raised a finger and pointed at the middle of the crowd. The mayor and co-chair of the church club locked their eyes on Richie Wingmore, who was starting to stumble.

"How's this for an appetizer, darlin'?"

"I suppose it will do," huffed Mrs. Duquesne.

Mr. Duquesne climbed onto the dance floor and started sliding dancers out of his way as he struck a path for Richie. Just as he got near, Richie's knees buckled, and he fell, hard, to the floor. "W'hey there, Richie. Looks like you're our first loser of the night." Mr. Duquesne's body disassembled, revealing a mess of sinew, teeth, and bile. Richie's legs were gone in an instant, and his torso was tossed high above the dancers into Mrs. Duquesne's maw. Blood spattered the dancers as Richie's corpse flew overhead, and a smear where he fell started to make some dancers slip. Mr. Duquesne helped to keep them upright on his way back out of the throng. "Whoa, easy, now. No cheatin'!"

Another few hours passed. Doc Callgoon, Winston Kraz, and Loretta Y. Wojniak all parted the dance floor the same way Richie did. But the Duquesnes were not satisfied. Mr. Duquesne paced back and forth in front of Granmammy Josephine, his eyes glued to Bessie Lou as she wore down the soles of her shoes.

"I don't think she's gonna fall, darlin'," growled Mr. Duquesne.

"Give it time," Mrs. Duquesne said, consolingly, though she, herself, was eyeing the moon.

"There isn't much time left, *Mrs. Mayor.*"

"Do not use that tone with me. We both want her, I know."

"She's got what we need."

"I know."

"Can smell it like a pie on a windowsill."

"As can I."

"I want that meat pie."

"And you think I don't?"

Mr. Duquesne stopped pacing. "What if I ... ?"

"We can't."

"Just once!"

Mrs. Duquesne grabbed his shoulder and gestured discretely towards Seiqqbe. "And risk losing this whole thing?"

"But she's got what we need!"

"They all do."

"I get that. But this'd be like eating breakfast, lunch, supper, dinner, and a bedtime snack in one bite, darlin'! We'd be satiated for *eons!*"

Over the din of the dance, Lishteb Seiqqbe called to the Duquesnes. "You'd be outcasts if you touched her before she fell. It has to be natural."

Mr. Duquesne dropped his head in a huff, letting out a guttural tone. "Fine," he said. "She'll fall naturally." He climbed up onto the dance floor and positioned himself right next to Bessie Lou, no matter which way she spun. "Howdy, little meat pie," he said, studying her for signs of weakness. "Havin' a ball?"

Bessie Lou caught sight of Mr. Duquesne and blushed, even through the heat and sweat.

"You're doin' a wonderful job ... but I think you might be upstaged by one'a your peers. What's'er name? Reneé?"

He gestured over to Reneé, who was also still giving it her all. A small fire lit under Bessie Lou's behind.

"She's pretty good in school, ain't that right? I hear Miss Gretta was gonna give her some kinda reward for her hard work. Don't seem fair to me, givin' a reward for studyin' hard. But dancin' – well, dancin's for everyone! If you dance real good, well, I could might see fit to puttin' your name on somethin' shiny. How'd y'like that?"

Shiny? Shiny! Reward! Bessie Lou danced with all her might. Mr. Duquesne stared, willing her small frame to give out. Surely, her consciousness would give in. Surely, darkness would fade out the light in her eyes, making her the freshest apple on the tree. Surely. No?

Reneé Gallifort's head cracked on the dance floor. Bessie Lou threw up her hands, planting both feet on the ground in stillness. Panting furiously, she pointed at Reneé in victory. She, Bessie Lou, had won the dance! She'd won her reward! This calls for punch! Bessie Lou stumbled off the dance floor on weak legs and fetched herself a refreshing glass. Overhead, the moon began to shift out of place. It was resuming its journey across the night sky.

"Hurry!" shouted Mrs. Duquesne to Mr. Duquesne.

The town mayor could hardly comprehend their misfortune. He almost didn't split the know-it-all with Mrs. Duquesne in time. Almost. When Reneé was no more, they slinked back to town hall, leaving the monitor to clean the blood off the floor and its dancers, and quietly discussing with one another the possibilities of changing the dance's schedule.

The next morning, Momma made oatmeal. Bessie Lou rolled to school in an old wheelchair, holding no thoughts of any kind of reward. Despite needing time to recuperate from all that dancing, she could hardly help talking with Fannie about how proud she was of her time on the dancefloor. Of course, Miss Gretta interrupted them to keep them on track. Before dismissal, she informed the class that Loretta, Reneé, and some others had moved to another town. All of the kids thought to themselves that those who had left were definitely missing out with the annual dance. Who would ever want to leave Duquesne?

INDEPENDENCE DAY, 1992
BY CHARLIE JONES

Saturday, Fourth of July. Tonight, fireworks. But this morning, a corpse.

McSweeney pulled the blanket back to show me the face. I hate this part of the job, identifying dead bodies. Most people only see a dead body at a funeral, but in my job, it's almost commonplace. A few times a year.

"How long she been dead, Lieutenant?" I asked.

McSweeney pulled the butt end of last night's cigar out of his mouth. "Since last night. Lucky no animals got to her."

I crouched and brushed the flies away from the face. Clothed. Chalk-white skin. Brown hair. Purple bruises on the jaw and under the left eye. Somebody pummeled her before they put two in the back of her head. They wanted to hurt her before they killed her. In life, when I knew her, she was fairly attractive and well-bred. Now she was just dead.

I was about to tell McSweeney whom she used to be, when the corpse opened her eyes, turned her head to me, and mouthed a few words. One of them was my name, Mike.

I fell backward on my butt and scrambled away from the body.

"Mike! What the ...?" McSweeney swore.

"Did you see that?" I stammered.

"See what? All I saw was you trying to get away from the body. What gives?"

"She...she..." I knew how crazy this was going to sound. "She spoke to me."

"Maxwell, you been drinking?"

I stood and brushed myself off. The corpse looked like it did a moment ago. "Not yet, but I think I need one."

He shook his head. "Okay, she spoke to you. What did she say?"

"I don't know. She just mouthed the words. No sound."

"Right. She spoke to you but made no sounds. I don't know whether I can take an ID from somebody who's hallucinating. Geez, why is it never simple with you, Mike?"

"Okay. I know it sounds nuts, but I saw what I saw." I see enough dead people in my dreams, I don't need them when I'm awake, too. "She was Millie Sparks."

He wrote that in his notebook. "How'd ya know her, Mike?"

"Client."

"Current or in the past?"

"Current."

"What were you doing for her?"

Normally a PI wouldn't tell a cop what he was doing or why a client hired him, or even the client's name, but I didn't think she'd mind. "She hired me to keep an eye on her ex-husband."

"Why?"

"He just got sprung from Graterford last week, and she was afraid he was going to come after her. She told me that he blamed her for him being locked up."

He pointed at the body. "Think he's good for this?"

"Don't know. Never met him. But from what I saw, he didn't come near her."

"What was he in for?"

I bent and covered her face. "ADW, attempted murder, resisting arrest."

"Why do you think she wound up here?" He motioned at the overgrown vacant lot we were standing in, just off Lehigh, not far from where Connie Mack Stadium used to be.

"Don't know. She was a nurse at Temple Hospital for the past ten years. No enemies, as far as I could tell."

"When'd you see her last?"

"Monday night. I met her at her home when she hired me. I've spoken to her every day since."

"How about him?"

"Yesterday afternoon. He went back to the Bryant halfway house."

McSweeney motioned for the ME guys to take the body. They scrambled over and around the piles of trash strewn around the lot.

"What do you know about the husband.?"

"Vincent Sparks. Forty-five, five-ten, one-seventy, brown and brown. Wears black horn-rimmed glasses. Walks with a limp from a traffic accident a few years ago. Grew up in the Northeast."

McSweeney was scribbling furiously. "What do you know about his arrest?"

"He pistol-whipped the owner of a corner store at 31st and Girard. Sparks said the guy short-changed him. Then he held the guy hostage inside the store and kept the cops at bay for three hours. When the cops finally broke in, they found the clerk with a skull fracture and a broken jaw. Another hour and the guy would have been dead."

"When did this happen?"

I scratched the stubble on my jaw. "Seven or eight years ago."

He motioned to the body. "How's the wife involved?"

"She talked him into surrendering."

"Ah. Do you think that's enough to kill her?'

"Don't know. When you find him, you can ask him, Lieutenant. How'd you know to call me to ID the body?"

"Found your card in her purse."

"If you have her purse, why'd you need me to ID the body?"

"I wanted to find out how you knew her, and if you could tell us anything helpful."

"Did I?"

He squinted at me. "Yeah. It would have taken us a half-day to link her with her jailbird husband. So, you saved us some time."

I continued to stare at the ground where she had been laying. What had she said?

McSweeney was talking but I wasn't hearing him.

"Mike!"

"Yeah, I'm here, Lieutenant."

"Thanks for your help. If I need anything else, I'll call. He pointed the dark butt at me. "A piece of advice. Don't be telling people that dead bodies are talking to you. Okay?"

"Sure thing, Lieutenant."

On my way out of the lot, I avoided piles of garbage and other unidentifiable stuff. It took me a moment to find my car. I sold the Cutlass the other day to a corner boy for $100 and bought a five-year-old dark blue Malibu. I sat there for a few minutes before I started the car. What did she say to me? She said my name twice with a few words in between. What was she trying to tell me? And why was I seeing things? And how did she end up dead in north Philly? Too many questions. But the real question, which McSweeney didn't ask, was why would a reasonably sane man nearly beat a stranger to death? That never sounded right to me. And why would another reasonably sane man see a corpse talk to him?

On the ride back to the office on the streets of North Philadelphia, I dodged potholes, barriers, and even a sinkhole where a sewer pipe broke a few weeks ago. The sidewalks weren't much better, strewn with trash bags in front of every rowhouse. I kept the windows up to try to avoid the odor. Made you wonder if the Streets Department ever got away from a few choice neighborhoods around Center City.

Downtown was quiet. The tall buildings dozed in the morning sunlight; the sidewalks were late getting rolled out. The parade and speeches happened by Independence Hall, and the fireworks over the Art Museum, on the other side of town, weren't until tonight.

I found an open cafe and ordered the breakfast special and coffee. The coffee was good, and I sipped it as I tried to figure out what Millie said to me. At least four words, maybe five. My name twice. The words in between were a mystery. I wrote it on a piece of blank paper.

Mike ____ ____ Mike.

What was she trying to tell me? I scribbled a few guesses.

Mike, it's all right, Mike.

That didn't make sense.

Mike, find him, Mike.

Maybe. Picturing her speaking rattled me. But I knew she'd haunt me until I figured it out. I tried until my meal arrived. I folded the piece of paper and stuck it in my jacket pocket to try later on.

After breakfast, I headed toward the scene of Vincent's crime to talk to the shop owner whom Vincent beat. The trolley tracks and islands along Girard Avenue made navigation a little tougher, but the traffic was light. I got to 31st Street and parked around the corner from the shop. I sat in the car for a moment, trying to clear my mind of the talking corpse, and figured out how to approach Emmitt Wylie. As I sat there, two young guys, one black and one white went inside and came out in a minute with nothing to show for their effort.

Millie had told me that Emmitt recovered from his injuries and reopened the shop a year after the attack. But she could never say if Vincent and Emmitt were involved in anything together. I walked into the shop and immediately felt claustrophobic.

The 31st Street Market contained about the same amount of stuff as an Acme supermarket in about a tenth of the space. Shelving reached to the ceiling crammed with all sorts of stuff. The shop catered to the neighborhood, in the absence of any other markets.

Emmitt sat behind an inch-thick sheet of plexiglass with only about a three-inch opening to pass through money or packs of cigarettes and condoms to the customers. He probably invested in the protection after Vincent nearly beat him to death eight years ago. He sat reading a detective novel. A white guy, shaved head over dark eyes and two-day growth. He wore a flannel shirt to ward off the air conditioning which was on full blast. The landlord must pay for that.

The most notable thing in the store was a stuffed shark that hung above the closed-in booth. The shark was about twelve feet long and must have weighed 250 pounds. It had a sharp snout and a mouth slightly open showing rows of sharper teeth. A round black eye stared at me. The top fin was a bit short like they trimmed it to fit in the store. The body was gray, with the top half darker than the bottom. It looked like a sleek killing machine.

"Mr. Wylie?"

"You a cop?"

"No. My name is Mike Maxwell." I pointed to the creature hanging above his head. "Is that a great white I hear so much about?"

He softened a little. "No, it's a Mako shark. I caught it off Townsends Inlet a while back. Wifey wouldn't let me put it up at the house, so it had to come here."

"Tough catch?"

"Yeah, a few hours. My arms hurt for a week. And I was a lot younger back then. You fish?"

"Yeah, when I get the time. A Mako. That's a maneater, isn't it?"

He liked talking about it. "Damn right it is. That's how I got my nickname. The kids started calling the place Mako's. It didn't take long for them to call me Mako."

"Good story. Look, Mr. Wylie, I'm a private detective and I'm inquiring about Vincent Sparks."

Wylie stood. He was about five-eight, two hundred pounds, most of it muscle. "That sonofabitch. He nearly killed me." He turned his head and pointed to a dent in the left side of his head above the ear. "That cocksucker better look out if I ever get the drop on him. I'll bash his skull in."

"Yeah, that's a shame, Mr. Wylie. Why'd he do that."

Wylie looked at the floor. "He said I shortchanged him. That he gave me a twenty for a paper and a pack of smokes. He only gave me a dollar, so I gave him back a quarter. We got into it, and he reached over the counter and grabbed me by the throat. This was before I got this booth. He whipped out a pistol and I thought he was going to shoot me, but he just beat me in the side of the head with the butt of the gun. You can still see the depression the gun made." He rubbed the side of his head as if remembering the beating he took that day.

"Yeah, I'm sorry to hear that, Mr. Wylie. I don't want to alarm you, but Sparks got out a few weeks ago. Have you seen him?"

He shook his head. "Nope. But if you see him, tell him I'll kill him if we cross paths. And tell that crazy wife of his to leave me alone, too."

"Fine. And if you see him, tell him I want to talk to him about his wife's death." I pushed a business card through the slot.

He looked at the card, then at me. "Dead, huh? She testified against him at his trial. I could see him coming after her."

I stepped back from the booth. "That's what I'm thinking, too. Let me ask you a question. Sparks drove the number 15 trolley by your place a few times a day. Did you know him before he tried to kill you?"

He looked to the left, then sat on his stool. "Maybe I seen him in here a few times. Smokes, gum, paper, maybe a scratcher if he felt lucky."

Not for the first time, a young black guy came to the door of the shop and peered in. Mako waved him off. The boy left.

I tried to measure my words here. "Ya see, Mr. Wylie, Sparks wasn't a violent man, and I wonder what made him snap and go off on you? Did you guys ever work together?"

His gaze shifted to over my head. The next thing he was going to say would be a lie.

"Nope, nothing like that. We weren't doing business if that's what you mean."

"I don't know what I mean." But that's exactly what I was thinking. "Were you?"

"I already said no." He raised his voice, trying to convince me. "Now get the fuck outa my store before I do to you what I wanna do to Sparks."

I left. I felt like there was more to the story than what I was hearing. It would be worth my while to give Mako a hard look to see if he unraveled at all.

The car was warm in the late morning sun. I opened the windows and sat there for a few minutes. In that time, three young men entered Mako's and left empty-handed. No snacks, no sodas, so there must be something else that attracted them to the store. It would bear looking into. In case anybody was watching, I drove off, north on 31st Street past rowhomes, garages, more plastic bags, and empty lots. I avoided large potholes left over from the Ford administration. As long as the tourists limited their visit to the Parkway and Independence Hall, they'd never get a sense of the real Philadelphia. Most of the city looked like this neighborhood, ignored or forgotten by City Hall, except when election time came.

I decided to check out the Sparks house and ask the neighbors if they knew anything. Millie deserved it. Traffic was light on the highway so I got to the Northeast in record time.

I pulled in front of Millie's Mayfair rowhome. There weren't any trash bags lining the sidewalks, and the roads were in good repair. It looked like this neighborhood and these people got the benefits from the city. All the brick rowhomes on the street flew bunting and flags, except the Sparks home. Windows and doors closed, no flags. Shut tight. I rang the bell. No answer. But I thought I detected some movement inside.

I walked around to the alley, counted off six homes, and looked at two stories above a garage door. A while back, somebody added a makeshift deck to the back of the house above the garage. It didn't look too sturdy, some of the support beams showed signs of rot. I guess L&I hadn't been around in a while. No steps, but easy enough to scale.

Next door to the Sparks house, a man was putting together a picnic table in the small fenced-in backyard that all the homes had. I walked down the alley and waited to see if anybody came out the back of the Sparks house, but after ten minutes, I gave up and went around to the front.

Two steps to their sparse front yard, then three steps to the door. I knocked on the door of the house to the right of the Sparks that shared their steps. A kid, about seven or eight, wearing cutoff jean shorts and a flag tank top opened the screen door. He gave me the eye. I guess he didn't see too many guys in a suit and tie in his neighborhood, especially on a holiday.

"Hiya, my name's Mike. Is your mom or dad home?"

"Mom! There's a guy at the door." And he ran towards the back of the house. The screen door slammed in my face.

A woman came toward the door. She spoke to me through the screen door. Her blue eyes gave me a once-over. "What are you selling?"

"I'm not selling anything. My name is Mike Maxwell and I'm a private investigator. Do you have a few minutes to answer some questions about Millie Sparks?"

She opened the screen door a bit and took the card I offered her. She looked at it, and I could see her trying to decide what to do, talk to me or close the door.

Her curiosity won. "What do you want to know? Did she do something wrong? Is she all right?"

Telling her she was dead would have changed the whole tenor of the conversation, so I put that aside. "She hired me to keep an eye on her husband. He just got out of Graterford."

Her round face darkened. "Yeah, she told me that. She was frightened that he was going to come after her."

"Yes, that's right. Have you seen Millie recently?"

The woman was about thirty, with long, light brown hair that she pulled back in a ponytail with a red, white and blue ribbon. She fixed a wisp of it behind her right ear. She wore a flag-colored all-in-one shorts-set that showed off her legs. For having kids, she looked in good shape. "No. What's today, Saturday? I saw her on Thursday at the bakery on Frankford Avenue. She was buying rolls for a party at work. She's a nurse at Temple Hospital, you know."

I nodded as if asking her to continue.

"She said she was off today for the Fourth. I told her to stop by if she wasn't doing anything. One more won't make much of a difference. Is she home? Did you try the bell?"

"I did, and nobody answered. Have you seen Mr. Sparks recently?"

"No. And I hope I don't. Millie was scared of him."

Another little boy, younger than the first one, came up and stood behind the woman. She held his head against her leg. She looked at him and asked, "Have you seen Miss Millie, Robbie?"

The boy looked at her and shook his head.

"Sorry, we can't help more. If you . . ."

"Mommy. I didn't see Miss Millie, but I saw a man go in her house."

The woman stopped. "When was that, Robbie?"

"Last night. I was looking out the window at some boys lighting firecrackers, and a man came up and went right inside."

"That's very good, Robbie. Why don't you go to the back and help Daddy with the chairs."

He turned and ran towards the back.

"Walk!" she called after him.

She looked at me with her eyes wider than before. "Should I be concerned that Vincent is next door? Should I call the cops?"

"No, let me look around some more. Maybe I missed something the first time."

I stepped next door and leaned on the bell. Once, twice, three times, telling anybody inside that I knew that they were in there. I peered through the front window. Nothing. I needed to get inside.

I walked around back and the man was still there, working on the table. He had three young boys, Robbie, and two others, helping him, running in the alley with his tools and hardware. The woman was standing on the back step. She told the man that I was looking for Sparks. He held my card.

Before I asked, he said, "Haven't seen Millie today, and I haven't seen Vincent since he went to jail. That was the best place for him. He always seemed a little off to me."

"How's that?"

"Who can afford a new Cadillac on a trolley driver's salary? A little off, know what I mean?"

He reached out over the fence and extended his hand. "I'm Bill Farnsworth." He pointed to the boys. "That's Junior, Robbie, and Bennie. Wife's Claire."

I shook his hand and told him my name. I pointed to the youngest. "Robbie said he saw a man go into the house yesterday. Seen any activity today?"

"Nah. I've been out here most of the morning, ain't seen nothing. You boys seen anything next door?"

Three No, sirs.

I looked at the Sparks home. "I sure wouldn't mind getting inside to take a look around. You wouldn't happen to have a key, would you?"

Bill looked at Claire, and she shook her head. "Sorry," he said. "But we have something as good as a key. Boys! Go inside with your mother for a few minutes. I'll tell you when you can come out." The three boys went inside, fighting to see who could get in first.

"Good kids," I said to Bill.

He went into the garage and brought out a twelve-foot aluminum ladder. He avoided the overhead wires and set it against the railing of the deck on the Sparks house. I took off my coat and hung it on a fence post. He held the bottom of the ladder as I climbed the ladder and clambered over the railing.

"Just come back on the deck and I'll put it up again." He walked away with the ladder in his hands.

The back of the house had a door and a window. I tried the door first, with no luck, but the closed window eased up. I climbed into a small kitchen. The PI Association frowns on breaking and entering, but as far as I knew the occupant of the house was in the morgue.

I stood still for a few minutes to listen if somebody else was in the house. I looked around. Mail was on the kitchen counter, dishes in the sink, and clutter on the table. I opened the basement door and decided to check the other floors first.

The house was warm and stuffy. I looked around for any evidence someone had been here. A man's jacket lay on a chair by the front door, so Robbie was right. Letters lay in a pile by the front door under the mail flap. I took the steps to the second floor slowly so that any squeaks would not alert anybody. Three bedrooms and a hall bath and nothing there. I retraced my steps to the basement door. My flashlight was still in my coat pocket, so I snapped on the light. As soon as I did, I heard movement. Either a big rat or a person trying to hide. I called down the steps. No answer.

Nobody ever called me smart, so I started down the steps. The stale air and moldy smell from the basement got stronger. I was halfway down when a man's voice told me to stop. I did. "Who's there," I called.

A voice came from the back of the basement near the garage. "Who are you?"

"My name is Mike Maxwell, I'm a PI, and I was working for your wife."

"She's dead."

"I know, I saw her body. I have a message for you. From her."

"That's bullshit. She's dead. She ain't leaving no messages anymore."

"Maybe so. But I need your help to figure it out. Can I come down to see you?"

I heard a change in his voice. "Hold on. Did Mako send you?"

"No. Like I said I was working for Millie."

He was scared. "You know Mako?"

"Yeah, I talked to him this morning trying to figure out what was going on between you two."

"What'd he tell you?"

I noted that he didn't deny that he was involved with Mako. "Not much, except he was going to kill you if he found you."

I continued down the steps. Cardboard boxes littered the basement. Most of them were marked 'Clothes,' some 'Tools,' others 'Stuff." Wires hung from the water-stained false ceiling. Weak light entered through the small, dirty windows in the front. Water stained the walls a foot up from the floor. The basement needed to be aired out and a good sweeping, and I noticed a used mousetrap in the corner.

A white guy came from the back of the basement. He walked with a limp and needed a good scrubbing with shoulder-length brown hair and pale skin, and brown eyes. Glasses. Blue jeans and a dirty white T-shirt. Low black Chucks. The same things he's been wearing all week.
We both stood there looking at one another. "A PI, huh? What do you want?" he said.

"I just want to talk to you. Vincent, I'm gonna level with you. It looks bad for you. You got out of jail and your wife, the woman you threatened, is found dead a few days later. I guess I want to hear your side of the story. Can you tell me first, what you and Mako were working on before you went away?"

"Nothing. He shortchanged me . . ."

"Don't give me that shit, Vincent. Nobody damn near kills a guy, then spends seven years in prison over change. What went on between you two?"

He used both hands to push his matted brown hair away from his face. He rubbed his week-old beard. Trying to figure out how much to tell me. He looked around the basement. "Can you believe my wife boxed all my stuff and stuck it in the basement with the mold and the mice?" He shook his head.

"At least she kept it. If it was me, I'd have tossed it years ago. She figured you'd be back someday. Now, tell me about Mako."

"Yeah, Mako. He's a bastard." He paused, trying to decide if he should continue. "You know, he runs a big drug operation out of that crappy little store. Retail and wholesale. Betcha didn't know that."

"No, I didn't." Now that I did, some of the things I saw earlier today made sense. "How were you involved?"

"I distributed to places on Girard Avenue up into Port Richmond, all along the route."

"Pretty handy," I said. And pretty stupid, I thought. "How'd you get involved?"

"Other trolley drivers brought me in when one guy retired. That guy has a beachfront condo in Boca. Sounded good to me."

And Cadillacs in the driveway. "Didn't the cops . . . "

"Mako had the cops in his hip pocket. Still does, because, he's still running the same operation."

"Tell me the details."

He scratched some more. He found a kitchen chair with a ripped seat cushion and sat on it. I leaned on the staircase.

"There were about a dozen drops along the route. We hit three or four on each run. We never hit all twelve on any loop, that would make somebody suspicious. We'd stop at Mako's to get our stuff and deliver it to the addresses marked on each bag. If you hadn't made the delivery by the time you were supposed to, you'd get a visit from one of Mako's goons who drove the route in big-ass Caddies."

"What were you delivering?"

"Garden variety stuff. Pills, marijuana, smack. Anything that was moving."

"How long did you do it?"

"Four years or so."

"Why'd you go after Mako?"

"He started giving us more stops and cut our take. A lot more risk with little payoff. That went on for a few months, and one of the other drivers would have smacked him around, but I got to him first."

"Where'd you get the gun?"

"Always carried one under my seat. Ever been at 63rd and Girard or in Port Richmond at four in the morning? You want a little friend."

"What kind?"

"Makarov 9 mill. Got it when I was stationed in Germany."

"Where were you last night, Vincent?"

"Why? Do you think I killed Millie?'

"You had a motive. You threatened her at the trial."

"I was here all night. I got a call last night at the halfway house from Mako saying Millie was dead and I was next. No way was I staying there where he knew I was. This was the only other place I knew."

"And you're sure Mako did it?"

Vincent looked at me with haunted eyes and guilt in his voice. "Either him or one of his guys. He was laughing about it. That I couldn't do anything about it because I'm an ex-con."

"You don't have any family?"

"A brother. He lives nearby. He's got kids. I didn't want to cause him any problems. You see what Mako does to people."

What he told me sounded kosher. I couldn't turn him in, he hadn't done anything wrong. But his wife was dead.

He looked at me. He wiped his eyes on his sleeves. "You said she had a message for me?"

"Yeah. I thought she said my name twice, with a few words in between."

"How'd she give it to you if she was dead?"

"Maybe she was trying to tell me who killed her."

He just gave me a quizzical look. "Now you're talking crazy."

"Maybe."

We were silent for a few minutes. I said, "We should probably talk to the cops about Millie's murder, tell them what you know."

He shook his head. "I don't want to talk to the cops. They'll get me for the drug charges."

"You haven't done anything since you got out, have you?"

"No, but they'll get me for the stuff before."

I scratched the back of my head. "I'm no lawyer, but I don't think they can get you for drug charges from seven years ago. Mako, on the other hand, he's still dealing, so they can get him for the drug charges and the murder charge."

He shook his head at me. I could tell he was reluctant to talk to the cops.

"Look, I know a cop, he's a good guy. He's working on Millie's murder so if you can give him Mako, he'd love to hear from you. It's the best way to get revenge for what happened to Millie."

"You know this cop?"

"Yeah, he's a stand-up guy. We went to high school together. I'll call him and tell him you're coming in, and that you need protection."
More head shaking. "I don't know."

"Look, if you don't get Mako off the street, you're going to be looking over your shoulder the rest of your life."

He rocked on the chair. "Can we talk to your cop friend today?"

"Yeah. I'm sure he's at the district doing the paperwork on Millie."

He finally nodded.

"Look, take some of these clothes, take a shower and meet me next door. They're having a picnic."

'Okay."

I pulled a shirt and a pair of clean jeans out of a box and handed them to him. "Fifteen minutes or I'm coming back in."

He nodded and went upstairs. I opened the back door next to the garage and stepped into the alley. I shielded my eyes from the noontime sun.

Farnsworth had finished the picnic table and chairs and was enjoying a cold one from a cooler. He sat in the shade by the back of the house. "I was getting worried; you were in there so long. He in there?"

"Yeah. He's cleaning up and then we're going to talk to the cops. He has an idea who killed Millie."

"Geez, Millie's dead. When? How? Did he do it?"

"No, but somebody he knows did. So, we gotta talk to the cops. The cops might be coming by here this afternoon. Keep your boys inside, okay? Best for everybody."

"Will do."

I looked at the PBR he had. He saw that and offered me one, which I gladly drank, to get the smell and sights of the basement out of my head. I asked if I could use his phone and he brought me inside and pointed at the yellow phone on the wall. Claire was stirring potato salad which looked good. I called McSweeney and told him that I was bringing in Vincent Sparks. He started asking questions, but I told him to hold off and ask them when I got to the district. I hung up, said goodbye to Claire, and stepped back outside.

A few minutes later, Vincent came out the back door. He chopped off most of his hair, shaved, and changed into new clothes. I hardly recognized him, but Farnsworth gave a brief wave, and Vincent nodded at him.

"Let's go, Vincent. They're waiting for us."

"I'm not sure about this. Mako has friends on the force."

"Not my guy." I thanked Bill for his help and Vincent and I walked around to the front, got in the Malibu, and headed back into town. We drove to the Central Detectives unit on 21st Street. A female police officer brought us into the unit and put us in an interview room.

Colin McSweeney came in a few minutes later. He turned on a tape recorder and introduced the three of us then let Vincent talk. Vincent told him the same story he told me, about Mako and the drug operation and the phone call that Mako said he killed Millie. McSweeney only asked a few clarifying questions, and when Vincent stopped talking, McSweeney snapped off the recorder and told Vincent to sit tight. McSweeney and I stepped out into the hallway and closed the door.

McSweeney had a look on his face that I'd seen before. He had questions, but he didn't know how to ask them, or in what order to get to where he wanted to be.

"Do you believe him, Lieutenant?"

He looked at me with hooded eyes. "Let's recap, Mike. Admitted drug dealer and ex-con comes into the station and tells us that an old accomplice, who's a drug dealer himself, killed his wife. The same wife that the first drug dealer threatened when he went to jail. How am I supposed to believe him?"

"I know it sounds preposterous, but I can verify that Mako is a drug dealer. I saw it myself this morning. Lots of guys going in and out of the store, scoring, and leaving."

"Okay, say I believe him. How am I gonna get a judge to issue an arrest warrant and a search warrant on the word of not one, but two, ex-cons?"

"I don't want to tell you how to do your job, Lieutenant, but maybe if you put somebody on the store, and watch the activity. Pick up any bus driver who makes a stop there and sweat him. The drivers aren't hard-asses, they'll break, and give up Mako quicker than you can say 'forfeited pension.'"

He reached for the doorknob of the interview room. "Yeah. Maybe." He stepped in and snapped on the recorder. He turned to Vincent. "Tell me the names of the other drivers who were involved in your distribution scheme." He pushed a pen and a legal pad toward Vincent.

"I didn't want to get those guys in trouble, just Mako."

"Those guys got in trouble the first time they made a pickup from Mako. They knew this day was coming. You've got a choice here, Sparks. Give me their names or get sent away for your wife's murder."

I knew he was bluffing about that last part. McSweeney had nothing linking Vincent to Millie's murder, but he was playing his cards as he saw fit.

Vincent looked at McSweeney, then me, then reached for the pen. Five minutes later, he gave McSweeney a list of six names of drivers who participated in Mako's scheme. McSweeney read them aloud for the tape. Probably most of them were down the shore for the holiday, but if McSweeney could find even one guy to talk, it would be enough to go after Mako. He told Vincent to stay put, that he wasn't under arrest, but that it would be best if he stayed at the district. McSweeney ran off to make arrangements to bring in the drivers.

I thought I'd try a different tack. I pointed the Malibu back towards Girard Avenue. My new camera with the long lens was sitting on the seat next to me. Maybe if I got a few pictures of his retail customers, that could be enough to get a warrant. I found a place to park where I had a view of the front of the store. The late afternoon sun shone directly on the storefront, making it ideal to snap a few pictures. I didn't have to wait long. Within a half-hour, I was changing a 24-picture roll of film to a thirty-six.

After an hour of snapping pictures, I had close to thirty customers. The cops should be able to find some of these guys to talk to about Mako. About six-thirty, a westbound 15 trolley stopped in front of the store. This was too good to be true! I got a couple of pictures of the driver going into the store, and a few minutes later, he came out with a large brown paper bag under his arm. He got back on the bus and continued his route.

I knew I'd catch hell from McSweeney, but I followed the bus across the bridge over the Schuylkill, past the zoo, and into West Philly. Just past 45th Street, he made an unscheduled stop and ran into a four-story warehouse on the north side of the street. He was in there for a minute or two, then came out and resumed his route. I drove ahead, past Lancaster Avenue, parked the car, and hustled to the corner, as if I was a passenger.

When the trolley pulled up, I got on, dropped a token in the farebox, and sat halfway back on the nearly empty trolley. A plan started to come to me. A block later, he made another unscheduled stop, jumped out with a small bag in his hand, and was back in a minute. When we passed 60th Street, I pulled the cord to get off at the next stop. I walked to the front and he opened the door for me. The driver wasn't much bigger than me, but he was a little soft from sitting all day. I told him he was getting off with me, and he refused.

The next few minutes were a blur to me. I grabbed him by his right shoulder and yanked him out of his seat. At first, he balked, then he came after me, and we both tumbled down the steps and out the door and landed on the street. My Marine Corps training kicked in and I was able to subdue him in a few seconds. I stood him up and plastered him against the side of the bus. He was as wobbly as I was.

Excited voices came through the open windows of the bus. I pulled a zip tie out of my jacket pocket and bound his hands. A woman on the bus was screaming at me, and I told her to hand me the paper bag that was next to the driver's seat. When she handed it to me, I told her the driver was a drug dealer and I was turning him in. We headed up 61st Street. The last thing I heard from the woman was her asking how she was going to get home from here.

The 19th Police district was a block or two away, and I manhandled him up the street, past the firemen sitting outside the firehouse. One guy asked, "Need any help, officer?" At times, the cop vibe helped. I told him that I had it under control. He tried to wrestle away a few times, but I finally got him into the lobby of the district. I pushed his face against the Plexiglas screen and told the woman at the desk to get in touch with Colin McSweeney of Central Detectives and tell him I corralled one of the drivers. It took about five minutes to convince her, but after she looked in the bag, she believed me. She took the driver back and locked him up and put the bag in the Evidence Room, and told me to stick around.

I stepped outside and lit a smoke and tried to clear my head. I must have fallen on my head, it felt like another concussion. I've had a few, the first in high school, then another one in Vietnam. This one didn't feel as bad as them.

I decided to take a stroll back to the trolley, what else was I going to do? The firemen saw me and asked if I took care of the guy I had earlier. Of course, I did, I told them. The bus was empty, except for one old drunk asleep in the back. As I looked around, a big, white guy pulled up in a Caddie. Muscle. Dressed all in black including a leather jacket on a warm day. He looked around the bus, too. When he saw me, he turned and walked away. I called after him, but he continued to walk toward his car. I sped up, and as he was about to open the car door, I put my hand on the door to keep him from opening it. He spun around and glared at me.

I looked into his face. His nose jutted to the left, and he sported a cauliflower ear. His jacket bulged under his left arm. I asked again, "Are you from SEPTA?"

"What are you? A cop?"

I pointed back to the police station. "No. But I saw somebody who looked like a cop take the driver to the district a few minutes ago. They haven't been back since. Do you know what's going on? The trolley is blocking the street."

He shook his head. "Nah, I don't know nothing. Get your hand off my car."

That would be the best thing to do, but the Irish in me was up, and I told him no.

"Get the fuck off my car," he roared.

He took a swing at me. I slipped it, ducked, and drove my right foot into the side of his left knee that had all his weight on it. I heard something pop. He tried to take a step toward me, but he collapsed. The pain kicked in, he screamed like a wounded animal, and, in a moment, his knee swelled to almost the side of his head. His screaming was loud enough to attract the firemen who came toward us. I figured I wouldn't have much time before the firemen separated me from the big guy. He was laying on his left side and was holding his bent knee in both hands. Sweat showed on his forehead. I extracted the gun, a cheap .38, and stuck it in my belt. I asked him if he worked for Mako, and he swore at me.

I stood and said, "Let's try this again." I put my foot on his left knee and pushed slightly. Another howl of pain. By this time the firemen arrived. I held up my hands and told them to wait.

"One more time. You work for Mako?" and I pushed harder. He screamed and sweat ran down his face. A little more pressure, until the knee was on the hot macadam.

"If I push any harder, they won't be able to fix this knee. They'll have to amputate the leg. What's it going to be? You working for Mako?"

Between gasps for breath, he nodded.

"I need you to say it," and I twisted my foot a little.

"Yeah. I work for Mako, cocksucker. Get off my knee!"

I lifted my foot off his knee. "That wasn't hard, was it? These firemen are going to take care of you, then the cops are going to want to talk to you. So just lie there for a few minutes."

He tried to get up but collapsed again with another yelp of pain. He'd need some help to move. I motioned for the firemen. I told them to immobilize his leg, then take him to the district.

I sat on the bottom step of the bus door and lit a cigarette. It made me feel woozy, so I tossed it away, and held my head in my hands. A fireman saw how I looked and he told me to take it easy, they'd have an emergency tech take

a look at me.

A few minutes later, McSweeney showed up. He looked at me, and I

guess he took pity on me. He didn't blast me for jumping the gun.

"What happened here?" he asked.

I recounted it as best I could, but I told him that the big guy did say he

worked for Mako and that I took a .38 from him. I handed it to the Lieutenant.

He took it with a pen through the trigger guard. He asked if I could stand, that I

needed to go to the district to make a statement about what happened with the

driver and the big guy.

I stood, and he grabbed my arm and escorted me to the district. A

question was buzzing around in my head, but I couldn't get it to come out. It

took almost five minutes for us to stumble into the district. He sat me on the

bench, and as he turned away, the question came to me. "Was Millie shot with a

.38?

He told me he didn't know, but that he'd call the ME's office to see if

they could tell us.

"You're probably holding the gun that killed her. I took it off him."

"Which one?"

"The big guy."

"Okay. Sit tight until we can get somebody to take your statement.

And, Mike?"

"Yeah, Lieutenant?"

"Part of me wants to say nice job, but another part, a much bigger part, wants to kick your ass for jumping in before we were ready. I'll leave that for later when you're feeling better. For now, nice job."

"Thanks, Lieutenant."

He walked away. I closed my eyes. Maybe things will clear up if I got some rest.

A hand was shaking my shoulder. I came to. A female officer with the clearest blue eyes was looking at me. She was standing in the last sunlight of the day coming through the window, and her eyes gleamed like sapphires. I imagined that's what angels' eyes looked like.

She spoke with an angel's voice. Her nameplate read Simmons. "The Lieutenant says I should take your statement." She handed me a legal pad. "Write what you know about the two men you brought in. Call me when you're done, and we'll go over it." She turned and went back into the squad room. Even in my diminished state, I could tell she was gorgeous.

It took me twenty minutes to write down about Mako, the driver, the big guy, Millie, and Vincent. I told the officer at the desk that Officer Simmons wanted my statement. He told me to hold on and made a call.

I sat on the bench. The cobwebs were clearing, and I could think and see straight without the swimming feeling. An officer came to the front and asked for my statement. Big, beefy guy with a dark complexion and the worst Philadelphia accent I ever heard.

"Ya done, Mac?"

I was confused. "Yeah. Where's Officer Simmons? She wanted my statement."

He stared at me for a moment. "I'm Simmons. I wanted it."

Maybe the cobwebs were bigger than I thought. I handed him the pad. He looked at me, then the pad, and turned and walked away without a word. I sat on the bench and wondered how bad off I was. Maybe I should go to the hospital.

A few minutes later, McSweeney came to the front. "You all right, Mike? You look like hell."

"Just a little woozy, like I'm underwater."

McSweeney nodded. "We'll get you looked at. But right now, we got a task force to take down Mako. According to Billings, the big guy, Mako has an arsenal at the market, so we're not going to take any chances. We're going to roll at ten, see if we can catch him at closing time."

"I'd like to come along if you don't mind."

"Sure. Don't go running off and try to do it yourself. You see where that gets you."

Around nine-thirty, Simmons brought me back to the squad room. Fifteen cops, the Stakeout Unit, all with bullet-proof vests, were listening to McSweeney. Some were holding semi-automatic weapons, some had shotguns. These guys were going in heavy.

"You all have his picture. He's armed and dangerous, but we want to take him alive. You all have your assignments. Work together and stay in communication. We all want to go home tonight. Be safe." He turned the cops over to Lieutenant Bradley, head of the Unit.

All the cops moved towards the doors, and McSweeney motioned for me. He handed me a vest. "I want you to stay away from the store. I'm doing this as a favor to you, but don't do anything stupid. I don't want you getting hurt any more than you are already. Promise me that, will you Mike?"

"Sure thing, Lieutenant."

We drove along Girard Avenue towards the store. Kids with sparklers ran around on the sidewalk, and when some of them saw a line of police cars, they tossed firecrackers and cherry bombs our way. We parked on the other end of the bridge by the Zoo. Traffic cops diverted the cars away from the bridge and the shop. As we got to the other end of the bridge, I saw that the cops blocked off Girard as far as I could see. Not one car or pedestrian in sight. Bradley spoke into the radio and got confirmation from the squad leaders that they were ready. "Move in," he said.

I stood about fifty yards away on a bridge over some railroad tracks. An officer stepped forward and shot a gas grenade into the shop through the front window. I heard the pop of the grenade and at the same time, the fireworks display over the Art Museum started with a huge bang, lighting the sky less than a mile away. A few seconds later, automatic rifle fire came from the shop, peppering the cars parked there, the street, and the sides of the bridge. I scrambled to the north side of the bridge to be out of the line of fire and it gave me a better look at the fireworks. I don't know which one interested me more, the life and death situation at the corner, or the annual celebration of our nation's birth. I sat on the sidewalk and watched the red, white, and blue fireworks, with occasional glances at the firefight. Mako held them off for fifteen minutes, but he either ran out of ammunition or willpower and gunfire from the store slowed. The fireworks culminated in an orgasm of pyrotechnics which lighted the sky for miles around and then died. Smoke from the fireworks and the firefight lingered over Girard Avenue and lessened the streetlights. A squad of cops moved in and brought out Mako. He was wearing a gas mask, a helmet, and a vest. He was prepared but was no match for the firepower of the cops. Only one cop suffered the ill effects of the tear gas, and he was fine in a few minutes. McSweeney understood that thousands of people leaving the fireworks would want to use the Girard Avenue bridge in a few minutes, so he broke down the roadblocks, and people leaving didn't even know that the cops assaulted the store while they were watching the display.

I walked over to where Mako was standing, in handcuffs and leg irons. A cop was at each shoulder, waiting to take him away. Dirt streaked his face, his eyes lined in red, and he looked like he lost a gunfight.

"Hi Mako, remember me?"

He looked at me with no recognition.

"I was in earlier asking about Millie and Vincent Sparks. Remember them?"

He shook his head and sighed.

My Christian attitude escaped me. I stuck my face right in his. "You killed an innocent woman, you bastard. Why? Why'd you have to kill her?"

In a smoke-ravaged voice, Mako sounded like a defeated man. "She was going to turn me in. I couldn't let her do that."

"I hope they fry your ass."

One of the cops pushed me back. They put him in the back of a car so I couldn't say any more to him. McSweeney came over and told the two cops where to take Mako. He turned to me, and said, "Feel better now, Mike. We got him off the street."

I nodded. "Maybe, but it's a hollow feeling. Millie's dead and nothing we do can bring her back. I hope they string them all up."

"Yeah. Look, a couple of men have to go to the hospital to get checked out. Heat, gas, that sort of thing. You want to go with them?"

That sounded tempting, but I asked for a ride back to my car. I told him that all I needed was some rest. He got a young cop to give me a lift. Before we left, I stuck my head inside the store. Disorder and chaos reigned. Even the shark was beaten up, missing his tail and his lower jaw, and most of his belly was gone.

The cop told me it was time to go. We rode in silence, and I tried to collect my thoughts. With all the traffic from the revelers, it would have taken a half-hour, but the young cop went lights and sirens, and we were back to my car quickly. I thanked him and got out.

I sat in my car for ten minutes or so, trying to collect my thoughts and figure out what I wanted to do. I realized I was hungry and hadn't eaten since breakfast. Maybe if I was thinking clearly, I'd have gone to the Duck Palace, and then home, for some rest. Instead, I headed toward the office. A lot of the partyers descended on Center City so I took my time. I finally got to the garage in the Fidelity building and parked on the third level.

It probably wasn't the best idea, but I walked over to Jimmy's. There were a few people in there still on a fireworks high. I sat in my usual seat at the end of the bar and tried to look interested.

Cleo came down and stood in front of me. "What'll it be, cowboy?"

"The usual, gorgeous."

She put a shot of rye and a High Life in front of me before the words were out of my mouth.

She peered at me with her dark eyes as she adjusted the clips in her brown hair. "Are you all right, Mike? You look like you're a million miles away."

"Yeah, I'm fine. This will help," and I pointed at the drinks. I ordered some food, a pastrami on rye. "And you know what else?" I went to the jukebox, dropped in a dime, and punched C24. I put in three more dimes and punched C25, C26, and C27. In a moment, Billie Holliday started singing. She had the floor for the next ten minutes, and when she took a break, I punched four more numbers and Sam Cooke showed up. I sat back and listened to them and tried to forget the day. A few more drinks and I let Cleo take me home. As I lay there, drifting off to sleep, it hit me, what Millie said. Not my name, somebody else's!

Mako killed me, Mike.

On my mother's grave, that's what she told me.

I got up and retrieved the piece of paper from my pocket and filled in the blanks. I stared at them the rest of the night, a message from beyond. Millie's words haunted me, that night and a lot of nights in the future. I failed her, and I'll never be able to make it up to her. I gotta find a new line of work where murder victims don't talk to me.

HUMAN, AND NOT-SO
BY JIM TOWNS

Luiz was about to close up his little corner bodega for the night and go home to his family, when the Stranger came in; he knew he was going to be home late— or not at all, maybe. Because the Stranger had to die.

One of Luiz's earliest memories was his abuela's funeral. She'd been closing up this same store one night back in 1987, when a stranger had come in and killed her. Not just killed her, he'd nearly ripped her throat out. Nothing had been taken, and the man had never been caught.

Some kind of maniac, he remembered his relatives saying at the wake, as he stood around in an ill-fitting Communion suit that had been his cousin's, not knowing what to do or say. He'd only been six.

Tonight, a now middle-aged Luiz watched the man as he wandered slowly through the small market—past the racks with the fresh produce Luiz always made sure to keep misted with water, past the cooler with a few pieces of assorted meats he bought straight from the butcher every other weekday, and past the racks stocked with dry goods like pasta and instant soup. The Stranger was short, with a haggard, pockmarked face and long stringy hair that reached his shoulders. His eyes were sunken into the sockets of his skull so far they seemed almost not there, but for the way they would occasionally catch the light with a reddish-tinged glint. He wore old, tattered clothing, beat-up cowboy boots and a ratty trenchcoat that nearly reached the floor.

Luiz's hand slowly reached for the shotgun he kept under the counter.

*

It was 2002, and Luiz had been twenty-one: he had just gotten his associate's degree in nursing—the first person in his family to get a post-high school diploma. His father had come to the commencement ceremony that afternoon, but he'd had to go back to the store that evening. The family had been celebrating back at their house only a couple blocks away, when there was a knock on the door and two Jersey City police officers were standing there. Alberto Flores had been viciously killed just before closing the store by a man in a long coat who was described as short, with bad skin and long, lank hair.

Nothing had been stolen.

*

That had been almost twenty years ago, and Luiz had been expecting the man to come back for the last few.

After his father's death, he'd put aside his plans for being an RN for a while, and had focused on keeping the store running. His mother was so grief-stricken by the brutality of her husband's death that she'd stopped being able to work, so Luiz had hired a local girl named Maria to help out. Soon he and Maria had fallen in love, and had a child together—little Camila. Years had passed quickly and Camila was now in high school, and Luiz never had a chance to pursue his career, but that was okay: he had kept the family business running.

The Stranger was opening the Plexiglas doors of the refrigerated racks now, one by one—looking at the sodas, the beers, the waters, but not selecting anything. He was taking his time, Luiz knew.

Under the counter, his hand gripped the handle of his shotgun.

"Hey, I'm closing soon, my friend."

When he spoke, the Stranger glanced up at him and grinned. His teeth were yellowed and jagged—several of them missing and at least one glinted gold.

"So, like, just do me a favor and grab what you need, okay?" Luiz mumbled. He had a strong feeling that the Stranger knew exactly what he was holding under the counter. The uncanny-looking man glanced all around the place, taking his time, before finally letting his eerie eyes once more come to rest on Luiz.

"You've been expecting me."

"You've been in this shop before."

The man nodded: "A couple years ago."

"And a couple years before that?"

"Possibly. I come by this way every once in a while." The Stranger was coming towards Luiz very slowly—almost imperceptibly. He noticed the man moved strangely: like he weighed nothing; like it required no physical effort to make his body move. His high-heeled cowboy boots should have clacked on the linoleum tile floor of the shop, but they didn't.

"You can stop right there," Luiz said when the Stranger was still a good six feet away. He half-pulled the shotgun out, so the man could see the stock and the trigger.

Unexpectedly, the Stranger burst into cackling laughter.

"You *have* been expecting me."

"A man murders your grandma, then your pops—you make plans for if he comes back."

A head cock: "They were your ancestors? Interesting." Luiz could see the Stranger's hands flexing, and noticed his fingernails were very long, and dirty.

It all made sense, now.

Luiz had given many late nights of thought to the killer of his father and grandmother: to the heinousness of their murders, but also the similarities. They'd been killed fifteen years apart, but in almost the same way—their throats slashed and mangled.

He'd read a lot about serial killers, and the patterns they follow. But this felt different. It was random, but there was also a certain syncopation: a poetry.

An awful, grotesque rhyme, but a rhyme all the same. So of course he knew the killer would come back to complete one final verse.

The Stranger made one or two more cautious steps forward, and Luiz's hands gripped the gun tighter. It was a two-barreled twelve-gauge: he'd had his friend Cameron use his Sawzall to cut the barrels and butt stock down, and he'd filed the cut edges smooth. It was now 18 inches back to front and totally illegal, but who gave a damn—this fiend had butchered two generations of his family.

"You think you'll whip your gun out, and get revenge on your forebears, son? Is that it? I'm sorry, that won't work... things may not be quite what they appear to be."

The Stranger was teasing him, but Luiz didn't care—he knew exactly how things were. The person standing before him was *el Muerto*—the Undead. He'd read all about these creatures from childhood, but it hadn't been until his father was killed that he'd put it together with the death of his abuela. Both had been found with their throats gashed, but very little blood had been spilled. Luiz himself had had to clean up after his father died, and that's when he'd come to the realization.

Whatever had killed him had taken his blood as well.

Both attacks had happened just after nightfall.

The attacker was fifteen years older when he'd killed Alberto, and yet the attack had had the same ferocity and violence and power—as though the attacker hadn't aged in the interim.

"I know what you are, fiend."

"And what pray tell is that?"

"You're *el Vampiro...* the undead."

The Stranger stopped—and bowed slightly: "I'm very impressed. The vast majority people can't come to grips with what I am, until the very end. I see the realization appear in their eyes, even as their life is draining away. It's sad. But also kind of beautiful."

The killer paused: "I'm wondering, son, what your eyes will look like as you die."

"You'll die wondering, fiend." Luiz raised the shotgun and pulled the trigger for the left barrel. The retort was deafening and the kickback nearly knocked him backwards into the shelves, filled floor to ceiling with a hundred types of liquor in a hundred different-shaped bottles. Through the smoke of the shot he heard a body fall hard to the ground.

He'd done it. He'd shot the thing that had taken his father, and his mother before him.

But then he heard the scrape of nails on tile—the rustle of an old coat—and out of the smoke the Stranger rose up. Part of his face was now blackened and burned, and his right ear hung loose by tendons. The eye on that side now glowed a dull deep red, its cornea ripped off by the shot.

"You little shit..." the Stranger croaked, and Luiz heard air escaping out the side of his torn cheek as he did: "You think *this* is going to stop what's going to happen to you?"

In a single leap, the Stranger launched himself six feet across the floor, up and onto the counter in front of Luiz, landing in a crouch—its tattered cloak flapping. A hand like a sledgehammer slapped the gun from his hand, and Luiz felt the other one grab him powerfully by the throat. The Stranger's haggard and bloodied face was close to him, and his breath was rank as rotting meat as he spoke:

"You know how many men have tried to stop me? Dozens. And are any of them still alive?" He shook his head slowly side to side, and shoved Luiz violently back against the shelves, shattering the bottles and spilling the liquor down the gashes in his burning back.

Next Luiz was shoved to the floor, and felt the Stranger's boot pinning him down even as claw-like nails slowly dug into the flesh of his neck. It was agony.

"You will die here tonight, and I'm sure that in short order, one of your own squalid brood will take over for you, as you did yours... a son, perhaps? Or, if I'm lucky—a daughter." Camila's face flittered through Luiz's mind even as blood ran from the gashes in his neck and pooled around the floor beneath him, mixing with sour-smelling bourbon and tequila.

His outstretched fingers touched the sawed-off handle of the shotgun.

"Perhaps I'll return this way sooner this time—so as to meet her while she's young and delicious... not old and tired like your grandma."
Luiz knew he would die tonight. But he silently swore to himself that this fiend would never hurt Camila.

His hand closed around the handle of the gun, and his finger felt the touch of the triggers, finding the second one. The right barrel.

And then the Stranger ripped out his larynx.

Luiz felt all the air in his body rush out of his lungs through the gaping hole in his throat, even as he saw the Stranger lift it up and let his blood drain into his mouth. That hideous face then sank down onto his neck and he felt a strong suction—it was taking all his blood. There was no more pain, and he felt his mind slipping away from his body, as he grew weaker and weaker. But there was still a moment, and he would make it count.

With every ounce of energy remaining in his shredded body, he raised the heavy gun into the air, turning it and pressing the barrel up under the Stranger's chin, forcing it up a few inches away from his own face.

The Stranger cackled once more: "Bullets won't help you anymore, son."

Luiz smiled through the blood, and squeezed the trigger. One and three-eights ounces of silver shot erupted out of the barrel into the Stranger's head. The silver had once been the rosary his abuela wore: the one his father had kept on his dresser his entire life until he, too, was killed by this monster. Luiz had had it melted down and recast as little pellets by his same friend who'd sawed off the gun. He'd packed it into a shotgun shell himself, and Father Evan had been kind enough to bless it, despite his misgivings.

The Stranger's skull erupted into a thousand fragments: coating the walls, floor and ceiling with dark, coagulated blood. The headless trunk wavered a moment, then toppled over on its side.

Luiz let the spent shotgun fall. He couldn't move, and he knew he'd lost too much blood now. They'd find him this way, next to the headless body of the fiend. The police would believe he'd killed a would-be robber in a fight, and that was okay with him. No one else needed to know that horrors like this thing still walked the earth.

Luiz let his head fall back as the last of his lifeblood poured into the sanguine halo of blood and booze surrounding his head. The store would go on. Maria would make sure of that. His customers, who were his friends and neighbors, would have a place to get their food and goods, and to meet and chat about what was happening in their little neighborhood.

Most of all, Camila would be safe. He knew it.

Luiz's eyes closed.

THE BOOK OF LIFE
BY
MICHAEL R. RITT

"And I saw the dead, great and small, standing before the throne, and books were opened. Then another book was opened, which is the book of life. And the dead were judged by what was written in the books, according to what they had done."

The sound of a barking dog woke Ben Lawton from his afternoon nap. He opened his eyes but remained still as he tuned his ears to the sound, which seemed to be coming from the yard two doors down and across the street. It took a moment for him to distinguish the barking that had awakened him from the barking and growling of the wolf pack that had surrounded him in his dream.

He looked from side to side as his surroundings became familiar to him once again. He was sitting in a lawn chair under an old maple tree in his granddaughter's front yard. Only a few seconds ago, he had been a much younger man, somewhere beside a river. There had been a young woman with him in his dream, and they had been fending off a pack of wolves that had surrounded them. He tried to remember more about his dream, but the details were already starting to fade away. He knew the dream was of another time and another place; sometime in the late eighteen hundreds. Maybe he was a lawman of some kind, tracking an outlaw through the mountains. He couldn't be sure, but it felt right. It felt real.

After stretching his arms and yawning, Ben picked up the glass of lemonade that was nestled in the glass holder in the arm of the lawn chair. The ice had long since melted and diluted the contents. He must have been asleep for over an hour.

Placing both hands on the ends of the armrests, he leaned forward and pushed in an effort to get to his feet. The first attempt failed, so he rocked his body and pushed harder. This time he was able to stand up, emitting a series of involuntary guttural sounds his wife used to call "old man noises" before she passed away two years ago.

It had been difficult without her. They had been married for over fifty years. At seventy-six years of age, he had been the one with all of the health issues. She had seemed to be in good health – active and even feisty at times – right up until the stroke that took her away from him. He had gotten out of bed one morning to the sound of her singing hymns as she made the morning coffee. She had just sung the first verse of "The Old Rugged Cross" while Ben was stepping into his slippers and tying his robe. The singing stopped suddenly as Ben walked out of the bedroom and into the kitchen.

"What's the matter, Beth? Did you forget the chorus?"

That's when he saw her body on the kitchen floor. She was gone just that fast, and they hadn't even said goodbye.

Ben heard the front door open and turned to see his granddaughter walking toward him.

"Are you alright, grandpa?"

Ben smiled as he considered how much Connie looked like her grandmother. She fussed over him, just like Beth had done. She had that same look on her face, with the outside ends of her eyebrows raised and her nose scrunched up, whenever she was worried about him.

"I'm fine, sweetheart," he said. "Just took a little nap, that's all."

She held out her hand to him. "It's time for your pills."

He held his hand out and she dropped the pills into his palm.

Ben frowned as he stared at the different medications he held. There were pills of all shapes and sizes and colors; for his thyroid, his heart, his blood pressure, his cholesterol...

Connie bent down and picked up the glass of lemonade and handed it to him as he brought his hand up to his mouth. He hated taking the pills, and always swallowed them all at once to get it over and done with.

It was mid-October. The red, orange, and gold leaves fell from the limbs of the huge old maples that lined their street. Like pieces of a shattered rainbow, they floated down to cover the ground in a plush fiery carpet that blurred the distinction between the road and the sidewalk.

Connie shivered and hugged herself against a short burst of the wind which rustled the leaves, freeing even more of them to join their companions on the ground below. "You should come inside now, grandpa. It's getting chilly out."

Ben looked down the street toward the center of town. "I think I'll go for a little walk." He started fumbling with the buttons on his cardigan.

Connie gently pushed his fingers aside and finished buttoning up the grey, wool sweater for him. "Alright, but be careful." She had that scrunched-up, worried look on her face again.

"I won't be very long."

Connie hugged him and started back toward the house. Halfway there, she turned and said, "I'm making white chicken chili for dinner."
Ben picked up his cane, which had been leaning against the side of the lawn chair, waved goodbye, and started down the street toward town.

The streets were quiet as Ben made his way toward the center of town. It was a weeknight and not much was going on – not that there was ever much going on in this unobtrusive little Midwestern town. Ben tried to remember the last time that anything really exciting had happened to break the monotony of living in this place, but he couldn't think of anything.

He wasn't complaining; it was a great place to raise a family. Children could ride their bikes up and down the streets, or they could play ball at the park and their parents would never have to worry about them. Everybody knew everybody in this town, and they watched out for everyone else. He had raised his family here. His granddaughter had grown up here. They had roots in the community; roots that anchored them firmly in place and nourished them with a sense of belonging and security that most people craved.

But Ben had been uneasy about something. It had been gnawing at him since his wife had died, and the feeling had only grown stronger over the past few months. It was a restlessness that was foreign to him. He had never wanted to live anywhere else, but lately, nothing satisfied him; not the town, or the people, or even his life.

He passed the courthouse which took up a whole block right in the center of town. The four-story structure was one of the oldest buildings in the county, having been built in 1882 from stone quarried just outside of town. The courthouse was surrounded by lawns and gardens, with oaks, maples, and elm trees scattered throughout.

He found his favorite bench and took a seat. Just walking the five blocks from Connie's house had made him short of breath and he needed to rest a few minutes before making the return trip. The sun was getting low in the sky and the streetlights were starting to turn on. While he rested, he watched a pair of squirrels tunneling through the fallen leaves, collecting acorns for the winter.

As he got to his feet to start back to Connie's, something across the street caught his eye. It was a small red neon sign that said "Open." Ben wasn't sure why he noticed it, except maybe it was the way the neon flickered through the tubes of the sign, as though it had just been turned on and was in the process of warming up.

Ben knew every business in town, but he couldn't remember which one was across the street. He looked to see if there was any other sign that would jog his memory and identify the place for him. Then he saw the sign above the door. "Reaper Books."

A bookstore, huh? I don't remember a bookstore being there.

He walked down to the corner and looked first one way, and then the other. There was no traffic on the street tonight, but a cool breeze met him head-on. He pulled his sweater close around his neck and started across the street toward the bookstore.

Ben took a deep breath as he opened the door and stepped inside. He loved the musty smell of old books. His granddaughter had her books on some kind of a computer gizmo that she carried with her. She said it would hold thousands of books. He stood in the doorway and took another deep breath. She might be able to carry a whole library at one time, but this wonderful, musty scent is something she could never get from some computer.

Reaper Books was a quaint shop that looked bigger on the inside than it did on the outside. There were rows and rows of shelves of used books piled, with little regard to organization, on every surface that would support the weight. The shop was dimly lit by the light of the waning sun through the window in the front of the building. The only other source of light was from a lamp sitting on top of a massive oak desk that sat in the middle of the shop. It also had stacks of books and newspapers cluttering its surface.

Ben couldn't see anyone else in the shop, so he started browsing through the shelves, pulling out first this book, then another, only reading the titles of some of them, but browsing through the pages of others that piqued his interest.

"Is there something in particular you're looking for?"

The voice startled Ben and he involuntarily slammed the book shut that he had been reading. When he turned around, he saw a man standing calmly at the end of the aisle with his hands folded in front of him. He was an attractive man, probably in his late thirties or early forties. He had a Mediterranean look about him with dark hair and eyes. He had a beard and mustache that were as black as crow's feathers and were short and neatly trimmed. His suit was also in black but was impeccably tailored.

Ben replaced the book on the shelf. "I didn't see anyone else in here. I was just browsing. I hope you don't mind."

"Not at all. You're more than welcomed to look around. I'm Mr. Reaper, the proprietor." He held out his hand and stepped forward. Ben shook hands and introduced himself. "I thought that I knew all of the businesses in town, but I guess that my memory isn't quite what it used to be," he said, apologetically. "Have you been here long?"

Mr. Reaper smiled. "I've been in this business for quite a few years, but this location is rather new for me."

"Well, it seems like a nice place you have here. You've got a lot of books, that's for sure." Ben said as he turned to look down the rows of shelves.

"I have something for everyone; mystery, romance, suspense, fantasy. Or perhaps you enjoy nonfiction; history, biography, theology, natural science. You can find it all on these shelves. What is it that you are looking for, Ben? What is your personal preference?"

"I like westerns. That's mostly what I read."

Mr. Reaper smiled and pointed at Ben. "I could have guessed that," he said knowingly, shaking his finger. "You have the look of rugged individualism about you." He motioned for Ben to follow him. "Come this way and I'll show you where the westerns are kept."

Ben followed as Mr. Reaper led him through a maze of shelves full of dusty-smelling books of all kinds. The light in the shop was dim and Ben got disoriented as they made their way to a little alcove.

"This section is dedicated to our western collection of books. Feel free to browse."

Ben started skimming over the titles of the books displayed on the shelves. He quickly recognized books by some of his favorite authors; Zane Grey, Louis L'Amour, and Jack Schaefer to name a few, but they all seemed to be books he had already read over and over again.

Mr. Reaper noticed Ben's lack of interest as he skimmed over the titles, but didn't pull any of the books off of the shelves. "I suppose you are already familiar with these books. They are classic westerns, after all."
Ben nodded, "Yes, I've read most of these several times. I like the old-time writers and their stories, but I guess I can only read them so many times."

"Have you tried any of the newer writers?"

Ben shrugged, "A few of them, but they're not the same."

"How so," asked Mr. Reaper. He pointed to a pair of overstuffed leather chairs that were to one side of the alcove. Between the chairs was a coffee table with a little lamp in the middle. The lamplight cast a warm glow that was just enough to envelope the two chairs. It was a comfortable, inviting spot, and both men took a seat while they continued.

"To me," said Ben, "when I read one of the newer books, it's like I'm watching the story unfold on a movie screen. But when I read one of the old-timers, it's like I'm actually inside the story." Ben was lost in thought for a moment remembering when he had read The Virginian for the first time as a kid. He remembered how he would ride with Trampas and the Virginian and the other cowhands on the Sunk Creek Ranch. He glanced over at Mr. Reaper who was smiling at him. "I guess that sounds pretty silly."

"Not at all. I know just what you mean. I think I have just the book you are looking for." He stood to his feet and walked over to a nearby shelf. There was a small step stool that he moved into position right in the center of the row of shelves. Climbing up onto the stool, he reached up to the uppermost shelf and pulled down a brown, leather-covered volume.

"Why don't you browse through this one," he said, handing the book to Ben. "I'll leave you alone while you look it over, but If you have any questions, just ring that bell." He pointed to a small handbell sitting on the table next to the lamp.

Ben looked where he was pointing, and when he looked back up, Mr. Reaper was gone.

He examined the book that had been handed to him. It wasn't like any of the other books that he had looked at. It seemed to be quite old. The leather cover was a little stiff and was cracking in places, and as he flipped through the pages, he saw that they were yellowed with age. The words, "The Book of Life," were stamped across the front of the cover in big gold letters. Ben examined the book further, but couldn't find the name of the author anywhere. There was also no copyright date or publisher.

*"This sure doesn't look like any western I've ever seen. "*Ben surprised himself as he realized he had said this out loud. He had begun to talk to himself

more and more sinse Beth's death and inwardly chastised himself for becoming a cliche.

He sunk back into the comfort of the chair, noticing how the aroma of the leather filled his nostrils. He loved the smell of leather. It reminded him of saddles and horse tack. There wasn't a whisper of a sound coming from anywhere in the shop. The warm glow of the lamp softly illuminated the little alcove. He was surrounded by books, from floor to ceiling. It was almost like being in a cave made out of books.

He opened the book to the first page and started reading...

*

He saw the dark plume of smoke rising in the distance and pulled back on the reins. The solitary rider on the blue roan shielded his eyes from the waning sun and set his gaze on the horizon to the southwest. There was but the slightest breeze, so the smoke rose straight into the air before wafting slowly to the east. It stood out in sharp contrast to the perfectly blue and cloudless June sky.

The rider scanned the prairie in every direction without spotting any sign of movement from anything, anywhere. Except for the fact that someone had started the fire, it would have been easy for him to imagine that he was alone in the vast sea of grass.

He patted the gelding on the neck and pointed him in the direction of the smoke. "I guess we better go find out what that's all about."

Nearly thirty minutes later, the source of the smoke became apparent as he rode up to the smoldering ruins of a prairie schooner. He looked carefully around before dismounting to search the area. Pieces of furniture, articles of clothing, and other personal belongings were strewn all over the ground, trampled by horses and men. From as best as he could make out, there had been at least five unshod horses. It was when he walked around the far side of the wagon that he saw the body.

It was that of a man in his early thirties who was laying on his side. He had an arrow protruding from one of his legs and another that had entered the right side of his chest and was sticking out of his back. The man had also been scalped. Flys buzzed around the bloody skull cap as ants explored the ears and nose.

He bent down to examine the arrows. *Kiowa.* The previous year's treaty at Medicine Lodge was supposed to have relocated the Kiowa to a reservation below the Washita River in Indian Territory, but there were still plenty of Indians that didn't like the idea of leaving the Kansas plains.

He located a shovel from among the scattered debris and dug a grave in the dark, rich Kansas soil for the deceased man. There were no papers on the man to help identify who he was, so he didn't bother with any kind of marker for the grave.

He tossed the last shovel full of dirt onto the man-sized mound of earth, then he threw the shovel to the side. Standing over the grave, he removed his hat and said, "Partner, I don't know who you were or where you were heading, but everyone's trail ends somewhere. Yours ended here. I hope the next leg of your journey brings you more peace than this one did. Amen."

Stepping into the stirrup, he threw his leg over the back of the roan and took one final look around. He knew what he had to do, for among the clothing scattered around the wagon were several dresses, however, there was no woman's body anywhere. That could only mean that there must have been a woman on the wagon who had been taken by the Kiowa.

He circled the wagon in ever-increasing concentric circles, casting for sign until he located the trail the Indians had used when they rode away. The trail headed south toward the Cimarron and Indian territory. He thought about riding back to Fort Dodge for the Army, but it was a three-day ride to the east. By the time he got back with a detachment of soldiers, the Kiowa could be almost a week ahead of them. As it was now, they only had about a two-hour head start. If he hurried, he might be able to catch up with them by nightfall.

*

Ben closed the book and looked up from his reading. *This story has potential.* He looked around the little dimly lit alcove of books in which he had been tucked away like a caterpillar in a cocoon. He realized that while he was winding his way through the maze of shelves in the store, he had lost his bearings and wasn't even sure where the door was. *Now, where did that Mr. Reaper get to?* Then he remembered the bell on the table next to him. The chair he was sitting in was so soft and plush, it took a little effort to move around in it, but he was able to stretch his arm out and ring the bell with the tip of his finger. When he looked up, he gave a start, for Mr. Reaper was standing right in front of him.

The book store owner must have seen the shocked expression on his face.

"I'm sorry if I startled you. I was just around the corner shelving some books."

Ben started to get up out of the chair, so Mr. Reaper took him by the arm and helped him to his feet. "I like the way this story is unfolding," Ben told the store's owner, "but I don't know…" He rubbed his chin thoughtfully. It was a negotiation tactic he always used when contemplating a purchase. "It's kind of a strange book; no author or publisher mentioned; no copywrite either. How does a book like this get published?"

Mr. Reaper only smiled and said, "I agree, it is an unusual book and a bit of a mystery. All I can tell you is that I've had it a very long time."

Ben hesitated a moment, and then said, "Well, I'm interested if the price is right. I'm on a fixed income you understand."

"I'll tell you what I'll do," replied Mr. Reaper. "Because of the concerns that you've expressed about the book, why don't you take it home and look it over for a couple of days. If you decide that you like it, you can come back and we'll work out a price that's satisfactory to both of us."

Ben was hesitant, "Oh, I don't know. That doesn't seem right…"

"I insist," replied Mr. Reaper. "I make it a practice of mine to make sure that every customer is completely satisfied with his purchase."

"Well, if you insist."

"Excellent!" Mr. Reaper rubbed his hands together in satisfaction. "Let me show you the way out." He turned and led the way to the front of the store with Ben following close behind.

Once outside, Ben braced himself against the autumn breeze. Dusk had settled over the town. Leaves, caught in a whirlwind, rose from the curb, dancing and twirling a choreographed ballet down the center of the sidewalk. At last, the energy of the movement waned, and the dancers fell exhausted to the stage.

Ben, book in hand, lowered his head against the wind and headed home.

It was afternoon the next day when Ben decided to take the book out to his spot in the front yard to read. He lowered his frail body into the lawn chair, letting gravity do most of the work for him. He had had a good night's sleep but still felt tired when he finally crawled out of bed that morning. Just the effort of getting dressed and making his way to the kitchen exhausted him. He felt a little better after his usual breakfast of black coffee and a piece of toast with Connie's homemade plum jam.

Connie brought out a blanket and a travel mug of hot coffee for him. She placed the mug in the cup holder of the lawn chair, and then spread the blanket across his legs and tucked it underneath him.

"Stop making such a fuss over me," he complained. But in reality, he loved having Connie dote on him.

"I just want you to stay warm if you're going to sit out here and read." She finished tucking the blanket in around his legs. "I'm going to go back inside and start the laundry. I'll be out to check on you in a little while."

"Thank you, sweetheart. I'll be fine."

Connie bent down and kissed him on the forehead before heading inside.

Ben opened the book to the place he had left off the day before and began to read...

*

The next morning, he watched through a pair of field glasses from the top of a small sandstone ridge. The Kiowa had made camp last night about a half-mile south of him between the ridge and the Cimarron. It had been easy to follow their trail through the prairie grass, and he had almost caught up with them by the time they had stopped for the night.

The good news is that he could see the woman sitting by herself in the middle of the Kiowa camp. She didn't appear to be injured. In fact, she appeared to be the recipient of special protection from one brave in particular. He was a huge man with a long scar down the left side of his face. He hovered close by, discouraging the other braves from getting too close to the woman.

The bad news is that the band of five or six Indians had joined up with a larger group. There was now close to fifty Kiowa in the encampment below. The army would want to know about this many Indians who had jumped the reservation, unfortunately, he would have to wait to inform them until after he rescued the woman—that is "if" he could rescue her. His odds were getting worse as time went by.

He knew he would need the cover of night to have any hope of effecting a rescue, so he waited on the ridge throughout the day, watching the camp below. They didn't seem to be in any hurry to break camp and cross the Cimarron, and that was a little puzzling. It could mean that they were waiting to be joined by even more Indians and that could be a real problem if he didn't act tonight.

By the time the sun had set, and the stars had begun to pop out in the east, he had formulated the rudiments of a plan. It was risky, but with the right timing and a little luck it could work.

There was a small gully between him and the Kiowa camp. It ran east to west and looked like it might be a dry wash that would empty into the Cimarron when it was running with water. The captive woman had been placed in a tipi just on the opposite side of the wash on the east side of the camp. He didn't know if there was anyone inside the tipi besides the woman. If so, he would have to deal with that when the time arose.

He decided to get a few hours of sleep. There might not be time to do much sleeping if the rescue was a success and they were on the run. He woke up a couple of hours after midnight. The stars twinkled like fireflies in the cloudless night sky. A quarter moon gave him enough light to move around in, but not so much that anyone guarding the camp could spot his approach.

He and his horse picked their way quietly off of the ledge towards the east side of the camp. There was a small copse of willow on the north side of the wash. He walked the roan into the trees and tied the reins to a low-hanging branch, then, making sure there was no one around, he crawled into the wash and, keeping himself bent low, made his way up the wash to the west side of the camp. Keeping low and quiet, his movement had to be slow. He didn't want to trip or kick a rock that might alert the camp to his presence. Even though he was only a couple of hundred feet to his destination, it felt more like a mile.

He arrived at the western side of the Kiowa camp and slowly stood up enough to look over the edge of the gully. So far, so good. No one seemed to be aware of his presence. There were a couple of campfires burning near the center of the camp, but it appeared as though most of the Kiowa had settled in for the night.

He carefully crawled up the side of the wash toward a tipi that had been pitched on the most westerly side of the camp. Crouching low behind the tipi, he gathered some brush and piled it against the buffalo hides that covered the structure. Striking a match, he held it to the dry wood until it caught hold. Within seconds, a small flame appeared, growing larger as the wood popped and sparks began to jump out of the flames. When he was convinced that the fire would continue to grow, he quickly made his way back into the wash and headed to the other side of the camp.

He was a little more than halfway when he heard a scream coming from somewhere in the camp behind him. Soon, other Indians were coming out of their tipis to see what the commotion was. Before long, it seemed as though the whole camp was in motion, rushing toward the fire, which by now had nearly engulfed the entire tipi and was threatening to spread.

*

This is a smart guy. He created a diversion to keep the Kiowa occupied while he rescues the woman. That's just what I would have done. Ben continued reading...

*

With the Kiowa distracted by the fire, he quickened his pace and sprinted the last twenty yards. He crawled back out of the gully and made his way to the back of the tipi where he knew that the woman was being held. He tried to listen for any sounds coming from inside, but couldn't hear anything. He didn't know if she was alone inside or if there were a dozen Indians. He had to take the chance now while the camp was occupied with the fire.

He pulled his knife from its sheath and plunged it into the back of the tipi, cutting downward. Sticking his head through the opening, he scanned the inside of the tipi. A small fire illuminated the inside. Shadows danced on the walls with each flicker of the flames.

The woman was there alone with her hands and feet bound. When she saw him, her eyes went wide and her mouth opened to scream, but he quickly put his finger up to his lips in a gesture to quiet her. At once, the fear in her eyes was replaced by a glimmer of hope.

He moved quickly and with agility as he made his way to her side; his knife in hand, it only took a second or two to cut through the leather thongs that bound her hands and feet.

"My name is Ben Lawton. I'm here to rescue you."

*

Ben's mouth hung open as he read that last sentence. He read it over again three more times to make sure he had read it correctly. *This guy has the same name as me! That's strange. What are the chances?*

*

The woman was beautiful. Ben had noticed that the first time he viewed her through his field glasses. She had been misused by the Kiowa brave, but even after having been treated roughly—with her torn, dirty clothes, and her hair mussed up with pieces of grass hanging from it—she was still beautiful. She had blond hair that hung down loosely over her shoulders. Ben couldn't make out much more about her, like the color of her eyes or of the clothes she wore. The dim light barely illuminated the inside of the tipi, obscuring all details.

Without saying another word, he took her by the hand and led her to the opening he had made in the back of the tipi. He led the way out and down into the wash. His horse was only about twenty feet away, up the other side of the wash, hidden in the willows.

He was just about to head up the embankment when he heard a scream behind him that froze the blood in his veins. It was a terrifying war cry. He turned to see the Kiowa brave with the scar hurl himself off the edge of the wash, into the air straight towards him. The Indian landed on top of him, knocking him to the ground, forcing the air from him. The impact must have knocked some of the air out of the brave as well because he was a little slow getting up. Ben was able to push him off as both men struggled to their feet. They stood facing each other, looking for their next move.

Scar face pulled a knife out of a sheath that he had hanging around his neck. Ben quickly drew his knife as well. He could have drawn his gun, but so far, no one else had seemed to notice their struggle. A gunshot would have surely put an end to that and drawn every Indian in the camp to where they were.

The brave made the first move, lunging forward. The moonlight glinted off of the steel blade as he made an upward slashing motion that cut through the front of Ben's shirt, leaving a thin line of crimson where the tip of the knife made a shallow cut across Ben's stomach. Emboldened, he charged again, and then a third time. Each time, Ben skillfully parried the attack. Then Ben went on the offensive, thrusting forward several times, forcing the Kiowa to back up with each advance. The clicking of the steel blades against each other, the grunting of the two men as they battled back and forth, and the shuffling of the gravel beneath their feet in the bottom of the wash were the only sounds made.

They continued like this, thrusting and deflecting. Each man circling the other, looking for a weakness to exploit. Both men seemed to have equal skill with the blade. Suddenly, the Kiowa drew his arm back and threw his knife at Ben. The action caught Ben by surprise. He tried to turn his body to avoid the blade that was streaking through the air, but he couldn't get out of the way in time. The knife embedded itself into his right side.

Ben stumbled backward, dropping his knife in the process. The Indian brave, having seen Ben drop his knife, lunged toward him, throwing himself on top of Ben in an effort to finish him off. There was a loud grunt, then both men lay still without making a sound. Finally, the body of the brave rolled off of Ben, onto the gravel in the bottom of the wash. He remained motionless.

Ben rolled onto his side, slowly, and got to his feet. After losing his knife and falling onto his back, he had seen the Indian brave charging him. At the last moment, he pulled the Kiowa's knife from his side and held it up. The brave fell on it when he threw himself on Ben.

Ben stood, panting, trying to catch his breath. He placed his hand on his side where the knife had penetrated between two of his ribs. The blood oozed out from between his fingers. He stumbled over to the edge of the wash where the woman helped him up the side and into the trees where his horse waited.

"You're bleeding!"

"We can't worry about that now. We've got to get some miles behind us. We're not safe here." Ben put his foot in the stirrup, wincing as he pulled himself into the saddle. Then he reached down to pull the woman up behind him. When they were both settled into place, he kicked his heels into the side of the gelding and headed north.

*

Ben closed the book and picked up his coffee mug. He had already drained it of its contents and he debated going inside to get it refilled. He just didn't have the energy right now to get up, so he remained in his lawn chair. He closed his eyes and felt the sun on his face. A gentle breeze brought the scent of earth and grass. He could imagine that he was riding a horse across the Kansas prairie, being pursued by Indians. It was more than imagination. It seemed so real. It seemed so right. It seemed like the thing that had been missing for the past two years.

He opened his eyes and returned to the book. It was a strange book, that was sure. It wasn't just that the main character had the same name as him, but there was an odd familiarity about it that he couldn't quite put his finger on. He continued to read...

*

They rode hard for the first hour with no words spoken. Then they slowed their pace but kept their progress steady. After another hour, Ben pulled back on the reins. "We've got to stop and rest the horse." He helped the woman down, then half dismounted, half fell from the saddle. He steadied himself by leaning against the roan.

The woman helped him to the ground. "Let me take a look." She pulled up his shirt to inspect the wound. The bleeding had slowed, but not stopped completely. She lifted her skirt and began tearing at the petticoat beneath. After ripping off several long swaths, she folded up one of the pieces and placed it against the wound. "Here, hold this in place."

Ben did as he was told as she continued to wrap the rest of the cloth around his chest to hold the bandage in place.

The sky was turning pale blue in the east, and the stars were blinking out above them. Ben was able to get a better look at her in the growing light of day. She looked to be in her early twenties; maybe eight to ten years younger than he was. Her hair hung down past her shoulders and was the color of corn silk. She had pale blue eyes; almost grey. Ben didn't see any fear in her eyes or any pain. Only strength and determination.

She caught him staring at her and she smiled. "I want to thank you for getting me away from those Indians. How did you know I was there? Or do you just go around visiting Indian camps to see if there is anyone who needs rescuing?"

"I came across your wagon and saw what happened. I followed and waited for dark." He hesitated and then added, "I buried your husband."

She finished tying off the bandages. A single tear rolled down her cheek. She quickly wiped it away. "He was my brother. We were on our way to New Mexico."

"What's your name?"

"I'm so sorry," she exclaimed with some embarrassment, "I haven't introduced myself yet. I'm Elizabeth Miller from Missouri.

*

Beth! Ben couldn't believe what he had just read. Elizabeth Miller was Beth's name when he married her, and she was from a small town called Boonville in central Missouri. How was this possible. What was happening here? Ben didn't understand what was going on, but it was right there in black and white. Even her description matched Beth to a tee when they had first met.

He looked at the book, flipping through the pages, examining the cover front and back, trying to find some clue as to how this could be. He tried to convince himself that it was only a coincidence, but somehow he knew he could not make himself believe that; he knew that what he read was real. This odd book with no author or publisher; this strange, wonderful story could have been pulled right out of his dreams. As amazing as it was, and as hard as it was to believe, this Book of Life was about him and Beth. It was their names written inside. It was their story. His heart started to race as he opened the book to where he had left off and continued to read...

*

Ben shook her hand. "I'm Ben Lawton. I'm a scout for the army out of Fort Dodge."

Beth stood to her feet and looked around in every direction. "Do you think we're safe?"

Ben got slowly to his feet with the assistance of Beth. "I haven't noticed anyone following us, but I can't be sure. If we were lucky, it took them some time to discover you were gone, or to find the body of that brave in the wash. We might have been able to get a four or five hours jump on them. If that's the case, they might decide it isn't worth the effort to try to find you. Of course, that's all speculation. They might be just over the rise and will be coming upon us any minute. We should keep moving."

"What will we do? Where will we go?"

Ben had poured some water from a canteen into his hat and was letting the horse have a drink. "We're about three and a half days out of Fort Dodge, but the army has a patrol out south of the Arkansas River, between us and the fort. If we keep heading north, there's a good chance we'll run into them in a couple of days."

They mounted up and continued on their journey north.

After leaving the valley of the Cimmaron in the early morning hours, they traveled over relatively flat country—which worked out well for them considering the dim light that they had to travel by. Now that the sun was getting higher, and they had no trouble seeing where they were going, they found themselves entering hills, covered with pine and red cedar, rising over two thousand feet. A large whitetail buck with a new set of antlers coming in darted across the trail in front of them and disappeared into a thicket of green ash.

It was slow going, but Ben didn't want to push his horse any harder than was necessary.

The sun was almost overhead when they walked out of the hills into a valley with a small river running through it to the southeast. "This should be Crooked Creek," said Ben. "Back in fifty-nine, the Second Cavalry out of Fort Belknap had a scrape with the Comanche somewhere along here."

"Are those the Indians that took me and killed my brother?"

"No, those were the Kiowa. They're just as bad, if not worse."

They stopped to rest by the side of the creek. Ben was pale from the loss of blood and had to be helped out of the saddle. Beth led him to a cottonwood where he could recline in the shade. "There's some jerky in my saddlebags," he instructed.

Beth retrieved the jerky and joined him under the cottonwood. "You don't look very good," she remarked. Ben had beads of perspiration on his face although it was a nice day and not particularly hot. She placed her hand on his forehead and felt the side of his face. "You're burning up."

Beth unbuttoned his shirt to check on his bandages. The bleeding had stopped and the blood had formed a hard crust on the strips of cloth that were over the wound. The bandages had stuck to his skin so she peeled them off carefully. The wound in his side was red and inflamed. After washing the wound the best that she could, she tore more strips of cloth from her petticoat and replaced the dressings. The only thing she could do right now was to keep it clean and covered.

They were both pretty exhausted. Neither of them had had more than two or three hours of sleep the night before. They ate their fill of jerky and rested while the horse munched on lush grass along the creek's banks.

Ben awoke and opened his eyes. He was momentarily disoriented. The position of the sun told him that he had slept about three hours, though he didn't feel much rested. He was still perspiring from fever and he felt nauseated. He saw Beth down by the river filling their canteens while she waded in the water. She hiked her skirt up to avoid getting it wet as she splashed barefoot up onto the grassy shore.

"How are you feeling?" she asked, as she approached where Ben still reclined under the cottonwood.

"Good enough to ride." Ben attempted to get to his feet. His legs were a little wobbly, so he leaned against the tree for support.

Beth hurried to his side to help him stand. She felt his forehead again and frowned. "You still have a fever. Your wound is infected. I hope we can find that army patrol soon. You're going to need a doctor."

"If that's going to happen, we need to keep riding."

With Beth's help, Ben made it over to the horse, and with some effort, he managed to pull himself into the saddle. Beth climbed up behind him.

"We'll cross over to the other side of the river and follow it north. I've got a feeling that the patrol will be following this river south. There's plenty of water for their horses, and it's easier traveling than picking their way through the hills on either side."

"Do you think that the Kiowa are following us?" Beth asked as she scanned the trail behind them.

Ben turned to look over his shoulder at her and smiled weakly. "I doubt it, but out here, you don't take anything for granted."

They forded the shallow river and climbed up the opposite bank. Then they turned and headed upstream.

*

Ben looked up from his reading when he heard the front door open. He saw his granddaughter approaching down the little flower-lined walkway that led to the front sidewalk. She stopped next to his chair and squatted down so they were at eye level with each other.

"How are you doing, Grandpa? You look a little tired. Can I get you anything?"

She always took such good care of him. He smiled and reached out his hand and placed it tenderly on the side of her face. She smiled back and leaned her head into his hand. Then she pressed her lips into his palm and kissed him.

"I'm doing fine, Connie. I think I'll be able to finish my book by dinner time."

"Are you hungry? I can fix you a snack."

"No, I'm not hungry at all. I'm fine. Really, I am."

Connie spied his empty coffee cup. "How about another cup of coffee? Or some lemonade?"

"Actually, some lemonade would be nice. Thank you."

Connie left with his empty mug and returned a moment later with a tall glass of lemonade. She kissed her grandfather on the forehead and returned to the house.

Ben watched her go back inside. The truth was that he wasn't feeling very well at all, but he didn't want Connie to worry. He felt not just tired, but weak. He had also become aware of a pain in his side that wasn't there when he woke up. He knew that there was something wrong with him, and he knew that he should tell Connie, but it didn't seem to matter. The only thing he wanted to do was finish the book. So he continued reading.

He read on into the afternoon as Ben and Beth made their way north along Crooked Creek. Ben grew increasingly weak as the infection from his wound took over his body. Beth had wrapped her arms around him and taken the reins from him to guide their mount upriver. At some point in their journey, Ben lost consciousness and Beth had an increasingly difficult time keeping him upright in the saddle.

*

Beth kept the horse headed in the right direction, barely able to keep the unconscious Ben from toppling off of the horse. As darkness began to settle, she knew they were going to have to stop. The horse needed to rest and so did she. Her arms and shoulders ached from the effort of keeping Ben in the saddle. She was afraid that if they stopped, Ben would not regain consciousness and she would not be able to get him back on the horse.

She found a grassy spot under some willows about a hundred yards from the river and pulled back on the reins. Hanging onto Ben, she swung her leg over the rear of the horse and slid down to the ground. Then she guided him the best she could as his body fell out of the saddle onto the grass. He moaned as he hit the ground, so she took heart knowing that he was still alive.

She worked to get the saddle and blanket off of the horse. Then she hobbled his hind legs and let him loose to forage for his dinner.

She rolled up the saddle blanket and placed it under Ben's head. Then she untied his bedroll and covered him up. He was shivering even though sweat rolled down his face. She was able to get a little water down him, but he never opened his eyes, and the only sounds he made were occasional moans.

Beth debated about starting a fire, but decided against it. If the Kiowa were trailing them she didn't want to give away their position. She poured some water from the canteen onto a strip of cloth and bathed Ben's forehead. He was still perspiring and shivering at the same time. She checked on his wound and did what she could to clean it, but it was looking even worse than it had earlier in the day.

The sky had gone from blue to purple to black. As the light retreated, the stars came out of hiding until they covered the dome of the heavens above. The quarter moon seemed brighter than normal, and Beth was grateful that they would not have to spend this night on the Kansas prairie in total darkness. She laid down next to Ben and pulled the edge of the blanket over her body. Soon, she was lulled to sleep by the chirping of crickets and the occasional swishing of the horse's tail.

She opened her eyes suddenly some hours later. Something inside of her told her to remain silent and still. She thought she heard something rustle out in the grass. She listened closely. The horse seemed agitated. Before Beth knew what was happening, the horse screamed and reared up. Something shadowy streaked across her line of sight and landed on the gelding's back. Another flash of grey, and then a third, and the horse was on its side, thrashing and screaming as the pack of wolves attacked.

Beth hurried to her feet, grabbing the Spencer rifle that was on the ground between her and Ben. She cocked the lever to chamber a round. Then she pulled back on the hammer and aimed as yet another wolf slinked toward her, head down, fangs bared. She pulled the trigger just as he hunched to lunge at her. The shot caught him in the chest in mid-air. The huge beast fell to the ground and rolled to the side. He twitched a few times before becoming motionless.

The blast from the rifle startled the other members of the pack who all ran off toward the river. Beth sent three more rounds after them for good measure.

As the sun began to peek up over the eastern horizon, Beth stood staring out into the dim morning light in the direction the wolves had gone. Her rifle remained pointed at their retreat, ready, in case they returned for their prey. She remained there like a statue, afraid to move; afraid to lower her gaze. Finally, her arm ached from the weight of the rifle and she sank to the ground, shaking like an aspen leaf.

The horse was dead. Ben was near to death. There was a pack of wolves somewhere out there, and on top of all that, the Kiowa may be on their trail as well. Now, what would she do?

*

Ben stopped his reading and closed the book. Something very strange was going on and he didn't have an explanation for it. He felt his heart pounding with excitement and fear as he had read through the chapter describing the wolf attack because he realized that he was reading exactly what he had dreamt about the day before when he had fallen asleep in this very chair. It was Beth that he had dreamt about, and it was him. It was the two of them in the book. It didn't seem possible, but he knew it was them. They weren't just characters in a book. Somehow, it was real.

The pain in his side had become worse throughout the day. He shivered as he pulled his blanket up and tucked it in around him. Ben realized he was growing weaker just as Ben in the book had grown weaker. He thought about calling out to Connie, but a voice in his head told him he would be alright if he would finish the book. There were only a couple more chapters to go, so he read on.

*

Beth knew that their situation was desperate, but she had a strong faith that would not allow her to lose hope. *Do what you can, have faith, and leave the rest in God's hands.* She had lived by this standard all of her life, and she had repeated it over and over throughout the last couple of days.

She took inventory of their provisions. There was still a little jerky left, along with a small amount of beans, some coffee, sugar, and a little flour. Probably enough food for two more days—if they rationed it out. Of course, there was the horse if they got desperate, that is if she could keep the vultures away from it. They had already pecked out its eyes and torn open the stomach. Two of the vile creatures were dragging the intestines across the ground and fighting over them. There was plenty of water in the river, so that wasn't a concern.

What she worried about most was Ben. He had become delirious from his fever. Most of the time, he slept and moaned and occasionally shouted out some unintelligible thing. At one point, however, while she was bathing his forehead, he suddenly opened his eyes and grabbed her arm. "Connie misses you," he said. Then he was unconscious again.

She had worked for the better part of an hour to drag his body, inch by inch, further back about fifty yards into the trees. Mostly it was for their safety, but also it was to put some distance between them and the disgusting vultures and the dead horse. One of the willows had been split in two by lightning and half had fallen to the ground, so she dragged his body behind the fallen trunk. Then she piled more branches and brush against the log to create a small wall between them and the river. Being better concealed, she would be able to start a fire that would help to keep the wolves from returning during the night.

She spent the day tending to Ben, keeping a wet cloth on his forehead, and shoeing flies away when they landed on his face. She started a little fire and boiled some of the jerky to make a broth, and was able to get Ben to swallow a few spoonfuls. Just before nightfall, she took their two canteens down to the river to refill. On her way back, she chased the vultures away from the horse and stopped long enough to cut some meat away from the rump. She would roast part of it over the fire for her dinner. She would cut the rest into strips and dry it to replenish their jerky supply. It would be the first time she had eaten horse meat, but she knew people who had eaten it and considered it a delicacy.

That evening, she couldn't sleep worrying about the return of the wolves. Every sound made her jump. With every snap of a twig or every rustle of a branch in the wind, she was sure that they were about to be overrun by the pack. She kept the fire stoked and sat next to Ben, the Spencer lying across her lap. Sometime, late in the night, her exhaustion got the better of her and she closed her eyes, only for a moment...

When she opened her eyes, it was light out. She sat up with a start and looked around. She hadn't meant to fall asleep, but she had been so tired. Everything appeared to be just as she had left it last night. The fire had gone out and only a few small embers remained half-buried in the ashes.

She looked at Ben. He was so still and quiet she thought that he must have passed on during the night, but closer inspection revealed that he was still breathing—although his breaths were shallow and there was a raspy sound in his chest whenever he took a breath.

She was about to get to her feet to gather more wood for the fire when something told her to be still. She stayed low to the ground as she crawled closer to the wall of branches that she had piled up. Peering through an opening in the branches, she could make out five mounted Kiowa braves walking their horses across the river, headed in her direction. One by one they entered the river and waded through the current in a single file until their horses stepped up on the bank nearest her. She took the rifle and stuck the barrel through the brush. Then she waited.

The Kiowa had been drawn by the activity of the vultures circling overhead. Within minutes, they located the dead horse. Two of the braves dismounted to investigate. They were close enough for Beth to hear what they were saying even though she didn't understand what they said. One of the braves walked around, his eyes on the ground, searching for something, and Beth knew just what he would find. Sure enough, she watched from concealment as the brave bent down to examine the drag marks in the grass where she had struggled to pull Ben into the trees. He said something to the other braves and they all looked in her direction.

Beth didn't believe that they could see her behind the brush pile, but they certainly looked curious. One of the braves started walking in her direction while the others looked on. She waited until he had taken a dozen steps, then she aimed the rifle and fired. The Kiowa brave was hit in the chest, his body pierced and pushed backward by the force of the .56 caliber slug.

The other brave who had dismounted made a mad dash toward his horse, while the three mounted braves turned and kicked their horses into a gallop back towards the river to try to find some cover along the bank.

Then Beth heard a shot ring out, followed by a second shot. Then a volley of gunfire erupted. She watched as two of the Kiowa fell from their horses. The remaining two tried to make it across the river. She watched as several men dressed in blue army uniforms appeared out of nowhere in pursuit of the Indians. More gunfire rang out and the last of the Kiowa braves fell from their horses into the river, their bodies motionless as they floated downstream.

Beth stood to her feet and came out from her hiding place behind the brush pile as a dozen mounted soldiers came into view between her and the river.

One of the soldiers closest to her noticed her standing in the trees and called out, "Sergeant. Over here."

A burly, red-headed man with sergeant's stripes spurred his horse toward her, then abruptly pulled back on the reins and dismounted. "Ma'am. I'm Sergeant Doyle out of Fort Dodge. Are you all right?"

"I am now, sergeant. You and your men showed up just in time."

"We were camped upriver last night, only about a half-mile from here. This morning we saw the vultures and heard a gunshot, so we decided to check into it."

Beth's eyes were like saucers. "You were only a half-mile away from me last night?"

"Yes, ma'am." The sergeant looked around and asked, "Are you out here by yourself?"

Beth took him by the arm and said, "No, Sergeant Doyle, I'm not. We need your help." She led him back behind the brush pile where Ben was hidden.

"That's Ben Lawton," exclaimed the sergeant. He bent down to have a closer look. "What happened?"

Beth quickly related the whole story.

"He's in pretty bad shape. We'll have to get him back to Fort Dodge so the Regimental Doc can have a look at him.

Three days later, Beth sat next to him while he was lying in the hospital bed. Other than taking time to bathe and change into some clean clothes that one of the officer's wives had given her, she hadn't left his side since they had arrived the day before. The doctor had washed and sewed up his wound and put clean bandages on it to which he had applied a mixture of bromine and bromide of potassium to fight the infection. She had a basin of water that she used to keep his forehead cooled, but the fever remained and he struggled to breathe. The doctor said that he had developed pneumonia. All she could do was sit by his side and watch him die. She bent down and kissed him gently on the cheek. "Don't die on me, Ben. Don't leave me without saying goodby."

Beth looked up as the door opened and the doctor stepped into the room. He was a handsome, swarthy man in his mid-thirties. He had dark hair and a neatly trimmed beard to match. "Doctor Reaper, I don't think he's getting any better." She pulled a handkerchief from inside her sleeve and dabbed at a tear that had pooled in the corner of her eye.

*

Doctor Reaper! That's the same name as the man who owns the bookstore. Ben thought that he should be surprised by this new turn of events, but so many strange things were connected to this book—like Ben mentioning Connie during his delirium. He was more thrilled than surprised. He knew that this was not a normal book and that somehow he and Beth were together again. He didn't understand it, but he knew that it was as real as the chair that he sat on. It was as real as the wind on his face or the pain in his heart that he had lived with ever since Beth had left him two years ago. A pain that...

Ben grasped his left arm as a sharp pain shot through it. A real, physical pain ran up and down the arm and seemed to explode in his chest. He dropped the book to the ground and closed his eyes.

*

Doctor Reaper took Beth by the shoulders and smiled. "He's in bad shape, my dear, but I have at least one more trick up my sleeve. You haven't eaten all day. You need to keep up your strength, too. Go get something to eat, then get some rest and leave Ben in my care. I'll let you know if there's any change."

Beth sniffled, wiping away yet another tear. "Alright, doctor." She started to leave, then turned and said, "Any change at all."

"I promise."

After she had left, the doctor locked the latch on the door and walked over to Ben. He pulled up a chair and sat next to the bed. Leaning forward, he placed one hand on Ben's head and brushed his hair back. Then he leaned even closer and whispered into his ear, "Ben, I know that you're in pain and that this has been a strange and confusing time for you. I'm speaking directly into your mind right now. You will no longer need the book to know what I am saying. You will hear my words in your head. Don't be afraid."

*

The pain in Ben's arm and chest grew stronger. He knew that he was having a heart attack. Although the pain continued, and he didn't even have the strength to open his eyes, the voice in his head was comforting and drove the fear away.

*

"It's time to let go, Ben. It's time to come home. It's time to be with Beth again. There are so many wonderful adventures waiting for you here. All you have to do is let go, Ben. Just let go."

With a moan, Ben opened his eyes and turned his head. He saw sunlight streaming through an open window. The sounds of men and horses greeted his ears in a way that was both strange and familiar at the same time. He was in a room with several other unoccupied beds. He turned his head and saw a man sitting next to his bed. "Where am I?"

The man smiled at him and said, "Welcome back, Ben. I'm glad you decided to join us. I'm Doctor Reaper. You're in the hospital at Fort Dodge. Do you remember what happened to you?"

Ben closed his eyes tightly, as though doing so might squeeze his memories to the surface. "Did I have a heart attack? I seem to remember a sharp pain in my arm and my chest."

"Not exactly. You suffered a badly infected knife wound. You had a fever and pneumonia. Don't worry, it will come back to you."

"Yeah, that's right. The Kiowa. I think I remember that."
He sat up slowly in bed. Doctor Reaper assisted him and cautioned him about tearing his sutures.

"How long have I been here?"

"The patrol brought you in yesterday, but you had been unconscious for three or four days before that."

Suddenly, Ben reached out and grabbed the doctor's arm. "Where's Beth? Is she alright?"

"Beth is fine and she'll be happy to see you're alright. Shall I go and get her for you?"

A broad smile creased his face. "Please do. It probably sounds strange to you, but it seems like I haven't seen her in years."

*

Connie had just finished checking the roast in the oven. It needed about another fifteen minutes. She went to the refrigerator to get the ingredients for her salad when she glanced out the kitchen window. *Grandfather must have fallen asleep again.* She had an uneasy feeling, so she opened the door and called outside. "Grandpa." Something wasn't right. She half ran to where he was sitting. "GRANDPA!"

*

Ida Harper pushed open the door and stepped inside the quaint little bookstore. In all of her eighty-seven years in this town, she had never noticed this shop before. She told herself that her memory wasn't what it used to be. At any rate, she loved books, and the musty smell of used books reminded her of her younger years as a librarian. That was a long time ago. Long before her children all grew up and moved away. Long before her grandson got married and had children of his own. And it was long before the stroke that took her dear William from her. All she had now were her books and her fading memories.

"Is there anything that I can help you with?"

A handsome man with dark hair and a dark suit appeared out of nowhere.

"Well," Ida hesitated while just a hint of a blush powdered her wrinkled cheeks, "what I really like are Victorian romances."

The man smiled, knowingly. "I think I have just the book for you."

ONE MORE TIME AROUND
BY EIRIK GUMENY

My LockStep starts vibrating against my wrist, just as the buzzer rattles across the apartment like a man being electrocuted.

My drugs are here.

"... and *early*," I murmur, turning from the gurgling coffee machine and tying closed my bathrobe. I consider grabbing something for underneath, something other than my boxers, but it's only Brad, and it'll only be a minute, so I don't.

Crossing my cramped one-room, I pull open the heavy circular hatch in the far corner of the ceiling, careful of the ladder that slides down. I begin making my way up the silo, past the hatches of my neighbors, until I reach the roof. It's not a short climb by any means, but the lower you are the cheaper the rent. And there ain't no one lower than me.

The early morning air is humid, the sky still heavy and hazy with fog, with the sulfurous gasses rising from the lavalands below. Squinting into the grey, I can't seem to find the sun; honestly, I'm not sure it's even risen yet.

My dealer – Brad No Last Names, Man – is standing near the buzzer block, a silver rectangle covered in buttons adorned with the names of all the building's tenants. A zipline pole is to his left, a half-dozen reinforced wires running to the other apartments of Vesuvius. The white, rectangular buildings stand like saltine sleeves on stilts, rising from the ever-roiling magma fields.

"Hey, man," Brad says.

"Hey," I mumble as I approach, still squinting.

"Nice weather this morning. Should be a good day to get out."

"Sure."

Brad gestures with his chin toward me, at the bathrobe that's almost entirely opened itself. I pull it closed and cinch the tie tight, making a knot I know I'm going to regret later.

"Hope you didn't get all dressed up on my account," he says.

I grunt out a laugh.

Brad makes a face. "You're usually more talkative than this."

"You're usually not here at six in the morning."

"Fair enough." He flips open his messenger bag and reaches inside, pulling out a tightly-wrapped brick of Tiger's Jackpot – mostly organically-grown marijuana, but with a top-secret blend of seven uppers and downers, too, all of 'em working in perfect balance. Was a time it was so popular it'd all but taken over the vaguely-illicit drug market. Now, not so much.

Brad bounces the brick in his hand.

"Hopefully this'll be enough to get you through the week," he says.

"You always do like to dream big," I say back.

I tap my LockStep a few times, transferring the funds; I hear Brad's ding and he starts towards me. But before he can hand the Jackpot over, before the two of us, hands reaching out for one another like that church ceiling with all the naked guys, can make physical contact – he's plucked off the rooftop by a screeching roc, one of the enormous murder-birds that lives in the nearby volcano.

Shit.

"Hey!" I yell, my bathrobe fluttering in the downdraft of the monster's massive wings. "Hey! I already paid you, man! What the hell kind of customer service is this?!"

"Sorry!" Brad yells back, his northern accent warping the vowel.

"Can't you throw it or –"

I watch in horror as the brick – as well as my dealer's arm, and a good part of his chest and ribs and all the squish underneath – plummet to the magma below. I rush to the edge of the roof; there's a little *poof* and scarcely a sizzle as my drugs and all the falling hunks of meat and bone are incinerated. There's another sizzle a moment later, maybe a quarter mile farther. Brad No Last Names, Man is unequivocally dead, killed before my very eyes, his body severed into puzzle pieces by the razored claws of the roc.

"C'mon!" I shout after the noticeably unburdened bird. "Now what am I supposed to do?" I throw my arms up in frustration. "You didn't even eat him!

What the hell? What was even the point, you stupid bird?!" I turn and scour the empty rooftop, hoping against reason that he left another brick of Jackpot somewhere. Obviously, I'm wrong.

"And now," I say to no one, "now I gotta go to work sober. Good. Great."

I stomp back toward the silo hatch, starting the fight with my knotted bathrobe on the way.

*

The name's Hodge. Rogen Hodgson if you're looking to give me money, or trying to get it. I'm 577 years old, but I don't look a day over 40. 45, maybe, if I'm being honest. Okay, 46, but that's it. Any more and my feelings're gonna get hurt. Even the losers, y'know? I'm not the oldest around, not by a longshot, but six centuries of breathing is an impressive feat for a human, all the same. I'm what they call a Prometheus, one of the last to get solid organ, flesh-and-blood transplants. Nowadays it's all cybernetics and synth parts, implants, sleek and shiny and new, most of which come with built-in fail-safes against "inhumanely advanced" old age.

Inhumane. Yeah, that was a fist to the nuts all right.

Not to say that the corporations were *wrong* precisely, but no one likes to be told they're a monster. Adding age limits for final surgeries wasn't even a controversy. Turns out that living forever ain't actually all that great. If everyone does it, you're looking at overpopulation, resource scarcity – and apartments built on top of lava flows – all those extra years turned into hardscrabble and hurt. And if no one does, if it's just you, then it's the constant death and crippling loneliness that'll screw you, and I mean poorly and ungently. Not exactly a lot of takers then. Go figure.

I didn't know any of this, of course, back when. I was just trying not to die young. Had my first transplant, lungs, at exactly the right time. Or exactly the wrong, depending on what day you ask. The easy explanation is that it was a perfect storm of the old ways and the new, a supercharged collision of science to increase human longevity way past the shelf-date. I'm one of the last of my kind, one of the last twenty or so Prometheans still walking. We're not immortal, not like most folks think anyway: shoot us or stab us or throw us in front of a maglev and we're as dead as the next guy. We're not invulnerable. Just old as the mountains and luckier'n shitting gold.

There's still a million ways to die out there, believe me.

I've seen most of 'em myself by now.

*

There's a little tinkle from the bell as I open the office door. We've got an office in a building of about a hundred others; third floor, windows out to the street. Older, all wood and glass and upkeep, not the pre-fab plastic or swanky plexichrome. Not the best, but definitely not the worst. Lights are already on and I can hear the comp-units thrumming, so I head for the kitchen. It's about the size of a closet, but there's a sink and a fridge and enough wall to keep it separate from the rest of the office, so.

I grab my coffee-stained mug from next to the sink only to discover that the coffee machine's not running. Pot's empty. Nothing's bubbling or hissing.

"You gotta fill it if you empty it," I say, loud enough that it carries. "That's like the only rule."

"I just got here," Roan says from behind the bathroom door. Her voice is like an earthquake, deep and rumbling. The bathroom's next to the kitchen, and even smaller. Not my favorite habit, talking through the door while she's dumping, but she's in there a lot. Four stomachs. If I always waited for her to be finished, we'd still be on our first case. You get used to what you have to.

Not to mention, if she's in there now, first thing, I'm guessing she didn't go home last night. Not about to begrudge her that.

Roan and I are partners, private investigators. She's a minotaur. Older than I am and younger at the same time. Not by much either way, though. Different mythologies age at different rates, and there's different beings within those mythologies – honestly, it's best not to think too much about it. Time gets real screwed real fast that way.

I grab the filters and the coffee and hit the switch. Bathroom door's so thin, Roan hears all of it, waits 'til I'm done to start talking again.

"We have two," she says. "On your desk."

I head over and lean my ass against the dense faux-oak, grabbing the print-outs as I do. We got a ticketing system, like tech support or ordering groceries; people just file a form online, filling in the pertinents. Turns out that honesty comes a lot easier through a screen, through impartial empty boxes instead of someone staring back at you. Saves everyone a lot of time and headache. You can even attach photos if you want, right from your LockStep, so you can just document and then start to scrubbing, 'out having to let those messes fester any fouler.

The tickets are streaked and sketchy – we've been running out of ink for a week now – but I can make out enough. Looks like a missing persons case on a mineral trawler up in the Rubble, the asteroid belt that used to be a moon, and a homicide out in the bergs of New Valhalla. Two in one morning's pretty good for us.

"Which one you want?" I ask.

"Homicide," Roan answers.

"You hate the cold."

"This is true," she says. "But those trawlers are built for gremlins and red dwarves. Low-orbit spacecraft were not designed with minotaurs in mind."

"Yeah, all right," I say. I squint at the paper-stub in my hands.

"Investigation or cover-up?"

"They're calling us aren't they?"

In theory, our office is open to everyone, all manner of services for all manner of beings in all manner of trouble – that's what our ads say, anyway – but in practice, we're cops for criminals, the law for anyone laying low from the corpos. Lending an impartial opinion when things get heated, or muddied, or outright dirty, for whatever the reasons. Happens more often than you'd think. The cops and the courts are all but owned by the corporations now, and so's the city for that matter. Divvied up like a board-game map. So you either fall in line, get branded by one of them, as one of theirs – or you get branded as something else entirely. Corporate life's an easy one, I get the appeal, I do, but you're around long enough, you see enough, it starts not to sit right anymore. Those kinds of brands burn, and they bleed, and that bleeding won't stop anytime soon. Plus, there's the simple and undeniable fact that the crooked pay better.

*

The metal pipe clangs despite the foamcore padding, the sound echoing down the narrow corridor. I look up: a dent, straight through the protective covering. I grumble. Already had a headache, a migraine starting, and this sure as shit isn't gonna help things. I raise a hand and, carefully, poke at my forehead.

Orbital spacecraft weren't designed with humans in mind, either. Here's what I know, why I'm up here: the ship's one of Honeycomb Global's, up on a routine resource run, and then one of the flight crew drops dead. Tragic, sure, but the air inside these things is thin even when everything's working, and I don't know I've ever heard of *everything* working. Industrial regulators were one of the first groups the corpos bought off and bought out, I don't even remember how long ago. Accidents on asteroids are as common as traffic reports. That's why I traded my wool duster for a safety suit, why I was willing to entrust my Oppenheimer 87MM with the security team – an accidental discharge up here'll be more than a problem. I've got an oxygen concentrator strapped to my hip, too, just in case.

Vic's a woman, human, older, name of Susie Q, according to the manifest. From Creedence, Clearwater. That's my first clue that not all of this is on the level: ain't no way those're her real pertinents. The song, the band, they're old, I'll give her that, before my time even during my time, but it's still sloppy.

Anyway, "Susie" drops and they ice her, shelving the body and grumbling about dealing with the paperwork when they get home. But then, like a week later, the onboard medical team discovers that the body's gone. And not just that but there's ashes and scorch marks on the slab. But not *enough* ashes to explain away an entire human. No sign of forced entry into the med lab or the freezer, and no sign of her, or even parts of her, anywhere on the ship. Lifeboat's still attached, too.

Enter me.

Captain's the one who logged the ticket, called me up here. Human, a Moreauvian, maybe, spliced with faunal DNA, or maybe he's just weird looking. Nervous as hell, definitely. Losing a crewmember isn't great, but losing the corpse'll get him in real bad with Honeycomb. You had one job, y'know? So I'm here, officially, to find out what went down – though we both know my *actual* objective is to clear his name. Right him of all wrongdoing. Med team's already floated the notion of spontaneous combustion, so all I need to do is get some statements and hope no one says anything that makes this any more difficult than it needs to be.

I duck beneath the next pipe, and the next, scrunching down into myself rather than leaning sideways – I am, conservatively, exactly corridor-sized. The sub-decks are even more cramped than the rest of the boat, built for the more technologically-adept mythologies that service them. Leaning – hell, tilting slightly – simply means I'll hit my head on something else, the wall, or one of the gauges or monitors or cable bundles that run between them.

I don't even want to think about what would happen if I sneezed. A few more careful steps and I knock on the hatch at the end of the corridor – small and rounded and not even as wide as my shoulders. I puff out my cheeks and exhale. Hopefully the engineers'll have the good sense not to try and invite me in.

*

Roan and I meet later that afternoon at the Empress Diner, a greasy little place in the undercity, the lower levels of Los Fantasmas, beneath the maglevs and the sunshine, to hash out the details of the day. I've already put away half a bottle of naprox and an entire pot of coffee, trying to stave off the crippling migraine I can still feel coming. The welt that's still throbbing.

My partner points to her forehead, fighting a smirk. "You've got a –"

"I know," I say.

We're in the back of the restaurant, in one of the reinforced booths. Minotaurs aren't exactly known for being small, and Roan's no slouch. Nearly killed her mother being born, the way Mama Xo tells the story; she thought she was delivering twins. Roan was a fighter once upon a time, too, a professional, until she lost one of her horns in a knockdown, drag-out with a cave troll. She keeps up the training even now, gets hired out as muscle a lot more than I do.

Her fur's red and short, shiny, with a couple of white spots, a thin stripe running between her black eyes, forehead to snout. Horn, and what's left of the other one, are black. Her suit's grey – and a wrinkled, battered mess. Trying to get clothes in her size is a hassle, so she tends to wear 'em into the ground. Plus she's so damn big and strong, just moving a shoulder's liable to tear a seam.

A first-gen 'bot, a dilapidated metal pedestal on wheels, rolls over with our orders: a salad the size of an end table for Roan, a green chile cheeseburger for me. Soy and veggie, not beef; I'm not that stupid, or rude. Not gonna say that I've never, but it's been a century, at least. I've heard the arguments, the savory specifics of real versus artificial, but all the surgeries have rerouted my nerves, dulled my sense of smell and taste. All I *really* get is the broad strokes, sweet or spicy or coffee or burger. Not about to pay extra just for the privilege of pissing off my friend. I'm only in it for the iron.

Roan's got her face in her bowl, so I spill, everything. I know plenty of investigators that don't go for the whole partner thing, but we work better together. Different eyes, different histories, different skillsets. Seems stupid to me trying to do the whole thing alone.

"Looking like a pretty routine spontaneous combustion," I say when I'm done. "All I got left is to file the report with Honeycomb."

She huffs out a laugh.

"What?" I ask.

"You and I both know that's a steaming pile," she answers. "I'll admit that the science on spon-comb is ... *sketchy*, to use your word, but all the research seems to agree that it stems from a miscommunication somewhere inside a *living* body. Shouldn't be possible after the fact, if there's nothing left alive to do the communicating."

I lower my eyes, sip my coffee so I don't say something I'll regret. Generally speaking, Roan and I are in agreement that any payment's a good one. We haven't gotten to it yet, but I'm willing to bet *her* stiff today was a centaur or a cyclops, someone proper ancient. Seeing "one of her own" on a slab always sends her reflecting on her own righteousness – at least recently, anyway. I know for a fact she's put more than a few of "her own" in the ground back when. But I'm not gonna push; friends, like I said. Plus, I know as well as anyone that dwelling on mortality when you're functionally immortal is always a little haywire.

"Could this Susie Q of yours have been a revenant?" Roan asks. "Or a draugr? Someone saw the corpse reanimate and set it on fire?"

"Maybe," I say, "but no one's copping to killing one. Fire plug in the med lab was still in the wall, too. And Honeycomb's got a bunch of exclusions in their contracts for reanimateds; no one's gonna get docked for putting down the living dead. I doubt the captain would've called me up there for that."

"What about a phoenix?"

I look at Roan, take a beat. Phoenixes are ancient, even by the most liberal definition of the word. Women capable of turning into extradimensional birds, and prone to burning themselves to death before coming back from the ashes. They're crossmyths, beings that come from a bunch of different places all at once. I've heard stories of various Egyptian and Greek factions both laying claim, trying to corral them into one syndicate or another, using all the usual lines about honor and blood. Don't think a single phoenix ever bought.

Hence the tale I'm about to tell.

"A phoenix," I repeat, flat. "What were you *just* saying about steaming piles?"

"Just because your limited human consciousness –"

"Limited?" I spit back. "Limited. *I'm* not the one forgetting that phoenixes were hunted into extinction by Osiris International two centuries back. Remember? That gang, what were they – the Society of Bennu, they were passing themselves off as humans, cashing in life insurance policies left and right, claiming fire damage and whatever else, every time they burned out. Made millions. Enough that word eventually climbed itself all the way up the ladder until Anubis himself found out and went absolutely ape, deciding that the best way to deny their claims was to *murder them all.*"

"Oh," she says. "Right."

"Right."

"So ... we are back to a body vanishing into slightly charred air."

"Or we just call it spon-comb, like I said."

Roan raises an enormous fuzzy eyebrow. "You know we charge by the hour, right?"

Now it's my turn to laugh.

Like I said, stupid trying to do this whole thing alone.

*

The headache and the tremors start, and hard, almost as soon as I leave the diner. Not so much withdrawal as the reasons I started with the Tiger's Jackpot in the first place.

I'm on a whole mess of meds, prescriptions, from actual doctors, to keep my body from chewing up all my replacement parts, from attacking my transplanted organs like they were viruses, foreign invaders. There's understandably some side effects. That'll happen when you're trying to chemically rewire an entire person. Synth organs don't have that problem: they're built to hide, to keep the immune system from realizing they're not supposed to be there. But I've got actual guts inside of me, from actual dead people, and my body is well aware. Unfortunately, there's no mix-and-matching, no switching from solid organs to synths. Not in humans, anyway. Throws too many systems into too much shock. So, the meds, and the resultant migraines, the hands twitching so bad it's hard to hold anything, and everything else. And so the Jackpot, to try and counteract the worst of 'em.

You'd think that the same pharmas making the immunosuppressants, the antivirals and the anti-rejection meds, would find a way to work out the kinks, come up with yet another scrip to sell us. But they don't, or more accurately *won't*: individually, the meds all work fine. The problem's in the combination, and that's limited exclusively to Prometheans. There's not much profit in creating miracles for less people than would fill a hoverbus.

Jackpot's the closest thing to a solution I've found, but even that's getting harder to come by. Facs – factory-manufactured chemicals – will get you a lot higher a lot faster and a lot longer. There's some that'll let you taste colors, see through walls, see the wind; a new one, something called Arthur's Lament, actually lets you levitate. Feet fully off the ground. Not much of a market for organics, especially the subtle ones, when there's shit out there makes you literally *fly*.

All of which means that while Roan's off on her own, having an actual life, I'm spending my evening scouring the undercity of Los Fantasmas for a dealer who specializes in the kinds of drugs no one wants.

I've got a triple-fiber antimicrobial mask pulled up over my nose and mouth, a red paisley that almost matches the tie hanging loose around my neck. Dark isn't the only thing trapped down here, down beneath the City of Ghosts. Decades of pollution, trash, neglect, are settled everywhere and, thanks to the meds, I'm susceptible to all of it, high-risk for every wayward bacterium out there. There's filters in the higher levels, air-scrubbers – just like on the orbital trawlers and all the other interstellar boats – and even artificial weather in places. But that's why you join up with the corporations and the crime syndicates. Better quality of life. Problem is it's only the one life – *their* life – that you get to live.

I was willing to gamble that once, try on that kind of life for a while. It was real nice actually, real quiet. 'til they found out I was a Prometheus. Then, all of a sudden, Consolidated Phukital starts refusing to pay not just for my Jackpot but basic anti-rejection meds. Then they start refusing to pay me at all. Went to punch in my numbers at the center one day only for the identiscanner to start screaming INVALID at me. Hit the button for Support, got a Security team instead, and that was that.

Guess I was more trouble than I was worth.

There's a window glowing warm up ahead, an old head shop that specializes in all-natural smokables and assorted paraphernalia. I'm hoping they'll have what I need, or at least a finger to point me in the right direction. Haven't been in a while. Used to know the owner, a heavyset, wild-haired gnome named Gary Garcia, but he's been dead at least fifty years now.

I open the door and there's a kid behind the counter – they're all kids at this point – a human, a cyberpunk. He's got his hair spiked into blue cones and a multi-spectrum exoplant in place of one eye. He's thin, got his knees up, leaning back on a stool, flipping a token between his fingers, too fast, a blur. Most likely he's got some kind of enhancement inside his wrist, too. Opposite side from his eye. The quick-draw combo. Hired gun, maybe, or just a kid settled into the graveyard shift. Either way, there's artillery pinned beneath the register.

No point screwing around, making like I'm looking at the bongs and the tie-dye, so I head straight to the counter, put my hands flat on the glass. So he knows I'm not up to anything. Just a customer. He cocks his one remaining eyebrow at me, a tacit *how can I help you?*

"You got any Tiger's Jackpot?" I ask.

"Yeah," he says, slow. "Not too many still asking for it, though." He slides his knees off the stool and hunches forward. "You're one of them, aren't you? A Frankenstein."

I'm warm with rage, quicker'n I can think.

"We prefer Prometheus," is all I say, smooth as silk.

"Sure, sure. You really got cadaver parts in there?" He pokes my chest. "A dead guy's heart? Going thump-thump, thump-thump." He pokes again with each word.

"And his lungs," I say, "and someone else's pancreas."

The cyberpunk leans back again. "What's it like, having a dead guy inside of you?"

"Probably about the same as having half a 'bot grafted to your face." I'm biting back real hard, trying to stay civil and not to get more specific with what part of the 'bot I'm talking about — the exhaust port, obviously. But telling someone he's got a robot's butthole on his face isn't going to make you any friends. Even if the kid doesn't shoot me, it'd slow things down and my head's killing me. I can't afford to keep searching tonight.

"Can you help me or what?" I ask.

"Yeah, I can help you," he answers. "On one condition ..."

Shit.

"The scars?"

"The scars."

Scars aren't a thing anymore, not since 'bots got better and started doing the surgeries, not since the processes got more specific and diseases started going away and healing got heaps easier. Hell, nowadays, implants are snaked in through existing orifices and printed inside of you. Some of the older mythologies still carry 'em, the scars, make a big deal out of showing 'em off, earning them in pitched battle or whatever. Roan and her Mayan minotaurs, for one, and the Greek minotaurs, too, the frost giants. Anyone born in the last century is endlessly fascinated.

"You're really gonna make me do this?" I ask. I can barely keep my eyes open.

"Only if you really want your Jackpot," he answers.

253

I stare at the kid, fighting to keep him in focus. I hate him. I hate this kid with the fire of a thousand dying suns. I hate his hair and his eye and his other eye and his stupid, smug, stupid face and I hear myself start grumbling, openly wishing a hundred messy and unsavory deaths upon him – even as my tie's already over my shoulder and I'm already struggling to unbutton my shirt.

*

I exit and don't even make it past the next window before I list to one side, slam my shoulder against the storefront, and slide down to the pavement. I'd say the pain is unlike anything I've ever felt before, but that ain't true – it's just something I'd like to never feel again. My vision's spotty and my stomach's somersaulting, everything inside trying to circus clown back out.

I pull the baggy the cyberpunk sold me from the inside pocket of my duster, the papers, then start rolling like my life depends on it. It doesn't – this ain't gonna kill me – but you try telling my body that. Shit's in a full-on revolt right now.

I find my lighter, heavy metal, in another pocket, light up with a shaking hand and take a long pull. I close my eyes, leaning back, feeling the hard cold of the wireglass on my skull, the brick against my back, and then I wait for the Jackpot to do its thing.

*

By the time I open my eyes again, it's dark – like, proper dark. Night, not just shadow. I can see the everlight of Los Fantasmas, blue and red and green and white, glowing above me, the neon not enough to do anything down here. An aurora of electricity. There's a very real chance I fell asleep, or maybe just blacked out.

Headache's gone, though, so.

I get to my feet, a hand on the window, and the world around me starts spinning in a brand-new way. I'm a lot looser than I should be, than I want to be, which leads me to believe the Jackpot the kid sold me wasn't quite as legit as he claimed. Surprised isn't the right word, but I'm missing Brad and Garcia something fierce right now.

Head down, I start back unsteadily toward the diner. Don't know if it's the drugs or the hours, maybe just a blood sugar thing, but I *absolutely* need something to eat before I try and grab a hoverbus back to Vesuvius, back to my empty apartment and my even emptier fridge.
I bump shoulders with someone, mumble an apology – a woman, human, near as I can tell. Eyes averted, all I really get a look at is everything from the knees down. She's barefoot, which is a little weird; her pants are scorched short. And the same gold as Honeycomb's safety suits.

I look up, turn, just in time to see her disappear into the head shop. Not much to work with and everything's fuzzy and dancing besides, but she's got bright red hair – fire red, you might even call it.

Son of a bitch.

I pull my Oppy, a snub-nosed atomic flayer, from my hip as I close in on the door. The pistol's highly illegal – it'll burn the wings off a manticore you're a good enough shot – but then so's most of what I do, and it's not like you can put a price on safety, right? I mean, you can, and a lot of people do, that's actually one of the services me and Roan offer, but you get the gist.

I push the stickered wireglass door open slow, the drag inaudible beneath all the plinky-plinky music, the conversation happening in front of me. The woman's talking to the cyberpunk at the counter. She looks a mess, covered in dust and ash, in a rash of fading burns, and the suit doesn't fit right, but it's definitely from the mining trawler. She's younger than I was looking for, but I guess that's the beauty of burning up before you come back. I'm a little jealous; every time *I* died, I felt ten years older.

Neither of them see me yet. The woman's keeping quiet, the kid's not, and I catch the word "ketadex," a nutra-ampheth they give to beings coming out of cryostatis, out of comas. Big surgeries. Gave it to me after my last transplant. Supposed to be everything a body needs after a long sleep.

And maybe after a rebirth, too.

It's a hunch, sure, but I've done more with less.

"Say that you'll be true and never leave me blue," I say, "Susie Q."

She's got her talons out, up, before she even turns, her hands shifted into gnarled knife blades. Wings, red and orange, feather and fire, tear through the back of her suit, spread halfway across the store. The cyberpunk, not wanting to be left out, pulls the shotgun from beneath the counter – sawed-off and old as shit, probably loaded with scatterslugs, real metal, the kind that'll hurt like hell and make a mess. The kind of weapon that'll make a point. But he's just kinda holding it, stepping off to the side, not quite sure what's going on and even less sure where to aim. But I've got everything I need, the haze of the drugs fading into a surge of adrenaline.

"Your captain's real worried about you, Susie," I say, gun low on my right, trained on her torso. "You left in an awful rush." I lift my left arm, my LockStep, all the digichannels she's gotta know I have access to, corporate and criminal alike. The standing bounties from Osiris International. "I'm willing to bet there's someone else looking, too."
The phoenix smiles sideways, her face flickering between woman and firebird.

"You're not wrong," she says, regal, a hint of aristocracy in her voice. "About that, anyway. But if you think you're going to be around long enough to cash in that hunch, if you think that glorified flamethrower is going to stop *me* – well, buddy, I got a bridge to Yuka to sell ya."

"I turn you in, I'll have enough to buy as many bridges as I want."

"That's a ... weird flex," says the cyberpunk.

"Stay out of this, child," the phoenix seethes, not looking.

I run my tongue over my teeth. Honeycomb's not gonna want it known that they employed a phoenix, and Anubis isn't the type to welch. I got options, is what I'm saying. Visions of cash-credits, of invoices and endless incidentals, rewards and corporate payoffs, dance through my head. Plexichrome offices and a crapper that's not inside the kitchen. An apartment not built over an active fucking volcano. Enough Jackpot I can forget what feeling bad even is.

The kid's still off to the side, shotgun in both hands, turning between us. His exoplant's scanning, I can hear it hum, but I'm guessing it doesn't know what to make of the phoenix. His finger's on the trigger, but he's not gonna shoot, not until he knows the bigger picture. He's a piece of shit, sure, but he's no fool.

I look at Susie's talons again – they're out, they could kill a man without a doubt, but they're angled up. For show. An intimidation tactic. If she were actually going to eviscerate me, I'd already be holding my intestines in my arms.

Which means that how this all plays out, which of the three of us walks out of here breathing and free, is up to me.

I lower my Oppy, just a little, from Susie's belly to her knees. Rage overtakes her as I do, a cry like a crow being strangled, fire in the air, and then the phoenix takes a step towards me, her wings reaching, stabbing outward, enough to startle the cyberpunk to the floor –

– but her talons are still up.

And that's when I get it. When I know for sure. There's fury on her face, but there's something else in her eyes: desperation. She *wants* me to shoot, to pull the trigger and see what happens. She wants this, all of this, the death and resurrection, the running and hiding and starting over and over again, the being hounded by shits like me, the incessant reinvention and the living forever and ever, to be *done*. To be gone. I've been there myself, once or twice.

Always is just too damn long a time.

I look at her, and I breathe – and then I holster my pistol.

There's a moment then, just long enough to regret, just heavy enough to fear – but the phoenix lowers her wings, the feathers and flame blinking back out of reality. The talons once again fingers, covered in blisters and ash. Her eyes are empty.

"Why didn't you?" is all she asks.

"Because I get it," I answer. "Because that feeling, that exhausted sense of surrender, it's fleeting. You want it all over, you want to give up, you want to go away and hope this time it sticks – but you want to be wrong, too. You *want* to change your mind. And you will. Maybe not immediately, or maybe you don't at all. I've got friends who've committed, gone all the way, and I miss 'em, I do, but I don't begrudge 'em what they did. Not this far into forever.

"But, still," I say, "I ain't about to make that call for you."

The woman laughs, short and sharp. "You say that," she says, shaking her head, small, then looking square at me, "but you're still making a call. You know that, right?"

"Yeah," I say back, slow. "I guess I am," I say. "And I'm sorry, I am. I got no idea if this is right or if it's wrong, but this call – this is one I can live with."

"And one I'm going to have to live with, too. Whether I want to or not."

"Yeah," I say again, the word barely one.

Silence settles then, nothing but the sounds of sitar whispering through the air.

"So," she says, a hitch in her voice, "where did we end up, you and I? I'm assuming you were after me for the disappearing act I pulled on the trawler, before you figured out ..." She doesn't finish the rest. "So, where does that leave us?"

I shrug in response. "I was hired to figure out what happened to a human, an older woman named Susie Q. Up on some Honeycomb boat. According to all the medical experts I spoke with, it was probably a spontaneous combustion," I say. "Haven't found nothing to convince me otherwise. Starting to think I won't ever."

She smiles, small. Then: "What about him?" she asks, pointing her chin at the cyberpunk on the floor. Kid's curled up and cradling the shotgun like a children's toy, trying to hide behind it. Got a wet shadow on his jeans, down both legs. His real eye's wide, darting between us; the exoplant's whirring, working overtime. A Frankenstein was one thing, but a phoenix?

I feel her take a step closer to me, beside me, see her stand a little taller as she stares at him, her burning wings a phantasm, there and not simultaneously.

"Him?" I say. "This piece of shit?"

"This piece of shit," she repeats.

"Well, believe it or not, it's his lucky day. He's about to become a wholesaler, and he's got two clients already lined up." I put my hand on my Oppenheimer and raise an eyebrow. "Assuming the discounts are deep enough, of course."

Maybe my dream of endless Jackpot's not so dead after all.

THE BOSS'S DAUGHTER
BY JAMES WHELPLEY

Adapted from the novel *Dancing in the Trap* for Starlite Pulp

Les Halles is the cheap, student area of Paris where eye-glassed bohemians in breathable clothes dress the windows and darken the doorways of boutiques and noisy cafes. Lately, it had become the kind of place you didn't want to find yourself after dark. It's also home to the busiest subway station in all of Paris and where I was to *rendezvous* with mademoiselle Durand, her letter and a bundle of bills burning a hole in my pocket. The letter hoped my client, a man named Robert Tremblay, was enjoying his time in Paris, insisted that he would be missed when he returned to America, and demanded a good sum of money. It was blackmail penned in letters so long and smooth they could have hailed a cab.

The letter instructed Tremblay to wait at an assigned metro stop, at a given hour, for three days in a row. Payment would be collected one of those three days – he was not to know which. I assumed mademoiselle Durand would be along to collect – and I assumed that *mademoiselle Durand* was an alias. Who in the hell signed a blackmail letter?

The metro station featured the same white-tiled bathroom look as stations in the States. I found the stop the letter described and took up what I thought was a strategic position. I nestled my face between the thick lapels of my pea coat and tried to think invisible. I shouldn't have taken the job, it wasn't in my line. I was a private investigator, and this wasn't an investigation. Robert Tremblay had come to me for help, said my reputation was that of a guy who knew how to keep it under his hat. Divorce work had been slow and I'd never been to Paris – so I took the gig.

Trains came into the station from both directions, spilled passengers over the platform, and vacuumed up as many. I watched dozens come and go before an older man arranging his grandchildren on either side of him stepped off the train trailed by a young woman in a purple skirt, with small red flowers in her hair. She stood, shoulders back, with posture you didn't find outside of a government typing pool. I watched her check her wristwatch. She looked nervous waiting alone on the platform. Maybe it was the way any young woman would look, waiting in a train station for the man she was blackmailing.

Her hair was short, dark, and turbulent. Her skin was olive and her eyes looked like they would glow in the dark. The sleeves of her fitted sweater ended just above her elbow and matched the color of her flowing skirt. She stood on top of tall red heels tied to her ankles. The shoes looked racy enough for the straps to be necessary and shared the same heavy gloss as her bright red lips.

"Mademoiselle Durand," I said while I was still some distance from her. I was the one who felt like a pigeon, but I didn't want her to flit away by making a lot of racket behind her. Maybe in Paris she was the girl next door but I didn't live in Paris. She was alarmingly pretty and a lot of ugly snares were baited as beautifully. When she turned around, it took me a second to make words. "I have your letter."

"I am sorry, monsieur, but I did not write you a letter," she said with a French-roasted kitten purr.

"Not me," I told her. "Tremblay."

"Who is monsieur Tremblay?" she said, but a smile was forming on her shiny red lips.

"Someone who couldn't make it. He sent me instead." She bid me good day and turned toward the stairs. You couldn't take your eyes off her, and I wasn't about to for a few thousand reasons. "I have the money," I announced.

She'd gotten to the foot of the stairs before she turned around. Her heels on the empty subway platform ticked like a clock. She looked me up and down as if our Halloween costumes didn't match. When she held out her hand, I took it. "Adrienne Durand," she said.

On its way out, the ungainly envelope tore my coat pocket. By its heft, I felt sure she was making out better on this deal than I was. I let her reach for it, then pulled it back and tucked it under my arm. Mademoiselle Durand did not view this with any level of menace. "I have been instructed to tell you, *mademoiselle*, that your business with my client is finished. You are not to contact him or any member of his family. Understand that this is the only payment you will ever receive."

She laughed out loud.

This beautiful woman made me hate the way beautiful women laughed, one hand on the opposite hip to keep her from falling to pieces, the other lazily draped over her heart as if it were in danger of arresting at any moment. By the time she regained herself, my teeth had ground to dust in my mouth. Whatever their dealings had been, it was obvious that Tremblay was a joke to her, and that I was a joke by proxy. Beautiful as she was, I considered punching her in the face.

The hard slap of the heavy envelope against her chest almost knocked her off her feet and did what my speech had failed to do. Her eyes grew wide and she looked at me for the first time with the level of seriousness I thought the occasion deserved.

"Listen sister," I said, keeping my voice low, "my client is willing to pay sucker-money provided you go away. But if you think you can bleed him beyond this, the next guy he hires to deal with you ain't gonna hand you no envelope." She clutched the money with both hands over her heart. "This was a successful little score, congrats. Go buy yourself a closet-full of new dresses and move on."

She began digging around in her purse. I half expected her to produce a gun from a balled-up tissue. She was visibly upset. Adrienne Durand didn't take being threatened as cavalierly as blackmail. She started to turn away and I grabbed her arm – I couldn't tell you why I did it. She looked back at me through wild, trembling eyes.

"Take your hands off me," she snarled.

I didn't.

"I'll scream."

I let her go. Extortion aside, I was in an empty subway station

manhandling a woman I didn't know from Adam, or whatever French for Adam

is. She closed her purse, said she hoped I would enjoy Paris, and called me an

asshole.

The job was over, I'd delivered the money. That should have been it,

but something didn't feel right. Adrienne Durand wasn't what I'd expected.

Blackmail was a crime for snivelers – for creatures who lived in the dark and

only came out when they wanted to get paid for doing nothing. She didn't strike

me as the type. I didn't believe for a minute I'd really scared her. And to top it

off, she was American. So was Tremblay and I wondered if that was a

coincidence. Her accent was good, she had obviously lived in France for some

time, but it's never long enough.

*

I walked down the street in Les Halles until I found a cheap hotel. I used my

real name, Eddie Hammond, to sign the registry, a long thin tome more supplely

upholstered than the lobby furniture. It was a touch of old-world style I felt

sure I was paying for, the kind of thing that caused tourists to nudge each other

in the ribs. I could have signed Jacques Cousteau for as long as the hotel clerk

looked at my ID.

The flight of stairs to the second floor made the handrail seem sturdy. I

hung the Do Not Disturb on the knob and turned the water on for a shower – it

came on with a whistle like shift-change at a steel-mill and rattled the

floorboards. I sat on the bed, it creaked. I took mademoiselle Durand's letter out of my coat pocket tucked it under the mattress. I tried to phone Robert Tremblay, tell him I'd delivered the money, but the line was dead. Someone had cut the phone cord where it led into the wall – cut it clean through – with a knife.

The metal bell inside the phone chimed faintly as I plunked it down in front of the desk man. "Monsieur has decided against having a telephone?" he mused.

"You'll have to add it to the bill." It was an old rotary job I hoped hadn't been appraised as an antique. I showed the clerk the cut cord. He didn't seem concerned and made it disappear behind the counter.

"*Baguette*," he motioned to the same basket of complimentary bread torpedoes I'd refused at check-in. I was hungry but wasn't interested in a scavenger hunt to find which hotel lobby had the rest of my sandwich.

The peal of a different bell, this one over the lobby door, announced the arrival of three Parisian police officers. I looked at the hotel clerk. "I said I'd pay for the phone."

The first *gendarme* stood in the center of the lobby, taking a mental inventory. The black and white tiled floor reflected in the luster of his motorcycle boots. The other two wore baggy nylon rain parkas and stood on either side of the door like ferns. Shiny Boots goose-stepped across the checkered floor with his helmet under his arm and showed the desk man the under-side of his chin. He produced a photograph from his chest pocket and held it out for the clerk's inspection. He spoke French with such force it could've been German. I understood *American, jeune femme,* and *metro.* When he was done, the clerk swallowed hard, and tilted his head at the American, fresh from *le metro*, standing before them.

Shiny Boots pivoted, referred to the picture in his black-gloved hand, and tried to determine if I were one or several people. "*Monsieur,*" was the first word out of his mouth and the last thing I understood. The desk man jumped in to translate. His name was Sergeant Something of the Paris police and I was to allow these officers to escort me to the local prefecture for questioning.

"Will there be someone there who speaks the King's or are you coming along?" I asked the clerk.

He mumbled apologetically to Sergeant Something's elbow. *Saltier* was the name embroidered on the left breast pocket of the man's motorcycle jacket. The *gendarme* cleared his throat, so I could better understand him, then continued in French. The clerk assured me that Sergeant Saltier's captain would be able to conduct the interview in English. As he said this, the two amoeba-like officers materialized at my side and led me to the backseat of their Citroen prowl car.

The Prefecture de Police is on the Ile de la Cite, an island in the middle of the Seine. Five-stories of ramparts surrounded a courtyard and spanned an entire city block. The building had been the scene of intense battles during WWII, so I kept my eyes peeled for German planes. The street outside was wet and my feet turned to fat mice on the tile floor of a long hallway. We came to a door with the number twenty-six stenciled on frosted glass. One of the amoeba produced a human fist, knocked lightly, and waited for "*Entre.*"

Inspector Dubois's name plate sat at the edge of his desk like the caption of a photograph. His office was ubiquitously paramilitary, four white walls, beige filing cabinets, and a light green tile floor. It was unclear whether Dubois was moving in or out. Boxes lay open on the ground and pictures of the inspector with assorted dignitaries leaned against each wall.

Dubois was shy of average height but his polyester uniform looked like it could stop a bullet. His black hair had white infiltrates and his mustache, judging from the pictures, was one he was re-growing. Dubois's age had infiltrated there as well.

When we were alone in his office, Inspector Dubois produced a small tape recorder from the top drawer of his desk, connected to it a small silver microphone which he laid on the blotter between us. He made eye contact, making certain my observance of his pushing *Record* with an exaggerated motion of his index finger. His hands moved with the deftness of routine over the file folder on his desk. He tapped loose a cigarette from a soft pack and lit it with a heavy desk lighter. He offered me the pack and just in case it was the last thing I would ever be offered, I took one. He pushed the lighter across the desk, leaning so far to do so, that I could see the top of his head.

Once we were back smoking in our chairs, he introduced himself as if it were necessary and asked me to state my name for the record. "Edgar Hammond," I said. Everyone calls me Eddie. A few who really know me, call me Gar.

"How do you find *Parie, monsieur Hammond?*" he asked.

"*C'est magnifique,*" I drawled through a plume of white smoke.

"*C'est magnifique. Bon.*" He asked if I'd had dinner. I said I hadn't.

He assured me there was a very good bistro across the street from my hotel. "Perhaps you have found it already." He waited for a response. I had none.

Two debts all civilization owe to the French are table manners and police procedure. I knew the tape recorder belonged on Dubois's left, juxtaposed with the salad fork, and I was familiar with this mode of questioning. The idea was to get me talking about anything, the subject didn't matter, then sooner or later, almost involuntarily, I'd spill my guts, tell him everything he ever wanted to know. But I didn't know what he wanted to know and I didn't feel like talking until I did.

"Monsieur Hammond, you were seen having an argument with a young woman in *le metro* earlier today." He placed a grainy picture from a security camera in front of me, a picture of me with my hand around the arm of mademoiselle Durand. "What was the nature of this argument?"

"She wanted to raise the children Catholic, but I'm a devout Hindu," I said.

"What was this young woman's name?" he asked.

"If she told me her name, we'd still be talking." But Dubois wasn't laughing. "Look," I explained, "I saw a pretty girl, I made the standard pitch, she didn't bite."

"And when she didn't bite?"

"We went our separate ways." I said.

"Monsieur Hammond, a young woman, fitting the description of the woman you are arguing with in this picture, was found dead earlier today. Her body was left in an alley outside of *le metro* in Les Halles, not far from where this picture was taken." Dubois produced two more photos from the file. The first was of a girl lying slack between an alley wall and a row of trashcans. Her bare legs glowed in the high contrast of the black and white snapshot, feet pointing in different directions, her body limp with the wilt of death. The second picture was of a face, washed clean, but very dead on an aluminum table.

It was going to be Adrienne Durand lying behind those trashcans. I had crossed an ocean to threaten a beautiful blackmailer in broad daylight. The *gendarme* had canvassed the area for an American man caught on a surveillance camera. Now a police inspector was showing me pictures of a dead girl. She was young, her body long and thin, made longer still by the perspective of the camera. She wore a sundress with flowers that buttoned up the front. The white petals and dark centers of the flowers stared at me like a thousand angry eyes.

The second photo, the morgue shot, didn't look like the girl from the metro – it didn't look like anyone. What I had seen of death always looked unnatural. How could anyone identify even a loved one from a photo like this. The girl's face was inanimate, like wet clay. Her hair was dark where still damp, lighter where it spread over the table, long and straight. The girl from the metro had been colorful and vital, this girl was gray and dead. But the peace of death had failed to make her look serene. The bruises at the base of her neck were fingermarks. Out of all this clay, someone had made a victim.

"It isn't her," I said. "This isn't the girl from the metro."

"We have reason to believe that it is," Dubois said. His fingers were tented just under his nose. His elbows rested somewhere unseen. The case file sat in front of him like an empty dinner plate and he waited patiently to be served. "Monsieur Hammond, did you kill this woman?"

I started to tell him how crazy he was. I told him how I watched the girl from the metro climb the stairs to the street and made sure to go the other way. "Besides, the girl in *this* picture," I pointed to the security camera photo, "is wearing a skirt and sweater." Dubois furrowed his eyebrows. "The girl in this picture is in a dress."

Dubois let out a large breath I had not seen him take and switched off the recorder. "Monsieur Hammond, I'm afraid I may have brought you here unnecessarily. Our medical examiner is placing this poor girl's time of death almost two hours before your little scene in the *le metro*. I hope you understand that a murder investigation is a serious matter, and that we must follow all leads to their conclusion." He clicked the tape recorder back on. "However, I am concerned why you chose to lie about your relationship to the woman in *le metro*. Also, the cut on the side of your head, I'm afraid is bleeding again." Dubois produced a folded handkerchief from his jacket pocket and held it toward me with a straight arm.

My blood soaked easily into the white linen.

"Monsieur Hammond, what exactly is the nature of your business here in Paris?"

I wanted to tell him I came to Paris to argue with pretty girls in subway stations, I wanted to ask him why his little confession had been omitted from the tape, but seeing as I was still being questioned in connection with a murder, I decided against it.

"I'm working," I said.

Dubois turned his attention to the manila envelope one of the amoeba had handed him. The envelope contained my wallet, passport, and the key to a train station locker that held my duffle. He dumped the contents onto his desk blotter and read them like tea leaves.

"I'm a detective," I offered.

"Like me!" he said with a mix of sarcasm and skepticism.

"Private," I said.

"And this young woman is party to an investigation?" he asked. I nodded and said that she was. "I assume you have credentials."

"Will they do me any good?" I asked. "I'm kinda far from home."

Dubois opened my wallet to the photostat that identified me as a licensed private investigator. He checked the photostat against my passport. Next, he opened the envelope that contained my return ticket aboard a freighter leaving La Havre and five hundred American dollars I'd yet to convert to francs, to cover any expenses. The bills, still bound by the bank band, caused Dubois to study me from under the bush of a raised eyebrow.

"Who is your client, monsieur Hammond?"

"You know I can't tell you that."

"Perhaps you can share the nature of your case?" he asked instead.

"Blackmail," I said. "My client received a letter demanding money. The letter didn't say what for. I assume my client knows what he did."

"And what exactly did he or she do?"

"I don't know," I said.

"You don't know, or you won't say?" asked the inspector.

"I don't know – because he won't say," I said. "He doesn't wish to open himself up to any more extortion."

"Your client believes if you knew this information, that you would try to blackmail him yourself?" the inspector asked. "Is it the information that is that bad – or is it you, monsieur Hammond, who is that bad?"

I didn't answer.

Dubois picked up the banded bills and fanned the edges. "Were you engaged by your client to break the law in order to clean up this blackmail situation?"

"No," I said. "I was hired to deliver the payment. That's it."

"What assurances can you offer?" he asked.

"None. Except that I've told you all of this willingly."

"I must warn you monsieur Hammond that any investigation of a French citizen must be done in conjunction with this office." The inspector replaced the contents of the envelope, including the money, and pushed it across the desk along with my wallet.

"Monsieur Hammond does the name Adrienne Durand mean anything to you?" he asked.

My blood ran cold. It couldn't be a coincidence. Adrienne Durand, the name of the girl from the metro, the name on the blackmail letter addressed to my client, the letter currently under the mattress in my hotel room, the letter that, if still in my possession, I would be struggling to explain to the inspector. My insides began a game of musical chairs. The cigarette was still burning in my face. I hoped the veritable smog cloud the strong French cigarettes had created between Dubois and myself was sufficient to cover any reaction I'd had to the name.

"Can I assume it belongs to the deceased?" I asked. Dubois nodded. I told him I'd never heard it.

"Would your duty to your client prevent you from telling me if you had?" he asked.

"Yes," I said. "It would."

He put his hand in the air to direct me to the door.

"Who was she?" I asked. "Adrienne Durand?"

Dubois's pen stopped on the form he was filling out. "The facts of this case will not be released to the public until such time as the victim's family can be notified." It was a rote statement and he recited like a prayer or the pledge of allegiance.

I reached for the small silver mic and threw a tiny switch on its side. "You can turn it off from here, too. Doesn't make that nasty sound on the tape."

Dubois made a noise in the back of his throat over the discovery of the tiny switch.

"Who was she?" I asked again.

"Adrienne Durand, twenty-three, only child of Martin and Catherine Durand. Monsieur Durand owns several local businesses, restaurants, a casino."

"You think someone was trying to get to him through his daughter?" I asked.

The inspector smiled like he would at a precocious child. "I think,"

Dubois said removing the tape recorder from his desk, "that we are not discussing this case." He leaned back in his chair and looked at the smog cloud hovering over his desk as if it obscured the answers to all life's questions. "She was but a child," he said. "It is a senseless world sometimes, is it not?" He sat up straight and cleared his throat. "The city of Paris appreciates your cooperation with this investigation." I thanked the inspector and got up to leave. As I reached the door, he added, "I must insist, monsieur Hammond, that until notified by this office, you are not to leave Paris."

*

I hailed a cab outside the police station. I asked the driver: "Do you know a casino owned by a man named Durand?"

"*Oui, monsiuer. Le Rouleau Chanceux,*" he said without giving it a second thought. My investigation had to start somewhere, it wouldn't be the first one to start in the back of a taxi cab. My driver's hack license read Remy, like Cher or Rasputin. He was very much on board with a trip to the *Chanceux*. There was a French military tattoo on his forearm and his English was plenty good for conversation, mostly about roulette.

Far from the *Palais de Festival* or the *Cote D'Azur*, the *Chanceux* was sandwiched between a travel agency and a flophouse. Above a garnet red awning were tall, iron-clad windows crowned by a hand of playing cards painted on the brick and splayed like false eyelashes. Inside was a parlor of six empty poker tables and light cane chairs. There wasn't so much as a hat-check girl between the felt on the tables and the street outside. The barred windows threw bright shafts of light in steep diagonals that illuminated the empty room. However spartanly adorned, it was clean, the felt on the tables was newly stretched, and the walls above the wainscoting freshly painted. I looked all over for the lever that made the floor turn over, and the real casino appear.

Remy explained this room was where the pit boss banished the serial losers, the turnips the *Chanceux* knew had no more blood to let. We pushed through a second set of double doors into the real casino, a grand room, three or four times the size of the first. It was long and narrow, with tables on either side of a tiled center aisle. The design on the floor mirrored a deco skylight that ran the length of the casino. The flood of celestial light made it seem that God might be watching and wouldn't let you lose too big. It wasn't Cesar's, but it was grand enough to make you feel you'd been bested by a superior foe, and were forgiven for going home empty-handed.

It was still early, there was no action aside from a skinny teenager pushing a twenty-year-old vacuum, and the autonomous rancor of unseen slots. At the end of the long room was a horseshoe shaped bar and a yeti putting a stool through hell. He spotted us and motioned for us to approach. Wherever you went, there was this guy, the big guy. Not fat, not muscular, just big. He's at the front door of every club and the back of every box truck. He never has hair, or a smile, or much to say. His face was wan, in contrast to the back of his head, which looked angry as hell.

I told him I wanted to speak to monsieur Durand. The palooka looked annoyed at my English and turned to Remy. I listened to them whisper dinner menus to each other – unsweet nothings in French I couldn't understand, but softly in case I could. "*Sa fille*," the lug croaked. *Daughter*, I understood. He reached behind the bar for a phone. The mouthpiece of the receiver disappeared in the deep folds of his hand. He felt for it with his lips, then moved the receiver to his ear to listen. He hung up and spoke to Remy. My driver threw up his hands, turned, and walked the long, tiled hall back to the turnip bin. I hadn't moved but was still met with "You. Stay." His English for the day.

The big guy was pawning me off. He pointed a fat finger into the adjacent room of slot machines and turned his attention back to a bowl of nuts. I could see another man strutting briskly toward us. He was buttoning the front of a tailored suit that fit him like a four-fingered glove. He came to a halt in front of me already looking unhappy. He was a small man and that seemed reason enough to be unhappy. His bald head looked as if he shaved it and his stubbled mug as if he couldn't. His chin was a sanding block and he stuck it up at me, every limb taut in his robin's egg blue suit.

"Who are you?" he demanded.

"I'd like to speak to Martin Durand," I told him. "His daughter was murdered yesterday and I have information that might help."

"Help what, bring her back to life?" He didn't laugh, he didn't so much as smirk.

"Help catch whoever did it."

"How do you know anybody *did it?*"

"Did you hear me say she was murdered?" I asked. "Strangled. You don't typically do that yourself." I watched the masseters in his jaw bulge. I didn't want a dumb crack to be the bone the little bulldog would latch on to but

I couldn't help myself around guys like this – pugs who played it tough from the jump.

"How do you know she was strangled?" he asked.

"The police," I said.

"I'm sure whatever you told the police, they will relay to monsieur Durand."

I stretched my neck in one direction, then the other. "I may not have told them everything," I admitted.

"Ah," his lips slid uncomfortably over an asymmetric smile that looked seldom-used. "You are American, yes?" I said that I was, it seemed to relax him a little. He unbuttoned his coat and put his hands on his waist. His belt was snake or lizard, something you'd step on – not very fashionable, not very French. "So, Mr. American, you would like to sell this information to monsieur Durand?"

"That's not what I said." The little man had turned our car down the wrong street. "I'm a private detective," I said. I regretted it as soon as I said it.

"A detective? Like on TV? Like Kojack?" This time he did laugh at his joke and turned to the Grape Ape, who was listening from his stool. Then the little man stopped laughing. "I will tell you what I think, Mr. American Kojack." He poked his finger into my chest, it found its way between my ribs. "I think you are very far from home. I think it was a mistake for you to come here." He left his finger where it was, I began to like it less.

"Can I talk to Durand now?" I kept calm, but let him know I was annoyed.

"No one talks to Durand without talking to me first," he said and twisted his finger in my ribs.

"That's great," I said, removing his hand from my rib cage. "But I don't feel like we're talking."

We stared at one another. The bells and sirens of the slot machines seemed to grow louder.

"Alright," he said and rubbed his square chin. "Let's go somewhere where we can talk." Without saying anything to the yeti, the little guy started back the way he came, through the cacophony of the gaming machines. I followed him through the arcade, checking more than once to make sure the big guy wasn't coming with us. He was still on his stool when we hung a left through an empty kitchen and out a steel door into the alley.

There was a cool breeze between the buildings which threatened to spoil the wet ground and garbage smell ubiquitous to all alleys. And I could finally think without the clangor of electric gaming all around us. I wondered what, or even if, the little man knew about Adrienne's death. Did Durand know? Inspector Dubois hadn't informed the family at the time of our interview – surely they knew by now. What did I really have to offer? That an American girl, posing as his murdered daughter, collected a blackmail payoff that she may or may not have helped extort from an American businessman.

The little man punched me hard in the pancreas. His fist felt like a crow bar as it smashed into my ribs. The punch doubled me up but I kept my feet. He stood sideways, taking great care with the placement of his feet. He held his fists in front of his face and his body disappeared behind his forearms. His gold watch caught the sun just before a fist smashed into my face. I felt the corner of his knuckle in the socket and was sure my eye had exploded. My face was instantly wet with what I knew was my own blood.

I'm no stranger to getting punched in the face – but we hadn't spoken in a while. A handful of barroom skirmishes are no introduction to the sweet science. The tough pug was half my size, but a learned pugilist, and he was gonna cut me to ribbons. The little man vanished for seconds at a time from my field of vision. When I finally located him, he dug two right hooks into my side, and I felt a rib snap. I put up my dukes with all the virtuosity of holding an accordion for the first time. He had no trouble slipping punches through my guard and stamped all my vital organs by order of importance.

I floated target-less punches his way. He alternated freely between slipping the punches and absorbing them into his guard with perfect technique. My blows fell as harmlessly as pats on the back, atta-boys for his fine work turning me into a Picasso. It was a left counter to my jaw that sent me spinning. I felt the power to my legs dim but come back online in time to keep me upright. As I stumbled, my right hand grasped the padded shoulder of his blazer. I dragged him toward me as I tried to regain my balance. I could hear the slick leather soles of his shoes skid on the grimy asphalt. My left hand found the corner of a dumpster and I righted myself in time to absorb an upper-cut that finished me.

Things were going black. I saw Robert Tremblay handing me an envelope of money bound for a blackmailer, I watched the amoeba-like policemen morph into Dubois suspicious eyebrows. I saw Adrienne Durand dead on a table and the silhouette of a mystery woman growing darker on a subway platform.

The tough pug had taken a deserved respite from destroying me to issue a half dozen threats I was sure not to remember. I could feel the damp grime of the alley floor seep through the back of my clothes. It was Remy who finally got me to my feet and into his cab. He let me know I looked like shit.

*

Remy returned me to my hotel like a truant child. We shook hands for a long time, but I hoped never to see him again. I was grateful to him for pulling me out of that alley, but in my mind, he was complicit – like blaming the Maître D for food-poisoning. Remy told me the tough pug who'd slapped me down in the alley was Ricard Moreau. Moreau had been a boxing champion as a teenager, moved from Marseilles to Paris to train as a Junior Olympian, and competed in the French Boxing Federation, akin to Gold Gloves in the States. Always the tough guy, he'd fallen in with other tough guys, was incarcerated, and had his back broken in a prison gang fight. Moreau belonged to that world of criminality and violence you only read about in the newspaper. He wasn't some loser in a bar, looking to throw haymakers after a couple of beers. He was an animal, without fear of the law, without fear of God. And Remy had left me with him, without a word.

The next morning, the sun pushed through the hotel room curtains with little impediment. The desk rang to ask if I intended to extend my stay. I told him to give me the rest of the week.

I was in no hurry to get up. I felt like a mark, no different than Robert Tremblay, even if I hadn't been party to the original act. And there had been an act, something worthy of blackmail. All things considered, wasn't the simplest explanation usually the correct one? If a guy's being blackmailed by a beautiful woman, it's going to be over sex. Or was that just the extent of my imagination?

I was examining the underside of the pillow when the phone rang again. An Anglican female voice told me that Mrs. Catherine Durand would like to speak with me. I was placed on hold for a long time with no music.

"This is Catherine." It was a practiced voice, belonging to someone who talked for a living, on TV or the radio.

I introduced myself only as far as being the gentleman she wished to speak to.

"I understand that you're looking into the death of my daughter, Adrienne."

"No ma'am, not exactly," I said. "May I ask who told you that?"

"I have my sources," she said.

"If Inspector Dubois – "

"It wasn't Dubois," she interjected. "I told you, I have sources of my own. Please, Mr. Hammond, if you have any information about who killed my Adrienne, I think I'm entitled to it."

I hadn't grown so hard that the mother of a murdered girl wouldn't soften me. "All I can say for sure is that her name was used in the perpetration of another crime. I couldn't say for sure it's related to her death."

"You're investigating a crime involving my murdered daughter," she said. "Isn't it reasonable to assume the two are related?"

It was a fair assumption. I offered Mrs. Durand my condolences. I was surprised how together she sounded. It was over the phone, but she'd kept it together even bringing herself to use the word "murdered." I asked again who had given her my name.

"I'd rather not discuss it over the phone, if that's alright with you."

Again, I relented. She gave me her address in Chaillot and I said I would come straight away. If her source wasn't Dubois, I didn't know who it could be. The only people who knew I was in Paris as anything other than a tourist were Dubois, the girl from the metro, and Ricard Moreau – and Moreau and I hadn't exactly exchanged business cards.

I showered and ran the electric over my face. My head looked like a bad piece of fruit, but knocking some stubble off was an improvement. I grabbed a croissant and a cup of coffee near the mouth of the metro. A couple of my teeth felt loose and it hurt to chew on one side.

I'd heard the Chaillot Quarter was fancy digs, with honest-to-goodness mansions, and some of the oldest money in all of France. Mrs. Durand instructed me to take the train to Passey or La Muette, but recommended Passey as the route would pass Balzac's house. I wasn't in the right humor for sight-seeing, and I didn't know or care who Balzac was. From the train, I walked along the Seine until I reached the park Mrs. Durand had described, the address was easy to find after that.

The Durand home was a squat, modern mansion. It shouldered its way between two large, dusty estates, whose high hedges obscured the Durand home completely from their view. The house itself was bright white, with cornices, pilasters, and tall rectangular windows. It wasn't a Roman ruin, on the contrary, the Durands were still waiting for the paint to dry. Compared to the estates on either side, it was small, but looked like it cost plenty.

The doorbell touched off an elaborate chorus inside. A brass name plate beside the bell read *Brugnol* and caused me to double check the address I'd scrawled on the hotel stationary. The woman who opened the door was in her fifties and wore the black broadcloth and white collar of a maid or a servant. I pointed to the plaque, "Is this the Durand residence?"

"Mr. Hammond, I presume. My name is Ilsa." She took my coat and escorted me down the hall to a sitting room. "It would be good of you to mention the name plate to Madame," she said. "No one ever does."

The sitting room was all white – white walls, white marble floors, and a tall white fireplace flanked by white vases filled with fresh flowers. The only spot of color belonged to a pair of rose-pink divans that faced one another and the long flowing auburn hair of Catherine Durand, who smiled at me from her wheelchair.

"Mr. Hammond, I appreciate you coming so quickly." The sudden volume of her own voice seemed to startle her.

"I thought for a second I had the wrong address," I told her. "It says Brugnol on your bell."

"Oh, that," she said and feigned a pretentious laugh. "Brugnol was the name Balzac posted on the front of his *maison* to hide from creditors. If only it were that easy these days."

Again with Balzac.

Mrs. Durand was an exceedingly attractive woman of indeterminate age. She was somewhere between thirty and fifty but the exact number seemed to change with the light in the room. She'd had Adrienne young and carried that physical immaturity into adulthood. Her skin was porcelain, with the same air of fragility. In the race for beauty, Mrs. Durand had arrived first, but was showing weariness at having been beautiful for so long.

"Ma'am, I can't help noticing you're American." I thought about Tremblay and the girl from the metro and wondered if there were any Parisians left in Paris.

"Canadian, actually." She motioned for me to sit on one of the divans and wheeled herself closer. She tossed wavy auburn hair over her shoulder. It was beautiful, bouncy, shampoo commercial hair, and it made the room smell like lavender. "I've lived here more than half my life, not that it makes any difference. If you're not Parisian, you may as well be from the moon." She made a motion, dismissing some long-remembered slight.

"I came to Paris to study ballet." She waited to note my surprise. "I wasn't always in this chair," she confessed. Mrs. Durand was petite and looked as though she always had been. The exact lines of her body were hidden beneath flowing satin and padded shoulders. "When I realized I couldn't dance, I picked up a brush. When I realized I couldn't paint, I got married." Her smile looked out of place. It belonged on a bear skin rug in front of a roaring fire. It wasn't a seduction, it was a performance. And it was a good line, I'm sure I wasn't the first to hear it.

I took a long look around the glowing white room. It was how Hollywood depicted heaven in the movies. "Have you always had money?" I asked. I didn't know how else to put it.

She laughed, her angular cheeks colored to match the divans. "The money belonged to my parents. I inherited it when they died. My father owned a nightclub, among other things. For a time, it was *the* place to be, maybe in all of Paris." Thinking about it transported her. I could see the movie playing behind her eyes. "It had the best music, the biggest dance floor, good food, and strong drinks. I went there on a date as soon as I was old enough. That's where I met my husband. Martin was the manager of the club. He came to our table with a bottle of champagne, looking just as dark and shiny as obsidian. I don't even remember the name of the boy I was with. Martin pulled me out of the booth, onto the dance floor, and that was that." She was looking at me again. The movie was over.

"He's the only man who ever treated me like I wasn't made of glass. Ironically, it wasn't long after we started seeing each other that I had my accident." She rubbed her hands back and forth on her thighs to console them. "Atop a horse is a bad place for an argument, Mr. Hammond," she said gaily. "So yes, I've always had money. Money is what I brought to the marriage."

"What about Mr. Durand," I asked. "What did he bring?"

She looked angry that we'd gotten off the topic of her so quickly. It passed. "The ability to do something with it," she said. "I'd never done anything with money other than spend it. My husband says it's because I never had to work for it. I suppose there's some truth to that. He's done a lot with my money, has my husband."

"How long after you were married did Adrienne come along?"

"Ah, Adrienne. That is why you're here," she wagged an accusing finger. "Martin married me, even after my accident. We didn't have a real wedding, not while I was in this chair. My vanity wouldn't allow it. Is that terrible?"

I said I understood.

"Adrienne came into the world not long after. Such an unloved child." I was taken aback. I waited for her to continue but she looked away to another part of the house. "That probably sounded terrible, too," she said, rejoining me.

I wanted to agree. "I've seen pictures of you daughter, she was very beautiful. She must have gotten a lot of attention from young men."

"A beautiful girl can garner a lot of attention from men without receiving anything close to love." She looked down at the glass in her hand. "I'm a lot of things, Mr. Hammond. Not one of them, however, is maternal. I never imagined I would be a good mother. And I don't know that Mr. Durand ever imagined himself a father. We never discussed children before we had one. Still haven't," she said with a wry smile. "So yes, I am afraid that Adrienne did not receive the love and attention that other children enjoyed."

Ilsa appeared with a tray. She set it down on the table between the divans and handed Mrs. Durand a tumbler of Campari buoying a lime wedge. I took a glass from the tray with a nod to Ilsa. Mrs. Durand said she hoped it wasn't too early for a drink. I lied and said it wasn't.

"I've never ridden a horse." I offered.

"Filthy beasts," she said. She took a long drink as if she needed it and began to speak before swallowing it completely. "Frankly, I'd trade the lot of them for lawn bowling." Mrs. Durand blushed as she blotted a drop of Campari from her chin.

"Did Adrienne live here with you and your husband?"

"She moved out when she was eighteen – like she was counting the minutes. It does hurt that she didn't want Martin or I to know where she was living. We would have let her be, even if we had known. Maybe that's why she didn't bother."

There was a long and awkward silence. It would have contributed it to the memory of her daughter, except that Mrs. Durand had not asked about my investigation, nor who I was working for. She seemed unconcerned with the cuts and bruises on my face, which had not escaped the notice of her maid. And she hadn't asked how her daughter was involved in something that would bring me across an ocean. Adrienne's murder seemed no more relevant to my business there than if I'd been selling encyclopedias. She spoke glowingly of her husband but had also been careful to insinuate that there were problems. Married or not, I got the feeling that Catherine Durand looked at me as a man who had come to call on her.

"Tell me something about yourself, Mr. Hammond. You know so much about me, I feel a bit silly. It's been so long since I've talked to anyone interesting."

I pretended not to hear the question and took a turn around the room. On the wall behind the divans were four large framed posters, the kind they hang at the entrances to movie theaters. "These are really something," I said.

"Are you going to the show tonight?" Catherine asked, her head down as she straightened the creases of her slacks.

I asked what show.

Catherine said their playhouse was putting on a production of *Medea*. "It's sold out," she said with some surprise. She admitted they'd suffered a couple of flops in a row, but they'd secured a new young director who was putting on the kind of performances people wanted to see. She asked if I knew the story. I said I didn't. "Medea is a powerful witch, but her husband Jason leaves her for a princess," she explained gleefully. "To get back at him, she kills the princess, then her own children."

"That would do it," I said. I hoped for Jason's sake, he'd taken it in stride. What I knew of Greek tragedies, people were always disfiguring themselves, doubling-down on grief.

"Of course, *posters* don't go with the décor, but Martin insisted we put them up."

I examined them more closely. The same woman appeared in every one, often as the heroine. I asked Catherine about her. She said the actress's name was Marguerite, though that was somewhat of a stage name.

"The old trollop is a survivor, I'll say that for her. There's a saying in the theater about knowing when to exit. I don't think she's heard it."

"To stick around that long, she must have some talent," I offered politely. "Does she get a lot of work?"

"She's ours exclusively," Catherine pronounced. "No one else will have her. She's a hack and a scandal." Catherine took a long drink, washing the taste of Marguerite from her mouth. "She's voluptuous, I suppose, in a vulgar sort of way. That still sells seats in old Paris."

I came back to the divans and replaced my drink on the tray. There was a book on the coffee table. The cover depicted an auburn-haired woman baring her chest, tempted by a devil holding a rose to her lips, and a skull behind her back.

"*Les Fleurs du Mal*," said Mrs. Durand. "The Flowers of Evil. Are you familiar with Baudelaire?"

I didn't know Balzac, and I didn't know Baudelaire. "I'm not an educated man, Mrs. Durand."

"It's poetry. Passionate, bitter, very Parisian. *Do not look for my heart anymore, the beasts have eaten it,*" she recited. "The book was given to me by a professor from the university. He gave the most dramatic recitation at one of our parties, I insisted he bring me a copy." Catherine wilted. "We used to throw the most wonderful parties. The house would be filled with actors, writers, socialites, even a few minor *célébrité*. Unfortunately, one need not be absent from society long to be forgotten."

Catherine Durand was not your average shut-in. She was cultured and beautiful, it was easy to imagine her at the height of her powers. But those gifts had become unnatural, like a colorful insect impaled in a display case. The lack of a proper audience had Mrs. Durand showing some rust at playing the old Catherine.

"Mrs. Durand, do you have a picture of your daughter?"

"Possibly in the girl's room," she said. Mrs. Durand showed me to the stairs and said she would meet me at the top. "I have a chair lift down the hall. It's only big enough for me, better that no one should have to see me in it."

She wheeled away as I took the stairs. There were several rooms but only one whose door stood open. I kept my feet in the hall but pushed the door wider. It was Adrienne's room, though it belonged to a much younger girl. White metal bed frame, pink curtains, bare walls. A single stuffed animal watched me from the bed. It was as if the room had been frozen in time before Adrienne was a teenager, or had been consciously restored to that time.

Mrs. Durand joined me in the hall, I followed her into the room. She fumbled through a few framed pictures stacked on top of a writing desk, then with the contents of a couple of drawers. She looked as unfamiliar with the room as I was and except for the speed with which she was doing it, didn't seem to know what she was looking for.

Her silken blouse was held closed by a single fabric-covered button at the nape of her neck and opened on her back. Her opalescent skin was marred by the smooth pink line of a surgical scar along her spine. I admired her longer than I should have.

"Ah ha." Mrs. Durand produced a photo of the girl and held it in the air as if she'd pulled it from the lake. Perspiration had begun to form under her powdered veneer. The picture was a few years old but I recognized Adrienne from Dubois's file. Her eyes were large and doe brown, not her mother's verdant green. She was tall, standing shoulder to shoulder with grown men. She wore a black and white gingham dress cut close to her body. Her unsmiling face wondered why her picture was being taken at all.

The men in the picture were older, her father's business associates. They'd had her surrounded but backed off long enough for someone to take the picture. One of those men was Ricard Moreau. While the other's looked obliquely at the camera, Ricard's eyes stayed trained on Adrienne.

"You must employ a lot of people," I said. "Any of them express an interest in your daughter?"

"No. Why would they?" she replied.

I let the question hang. "How did Adrienne support herself? Did she have a job?"

A grin developed on Catherine's face. "My daughter had no interest in starting at the bottom. Having a superior would have been beneath her dignity." Catherine said she wasn't sure but she thought her husband had been giving Adrienne an allowance.

"Did she ever mention a friend, an American girl?" I described the young woman from the metro with great restraint, in the least amorous terms I could muster.

Catherine had to stifle a guffaw. "Oh my, you really haven't gotten a picture of her at all. My daughter was an unrepentant snob, Mr. Hammond. She belonged to that class I spoke of, with no regard for anyone who did not *belong to Paris*. She would have laughed at the very suggestion."

I flipped through a few more pictures, mostly of Adrienne alone. "Catherine, do you know anyone who would want to hurt your daughter?"

"Mr. Hammond, I don't know anyone who knows my daughter." She rushed to compose herself, carefully blotting her hairline with the side of her index finger. "It's warm up here," she said fanning herself. "We should go back downstairs." I agreed and followed her into the hall. "Mr. Hammond, are you going to find the man who killed Adrienne?"

"I'm going to try, Mrs. Durand."

"Do the police have any leads?" she asked.

"They'd be more likely to share those with you than with me," I said. "I told them what I could."

"Which is what, exactly?"

I let her have it. "Mrs. Durand, I believe your daughter was involved in extorting thousands of dollars from my client and possibly others."

Catherine looked horrified. "Why would she do that?" She was visibly upset. She asked me to take her to the lift and pointed down the hall. She didn't speak and rested her forehead on tented fingers. When we reached the lift, I turned the chair around, grasped the armrests, and backed her into the narrow elevator. She whispered *merci* in my ear so softly I could have imagined it. I closed the iron grate and watched Mrs. Durand descended into the floor.

I considered ducking back into the girl's room to search but didn't. That room was no more hers than anyone else's. The girl that had lived there had been gone even longer than the young woman in the photo. I closed the door to the mausoleum of the most unloved girl in the world.

I met Catherine at the foot of the stairs. She seemed to have regained herself. "Please don't think I'm being melodramatic but it's my fault the way Adrienne turned out. I wasted years feeling sorry for myself because of my accident. I missed my daughter's whole life, not to mention twenty years of my own. I felt I'd lost so much, so much of who I was. I can't pretend I would have been the perfect mother but you're supposed to do the best you can for your child. If I'd have found a way to be a happier woman, that would have been the best I could have done for her."

"You're not responsible for her death," I told her.

"Aren't I?" She looked at me for confirmation, then chastised herself at the thought of it. "That's why I wanted to speak with you, Mr. Hammond." Catherine leaned towards me and lowered her voice. "My husband has not spoken a word since we learned of Adrienne's death. Not to me, not to Ilsa. He walks around like we're not even here."

I reminded her people grieved in different ways.

She sat up straight in her chair. "Do you think he could have had something to do with it?" Before I could answer, she continued, "I don't mean I think he did it. I just feel like he knows something he's not telling me. Me nor the Police."

I asked her what the police wanted to know. She said they asked Mr. Durand repeatedly if he'd received any threats, if Adrienne's death could have been some sort of retaliation. "*Retaliation*, they said. Retaliation for what?" Her eyes welled and she busied herself drying them.

"How long have you operated the casino?" I asked.

"For as long as we've been married. I sold my parents' club after they died. There were too many ghosts there for me. The casino was just one of the concerns Martin and I bought with the proceeds."

"A casino can be a tough business," I said. "It often brings people up against an unsavory element. Mrs. Durand, are all of your husband's business dealings legal?"

She laughed dismissively, "Mr. Hammond, you make him sound like a gangster."

"He runs with some pretty tough customers, men who can't hide what they are." I told her about my experience at the *Roleux Chanceux*, about my run-in with Ricard Moreau, what I knew about him, and how he'd left me flat on my back in the alley. She seemed to take notice of the cuts and bruises on my face for the first time and reached her hand out to touch them. I stopped her. Why did women feel the need to probe every wound?

"I'm sorry about your eye," she said.

"And my ribs, and my spleen," I said. "I wasn't supposed to walk out of there with my faculties, after no more provocation than the mention of your daughter's name. Catherine, if your husband were involved in something, if he were in trouble, would he tell you?"

"Is it my daughter or my husband you suspect of being a criminal, Mr. Hammond?" she said incredulously. "I swear you're worse than the police!"

Ilsa cleared her throat. The maid interrupted to ask Mrs. Durand if she would like anything else. Catherine stared daggers at the woman. She hid the expression beneath her beautiful hair as she straightened and smoothed her clothes.

"We should go back into the sitting room, Mr. Hammond, you still haven't told me anything about yourself," she said, trying hard to restore her composure.

"And I'm not going to," I told her.

Mrs. Durand didn't appreciate being countermanded her in front of the help and let me know it. "Do you not enjoy my company, Mr. Hammond?"

"You're a beautiful, interesting woman, Mrs. Durand." Superlatives always sounded disingenuous whether you meant them or not. "But this isn't a social call."

"Then you won't mind showing yourself out."

*

Maybe it was my bruised ego rather than my instincts that led me back to the *Chanceux.* It was late morning and I hoped to catch Ricard Moreau coming or going. I staked out the casino from across the street. At one p.m., Moreau stepped out the front door in a plum-colored jacket and turtleneck. I hoped I'd bled on his blue suit. Instead of climbing into a car, I followed him to the metro. The tough pug was a regular man-of-the-people. On the train, I listened to a couple argue. It was probably over the toilet seat or where to spend Bastille Day, but in French it sounded vital to the continuance of mankind. Moreau got off in Montparnasse. I followed him down the boulevard to an oddly-shaped block of apartment buildings. The block was a thin wedge, a pie-chart slice representing the number of lactose intolerant Parisians. A narrow street led to an inner ring of apartments with views of a park instead of the boulevard. Moreau climbed the stairs of one of the buildings.

The door to the lobby was glass with no lock or buzzer. I watched from

296

sidewalk as he mounted the stairs, then stepped inside. There were mail boxes with mis-delivered letters crammed into every available opening. None of the names on the letters meant anything to me. Moreau climbed to the fifth floor and entered an apartment to the left of the stairwell. I hurried to the fourth floor to listen to his movements. He stayed in the apartment for half an hour before coming out and knocking on the door across the hall. He was let in and stayed another half hour. When he started back down the stairs, I stood at the door to one of the fourth-floor apartments, with my back to the stairs. When Moreau passed through the lobby doors, I climbed to the fifth floor.

There were four apartments on each floor. I went to the apartment Moreau had entered and tried the knob – it opened. The lock was broken. The bolt had been carefully battened with paper, so it would stay closed. I stood listening for someone inside. If this was Moreau's apartment, I'd taken breaking in rather cavalierly. I didn't know if he lived alone, with a harem ready to scream like banshees, or a half-dozen cutthroat gunmen cleaning their rods. I stepped into the apartment and closed the door. The battened bolt worked as intended.

It was a typical one-bedroom flat, a living room and balcony, a galley kitchen, and a narrow hallway that led to the bedroom and bath. The edge of one couch cushion lay over the other like tectonic plates. A few of the drawers in the kitchen stood open, same with some cabinet doors. The bedroom and bathroom had been tossed with more passion. The contents of the medicine cabinet were in the sink and trash can. The cabinet beneath the sink had vomited its contents onto the rug. And the shower curtain had been torn from the rings, as if anyone hid valuables behind a shower curtain. A silver toothbrush holder, that looked like a pair of brass knuckles, was affixed to the wall and held one toothbrush loosely in its grip.

The mattress of the queen-size bed had been obliqued enough to allow a peek under each corner. The sheets lay puddled on the shag. The drawers from a bedside table had been emptied onto the mattress and the table kicked in, to insure there were no false backs. There hadn't been. A print of Van Gogh's *Café Terrace at Night* was removed from its thin plastic frame and torn from the backing. The contents of the closet had been evicted. Hat boxes lay open and empty. Shoes lay piled like small logs. These weren't Moreau's things, this was not Moreau's apartment.

I went back to the living room and fixed the sofa cushion before sitting down. To the right of the kitchen was a pedestal table, two heavy wooden chairs, and a piece of cabinetry that fit snuggly in the corner. The corner cabinet had three shelves and a base with a door. The top shelf was home to a company of porcelain ballet dancers. The tight, top-knotted hair and wan faces of the ballerinas troubled me. Beyond the beauty of their movements, their faces held only restrained anguish. Happy, pretty girls became cheerleaders – sad, masochistic beauties, ballerinas.

The second shelf housed a photographic exhibition, mostly pictures of the city in black and white. It was high-contrast art school stuff, no pics of friends or family. I took the backs off the framed photos – old detective trick. Behind a photograph of a bridge was a self-portrait of sorts, a young woman in front of a mirror, her face concealed by the camera. I would have been able to place the bedroom even if I hadn't recognized the gingham dress. This was

Adrienne's apartment. The furniture was more provincial than I thought would

appeal to a young Parisian woman of means. Maybe they were pieces that were

readily available, or maybe Adrienne was trying to build something worlds away

from her parents' gilded mansion.

This was a crime scene. The ransacking had been bloodless, but

Adrienne's death imbued the apartment with violence. The same hands that

opened her kitchen drawers, had held her neck until she couldn't breathe. The

same force that tore the shower curtain from its rings, had crushed the girl's

windpipe. Moreau had been looking for something. Pictures? Documents?

Money? Maybe he was looking for the same thing I was – the girl from the

metro.

I took the backs off the rest of the frames. Behind a picture of a merry-

go-round were ten one-hundred franc notes and a piece of paper with the word

Pigalle.

On the ground floor, the number for the super was spelled out in white

plastic numbers stuck in a felt bulletin board. One of the numbers had fallen off,

luckily only one. I could see it lying in the bottom of the case. I wrote the

number on my hand and walked to the park to find a pay phone. I called the

police, told them who I was, and asked to speak to Inspector Dubois. I kept my

eyes on the apartment stoop in case anyone showed.

"This is Inspector Dubois," he sounded as collected as he had the day of

our interview, but feigned surprise, as if taking unsolicited calls was highly

irregular.

"You're gonna get a call from a super saying he's got a missing tenant. You've already got the body but I bet you've been looking for the apartment. It's Adrienne Durand's."

I let him digest that. He took his time doing it. "*Monsieur* Hammond, I hope you have not been working my murder case?" he warned.

"No inspector, I haven't. I've been working my case, it just keeps bumping into yours." I gave him the address but withheld the details of my preliminary snooping. "I'm guessing it's not in her name since it doesn't look like your boys have been there yet. But somebody has, if you know what I mean. You've been looking for it, haven't you?" I gloated.

"We follow all routine procedures." His tight, clipped speech was meant to suggest his impending inability to provide me anything further.

"You think it has to do with Mr. Durand, don't you? He sounds like a real charmer, but I think his daughter had her own racket, enough like the old man's to get her killed." I knew he was going to cut me off, so I slid my question in before he could. "Have you looked at Adrienne's bank accounts? Anything fishy, like large cash deposits?"

"Fishy?" he repeated. Fishy didn't translate. "Thank you for the information, Mr. Hammond, but I am not at liberty to discuss this case with you."

I wondered if he was recording the conversation. "Well, someone gave my name to Catherine Durand and so far I've turned that into her daughter's apartment. I might have more for you later." I was sure he was about to tell me to stop my inquest, or even threaten me with obstruction, so I hung up. I looked at the number on my hand and called the super. After several rings, he

answered. He said he spoke English when I asked. "I need to know who rents

apartment 5B," I demanded.

"Why should I tell you?"

"If it's my daughter, she's underage." I tried the pushy asshole

approach.

"5B's a young woman, pays cash, months in advance. I don't have a

name," he croaked.

"Well, you better come up with one, because she's dead." I hung up.

There were already a couple of beat cops ascending the stoop of Adrienne's

building.

*

I walked to the main boulevard and flagged down a cab. "*Pigalle,*" was all I told

him and showed myself to the back seat of the idling car. We crossed the Seine

and headed toward the Champs-Élysées. He was savvy enough to skip the Arc

de Triomphe, whipping the car through side streets narrow enough to be alleys.

He didn't feel like idling through that mob, even with the meter running. The

car came to a screeching halt in front of a metro station in a large square.

The driver threw up his hands with a laconic, "*Voila.*"

I counted out the fare but didn't hand it to him. "This is Pigalle?" I

asked.

"*Regard, Pigalle,*" he made an exasperated motion toward the metro

stop with his right hand. "*Et, Rue de Pigalle,*" he said, pointing to the street leading away from the station. I handed him the fare and got out of the cab.

I studied the map outside of the metro, tracing Rue de Pigalle away from the station with my finger. At least twenty streets branched off Rue de Pigalle in every direction and every branch had several tributaries of its own. All but one, a short dead-end road called Cite Pigalle.

This area of the Champs-Élysées was lousy with night clubs and modern restaurants. At this time of day, they were filled with hustling wait staff, flurries of white shirts, foul language, and cigarette smoke. Like everywhere else in Paris, Cite Pigalle was two-hundred yards of restaurants and shops topped with walk-up apartments. I walked it twice finding nothing unusual, no giant X's marking spots. It was early, and Cite Pigalle was sure to look different when the sun went down.

I ate a good meal at a café on Rue de Pigalle and waited for the streets to fill with people. One of those people was Ricard Moreau, who emerged from the direction of the metro and turned onto Cite Pigalle. I followed him to the middle of the block where he disappeared behind door or a three-story walk-up. There were two doors to the street. The first belonged to an architectural firm on the ground floor. Behind the glass storefront, the walls were covered in canvas prints of the firm's finer work, bathed in track-lighting. In the dark, they glowed like movie screens. The second door had a glass pane which a drawn curtain turned into a black mirror. Stenciling on the window advertised the restaurant that consumed the third floor and rooftop. From the street below I could already hear the clink of dinnerware and bombilation of diners. Nothing on the door indicated what occupied the second floor. I took the stairs to the second floor landing, where I found a large man in a dark suit, standing by an unmarked door.

I'd seen him and he'd seen me. Turning back now was not an option. The man had a thick neck and cheeks as pink as Virginia ham. He stood with his hands folded in front of him like an altar boy. "*Bon Soir*," he said in a velvety baritone. He hadn't been an altar boy after all but a member of the choir. I returned a polite nod and reached for the door. The Ham barred my way with a sturdy arm. He demurred an apology in soothing French while he balled his other hand discreetly into a fist. His size alone served as a warning. I picked out the word "*prive*" from his apology, it meant private. I learned that word on the steps of a club in La Havre in the company of a couple drunken sailors.

"Vermouth," I said confidently. The Ham looked confused, like I'd handed him a wet handkerchief instead of the money I owed him. Places like this usually had a code word that changed periodically. It made sense to use a word that was pronounced the same in several languages, in deference to visiting perverts. There was no chance of guessing what tonight's word might be, but knowing I was supposed to have one, might weigh in my favor.

"Vermouth," I repeated.

The Ham waved over a second man who'd been sitting on a stool at the far end of the landing. I hadn't seen him until I'd reached the top of the stairs and he hadn't moved until now. He was an older man with a smooth head and dark glasses. His body looked like a pile of rocks, hastily stacked inside the same dark suit as the Ham. The first man whispered into his ear.

The second man gargled his orders. His voice didn't belong in the choir, it sounded like a tuna can in a garbage disposal. The Ham motioned for me to open my coat, which I did. He reached his balloon-animal hands around my back, under my arms, and tickled my waist. He stepped so close to me, I could feel his breathe on my face. He grunted in annoyance, then cupped my ass with both hands like it was the last song at a middle school dance. I could feel his thick, rough fingers moving deftly down my legs.

Tuna Can grumbled something dismissive on the way back to his stool and the Ham gave up his search at the back of my knees. I'd readied my fists to drive down the on the back of his porcine head when he looked up at me with a genuine smile. He straightened, opened the door, and bid me enter with a delicate flourish of his giant hand.

Inside, the club was not what I expected. The carpet, walls, and ceiling were deep red, lined with glossy black trim, like a wound bound in electrical tape. A full bar ran the length of the wall to my left. Behind it, stood a handsome fellow with butch-waxed hair and a mustache like a carnival strongman. He was tearing herbs to mottle for a tray of juleps. In front of the bar was a collection of upholstered chaise lounges arranged like diamond plate. One large oil painting hung on every wall with a consistent theme, a huntsman with a dog and a gun. I was expecting something dark and seedy, with thumping music stifling screams – instead the club looked like the set of a spaghetti western.

I scanned the room for Moreau but didn't see him. If he spotted me first, he'd tell the brutes at the door the place had rats, and I'd be in for a rough time. There were men of all ages, younger men pressed into modern clothes, and older gents ensconced in smoking jackets and leather slippers. No one here would recognize me and looking another man in the face was not encouraged. It was a private club, even to its members. The clientele averted their gazes, allowing each other to hide in plain sight. But this was just the waiting room, there were apartments deeper in the club, lurid little love-nests where a man's blood-lust could be quenched behind locked doors, willingly or not. Prostitution was legal here but exploitation was not. A simple brothel could operate in the open and every reason a place like this would need to remain clandestine made my skin crawl.

I walked to the corner of the bar and waited for Handsome Dan to finish gardening. He put down his pestle and wiped his hands. He was sinewy but tried to look broad, holding his arms wide and exaggerating the turning of his shoulders as he walked. "A Gibson," I growled before he could say anything in French. I nursed my drink while I got the lay of the place, then pushed my way deeper into the club. Two narrow hallways were decorated like the first room, like twenty feet of intestines. At the end of each was a painting of a man in knee-highs, holding a musket, flanked by a Braque Pointer. This was where the club stored their locked doors. Eight knobs and the only one that budged led to the restroom. I ducked inside.

There were three sinks with mirrors on the adjacent wall and three small windows above them. It looked to be the only way out. I climbed onto the sink farthest from the door and pushed on the rusted window lever as hard as I could. It didn't budge and felt like it might break off in my hand. I pushed against the sill but it was caked with paint and neglect. These windows hadn't opened in decades and weren't about to.

"Even if you got it open," a voice came from behind me, "there's no way down, just – ," Ricard Moreau made a long, slow, descending whistle.

"No dumpsters to aim for?" I asked, still standing on the sink.

"No dumpsters," he said. He shook a gold watch off his wrist and slipped it into his pocket. "I owe you one, Kojack."

"I'm fine with you owing me," I growled, climbing down from the sink. I didn't like Moreau's math. Our first scuffle had felt like a loss to me.

Moreau unbuttoned his sport coat, the lining was striped like ribbon candy – again, not very French. He crossed the length of the tiled floor, stopped short, and retreated a couple steps to have his picture taken with his fists up. No sucker punches this time, we both started when the bell rang. Moreau darted in, threw probing jabs, and ducked out again. I kept my left up to protect my eye but Moreau used that to hammer my exposed ribs. I took the blows and felt the air rush out of my body – but he'd taken the bait. I stepped on the tough pug's foot, pinning him to the ground. Unable to retreat, Moreau's eyes widened, his arms snapped closed in front of his face like a clam-shell.

I grabbed the smaller man with both hands, lifted him off the ground, and slammed him on top of one of the sinks. His feet kicked, trying desperately to find the floor. He hammered at the side of my face and my eyebrow opened like a zipper. I tried to crush his square jaw in my hand, his stubbled chin wrinkled like burlap under my fingers. I slammed his head into the mirror until it shattered. The shards stuck in the frame were jeweled red with Moreau's blood.

Suddenly, my arm was wrenched to the wrong side of my body, and a python coiled around my neck. It was impossible to breathe. "Take him into the office," a disembodied ordered right before the room went black.

*

When things go dark, a year can go by in a second, or a second can seem like a year. The voices around me were becoming clearer and the pinholes I'd been looking through began to widen. The first thing I made out was a sickly white face above the ruffles of a tuxedo shirt. "Are you back among the living, Mr. Hammond?" the white face asked from behind a large oak desk.

"Durand?" My own voice sounded strange, like my head was packed with cotton.

"No, Mr. Hammond," he said. He was an Englishman, with an affected accent common to Brits who've made their home somewhere off the island, in Africa, or India. "I am the Concierge. Welcome to my club."

"This isn't your club, it belongs to Martin Durand," I argued. I tried to stand, but two large hands slammed me back into the chair. The buttons of my shirt were missing. The air stung my chest like jellyfish welts. There were little black holes dotting my flesh – these jokers had been stubbing cigarettes out on my chest until I came around.

"The club has many owners, Mr. Hammond," said the Brit, coming out from behind the desk. "They entrust it to me. It's a responsibility I take very seriously." He was a thin older man in a neatly cut tux. His cheeks were hollow and his eyes colorless. His hair was sallow as corn-silk and slicked back on his head. The focal point of his bloodless face was a thin, black continental

mustache. "My associate, Mr. Moreau, would like to break your back. Do you

know why he hasn't?"

I said I didn't.

"Because you're on the team, Mr. Hammond." The Concierge leaned

against the front of the desk and crossed one ankle over the other. "Mr. Moreau

simply didn't realize who you were when you presented yourself at the casino.

After all, you went there quite unannounced. Dust-ups between teammates

aren't uncommon. Now that we've all been introduced, I trust it's water under

the bridge.

"From the look on your face, you don't have the slightest idea what I'm

talking about," the dapper man said. "Allow me to explain. You are aware

some unscrupulous individual has been blackmailing your client." He waited for

me to nod. I didn't. "Your client happens to be a member of our little club –

and, sadly, not the only one who was blackmailed. That, Mr. Hammond, is bad

for business. We serve a niche clientele here, provide them with discretion, at a

premium of course. In return they expect us to respond when someone is

fucking with them."

"How do they know it isn't you?" I said. "Getting 'em coming and

going. You think your clientele trusts a bunch of hoods?" Someone drove a

truck into the back of my skull. Even sitting in a chair, it nearly knocked me to

the ground. I'd know that over-stuffed, throw-pillow hand anywhere. It was

the Ham that had pulled me off Moreau in the men's room and it was the Ham

standing behind me now, waiting for me to misbehave so he could pull my arms off.

"I apologize for that, Mr. Hammond," the Concierge said.

"I thought we were teammates," I said.

"Teammates can disagree," he said. "Let's see that we have no more disagreements, shall we." Ire had brought color to the dapper man's face. He crossed the room and lifted the stopper from a crystal decanter. He poured himself a short drink and the color drained from his face again.

"As I was saying, we devised a plan to flush this unscrupulous individual out, put the whole business behind us. That's were you came in. You were the worm on the hook. When you walked into the casino and started asking questions, we were afraid you might be trying to pull the fisherman into the water."

Robert Tremblay set me up. He told this pack of vultures about being blackmailed, told them when and where the drop was. Best-case scenario, he used me to flush out a blackmailer. Worst-case, he'd supplied a fall-guy to take the rap when whoever showed to collect the money was found in a dumpster.

"Of course, you didn't know what you were doing. Since that time, you've been trying to avenge the death of an innocent. That's very noble. I might have done the same in your shoes." The tuxedoed man smirked knowing he would never. The lids thickened over his downcast eyes.

"As it turns out, we didn't need you after all," the Concierge said. The dapper man selected a cigar from a wooden humidor on his desk. "We found the culprit before the exchange." He lopped the end off using a cigar cutter, then stopped to admire the instrument. "Ugly business," he said, passing the cigar over the flame of a torch lighter. "But that's been dealt with. So now, all we need is the money," he said.

"I don't have it," I told him.

"Where is it, Mr. Hammond?"

"You haven't solved your problem. Someone's still out there," I said. "A woman, in the metro. She knew about the drop. I gave her the money."

"Oh, come now," he said and snapped the lid of the humidor closed like a trap. "You embarrass us both." He held the cigar in front of his face, studying it. I watched the embers glow, pulsing like the beating of a tiny heart. I listened to the spit and hiss of the leaves and followed the thin wisps of smoke, raptured to the ceiling.

The Ham wrenched my arms behind my back. The Concierge drove his thumb behind my collar bone, into the base of my neck. He knew what he was doing because it hurt like hell. Guys who've spent time in the slammer learn all about the human body. It's state-funded study-hall on what hurts, what maims, what kills, vital organs, pressure points, and nerve endings. Unwanted color was returning to the dapper man's face. A lock of hair fell in front of his eyes. My confessor took his thumb from my neck and smoothed his truant locks.

Sickness stirred in the pit of my stomach and spread to my unresponsive limbs. "I'm telling the truth," I said. "Adrienne Durand was blackmailing your members – but she wasn't alone."

The Concierge leaned against the desk again. His hand and the cigar covered the bottom half of his face. The Ham released me, I felt the blood rush back into my arms.

"Adrienne had a partner," I said. "Maybe more than one. They're still collecting."

I counted at least three in the room. The dapper man's bay rum failed to cover the odor of pine tar addressing a skin condition somewhere under his penguin suit. The Ham smelled like a lunch counter and I knew Ricard Moreau was somewhere close – bathed in Fragonard that would give him away at twenty paces.

"Adrienne's partner must have known about the trap," I said. "It's the only way they would have known to send someone else to collect the money." The Concierge looked confused and alarmed, like a sleepwalker waking up in the bathtub. "Who knew about the plan?" I asked.

Moreau appeared from somewhere behind me and went to stand next to the tuxedoed man, whispering in his ear. Despite the difference in their ages, he and the dapper man could have been brothers. Dickensian twins separated at birth. One polished like silver in English prep schools, the other steeped in grime on the streets of Marseilles. Their collected genteelness had been poured over the Concierge, the whole of their barbarity heaped onto Moreau. Both were poisonous as apple seeds. Despite disparate upbringings, they'd ended up two-bit gangsters, scraping enough off the luckless to afford a nice suit to be buried in.

"How did Durand take it when you told him Moreau killed his daughter?" I asked.

No one breathed. I had the attention of the dapper man and the tough pug.

"What did he tell you happened? Did he say that Adrienne confessed?"

I asked. "And you didn't ask yourself why the boss's daughter would spill to a foot soldier instead of Daddy Dearest."

Moreau again leaned into the dapper man's ear, but the Concierge pushed him away. He looked from me to Moreau, wondering which of our deaths might forestall his own. "I'm not a murderer, Mr. Hammond," the Concierge said, retying his bow tie. "I'm a good business man and an excellent host. And right now I have a room full of guests to attend to."

I'd overplayed my hand. If Moreau had been in league with Adrienne and fingered her as the scapegoat, turning him in now had diminishing returns. Adrienne having a partner might have convinced Martin Durand to spare his only child. But Adrienne was dead. Another head rolling now wouldn't bring her back. The dapper man's only play was to prevent Moreau's involvement from ever coming to light. That meant eliminating anyone who might want to pull back the curtain – namely, me.

The Concierge stood up straight and buttoned his jacket. "I'm going to leave you to Mr. Moreau now. I hope you won't hold any ill will against me for what he does to you."

The Ham grabbed the collar of my shirt, and the back of my pants, and slammed me prostrate across the big oak desk. Someone scurried around the side of the desk to grab my arms. It was the bartender! Handsome Dan had been in the room the whole time. The fear in his face and the trembling of his wide, apologetic eyes told me he'd been consigned to this duty. He held fast to my arms as if they were the difference between my death and his own.

When the Ham went for my legs, I kicked like a mule. I heard his big body crash into something behind. The wiry bartender was still holding onto my wrists. I pulled him across the desk and onto the floor. The Ham lowered his head and charged like a bull. He tripped over Handsome Dan and his big, bald head cracked against the desk like an ostrich egg. I grabbed the wooden humidor and savaged his skull until I was looking down at bone.

The Concierge watched the scene in horror with his hand frozen on the doorknob. Moreau hefted a length of pipe, the circumference of a grapefruit, that would have turned my spine to confetti. He inched toward me, salivating. His face twitched with a perpetual snarl, his tongue between his teeth anticipated the taste of blood. He'd intended to work me over, even maim me – but that was over. I knew now that Ricard Moreau was going to kill me. It was academic, if I didn't find a way out of this room, I would die in it.

I was almost glad to see the pipe in his hands. We'd done this bare-knuckled and both knew the outcome. Moreau seemed unfamiliar fighting with a weapon and that gave me a chance. He held the pipe like a fly-swatter and moved to his right, stalking me. I threw the humidor at his head and rushed him. Moreau ducked. He swung the pipe with everything he had – and connected with nothing. I put a shoulder into his chest and we wrestled for the pipe. When I got both my hands on it – his disappeared. In jockeying for position, I'd given him my back.

He slid his arm under my chin and around my throat. His bicep jammed against my carotid, his forearm was like steel and threatened to shear my head clean off. His hand on back of my skull pushed my throat deeper into the cleft of his arm and the lights began to dim. The blood left in my brain banged in my ears. I tried to flip Moreau over my head, but he'd widened his base, and his feet never left the floor.

I heard him laughing in my ear, felt his stubbled chin on the back of my head. His sweat mixed with the stink of his cologne. His forearm under my chin wouldn't budge. I tore the buttons from the sleeve of his blazer as I clawed at his arm. I tried to breathe but couldn't draw air into my lungs. I could no longer hear the blood pulsing in my ears – I couldn't hear anything.

I opened my eyes and saw the chair the Ham had pinned me to. I knew the desk was behind us. I drove Moreau backward with my legs, into the edge of the big wooden desk, and hoped I'd cut him in half. His arms came away from my neck and I spilled onto the floor.

The tough pug was still on his feet, his eyes trembled with frustration, like an animal in a cage. The pipe lay where I'd dropped it, in front of the big wooden desk. Moreau went for it. From my knees, I threw a right hand I wouldn't trade for an RBI single in the World Series. I caught the tough pug on the jaw and he slumped to the floor.

There was a commotion on the other side of the door and the Concierge moved away just in time for it to swing open. Sergeant Saltier stood in the doorway with his gun drawn. The room filled with *gendarmes*. I put my hands in the air. I heard the Concierge's voice ring above the clamor, "Don't give them anything, gentlemen. It's our word against his." Everyone got bracelets, except the Ham, who got an ambulance. Handsome Dan looked relieved and would have been just as happy being led away in stocks. It took several officers piling on top of Ricard Moreau to get him in cuffs. Dangerous as any three men in that room, he looked like a juvenile delinquent being led away with his coat sleeves bunched up around his shoulders.

That left only the dapper host, believed innocuous enough to be cuffed in front, he presented his interpretation of the events to Sergeant Saltier in perfect French. The Sergeant released him into the custody of two officers who escorted him from the room. "Water under the bridge, Mr. Hammond," was the last thing he said before disappearing into the hall, and the absolute last thing he meant.

*

"My wife thinks I am making you up," said Inspector Dubois as he set a cup of coffee in front of me.

"You had me followed?" I asked.

"*Oui,*" he said as he dropped into the chair across from me. "As a person of interest in the murder of Adrienne Durand, it was procedure to keep you under surveillance." The inspector lit a cigarette. He offered me the pack, but the burns on my chest had reduced my urge to smoke. Rumors of the club on Cite Pigalle had circulated for some time but even the most cooperative informants had refused to give up it's location. Dubois had me followed, let me go where my investigation took me, and used a trumped-up warrant for my arrest as an opportunity to raid the club. I wondered how many of the club's members knew how narrowly they had escaped being blackmailed by the opportunistic daughter of the very gangster who offered them protection.

As for the man who had introduced himself as the Concierge, Brun told me his name was Lavelle Nabors, though Interpol believed that to be an alias. He'd fled prosecution in South Africa for everything from burglary to racketeering. As much as I liked the idea of Nabors and Moreau sharing an eight by eight, there was a good chance the Concierge would be boxed up and mailed to Johannesburg.

"Monsieur Hammond," the inspector said, opening the case file in front of him, "what led you believe that the club on Cite Pigalle was owned by Martin Durand?"

"Isn't it?" I asked.

For my benefit, Dubois lifted the edges of a couple sheets of paper, feigning a search for the information he knew wasn't there. "The investigation is ongoing, but as of yet, we have found no link between the club and Martin Durand."

"I followed my nose," I said. I'd asked Remy to take me to the *Chanceux.* There I found Ricard Moreau, who thumped me for mentioning Adrienne's name. I didn't tell the inspector about the note with the word *Pigalle* hidden in the picture frame. Instead, I claimed I followed Moreau from the casino to the club, which from his surveillance, he would know was a lie. "I assumed wherever I found Moreau, Durand was at the top."

"That is the difference between the police and the vigilante," Dubois lectured. "The police do not have the luxury of assumptions." I didn't care for his use of the word *vigilante.* I wasn't trolling the streets with a baseball bat, busting up bodegas selling cigarettes to minors.

"How would Adrienne know about a club like that, unless her father was involved?" I posed.

"It is a good question," Dubois replied somewhat patronizingly. "Perhaps it was not her father that connected her to both places," he proffered, "but someone like your friend, monsieur Moreau."

So, that was it. Physical evidence would put the tough pug away for the murder of Adrienne Durand along with his involvement with the club on Cite Pigalle. For the cops and the courts, it ended there. But I wasn't the cops and I wasn't the courts.

*

I rode the metro to Chaillot. I didn't want to risk hiring a cabbie with a knack for remembering American fares. The gleaming white Durand mansion looked gray in the early morning light. I could hear Catherine Durand screaming from the front lawn, her voice sounded like she'd be at it a while. I didn't ring the bell. I'd facilitated the raid of his private club and the arrest of two of his lieutenants, I didn't want to meet Martin Durand for the first time at the front door, just to have it slammed in my face. I tried the knob. It turned and I entered cautiously as a cat burglar, which was one of several things I hoped not to be mistaken for.

Catherine was sitting in her chair at the foot of the stairs. She didn't rush to my side, or say a word when she saw me. She'd stopped screaming and the house was silent. Her head bobbed in front of her shoulders as if suspended by a reed. Her eyes were narrow, her jaw slack, tongue held for the moment between her teeth.

317

"Where is he?" I asked. I approached her like you would a stray dog. The Durand mansion wasn't so large that Martin could spring at me from any direction. There was the kitchen to my left, the staircase, and two passages to the right of the divans – one probably led to a study, the other to a master bedroom. I split my attention between the woman in the wheelchair and the passages to my right.

Catherine dangled a drink over the side of her chair. The heavy base of the octagonal tumbler had proven unwieldy and there was a pool of scotch on the tile beside her, more spilled in her lap. She saw me look at the glass and rolled her eyes. She went to lift it and it fell to the floor with a single loud plink. The tumbler had fallen on its side but the heavy base righted itself. A shard was missing from one of the octagonal facets but the drink sat erect – broken, jagged, and half-filled with booze.

"Oops," Catherine said flatly.

"Where is he?" I asked again.

She nodded toward the passage near the fireplace. "The bedroom," she slurred. "Not that he sleeps there. If he does sleep, it's not with me." The words echoed off the vaulted ceiling, the house sounded cavernous and empty. "He's leaving," she droned.

"Did he say that?"

"I told you he hasn't said anything in weeks." She looked for the drink her in her hand, then remembered she'd dropped it. "He's packing a bag."

"You told me he stopped talking after Adrienne's death," I reminded her.

She looked at me like I'd corrected her grammar. "How long is too long not to speak to your wife?" she asked.

"Have you heard from the police?" I asked. "They caught the man who killed your daughter."

"Who?" she slurred.

I didn't know to whom Catherine's *who* referred, the police, her daughter, or the murderer. I repeated the question.

"Is that all you're taking?" Catherine snapped. She wasn't looking at me. Her voice was shrill, not her practiced, throaty screen-test. Martin Durand stood in the passageway from the bedroom. His black turtleneck and dark blue suit were almost invisible in the unlit corridor, which left his head and hands floating, disembodied like a specter. He looked exactly how I'd imagined, his eyes were black onyx, his hair patent leather. His dark complexion and aquiline nose made him look like a Greek god. He had ten years on me but looked like he kept in shape crushing oil drums. He stared at me like I was leaning against the fender of his car.

"Go ahead and leave, you've been waiting to since the day we were married," Catherine accused. "He thinks I trapped him," she turned her attention to me. "*No one is pregnant for eleven months,* he said. What does he know? Women lose pregnancies all the time. I could have lost the first one without knowing." Catherine looked again for her missing drink. "Sure, I trapped you. It's what you do with apes. Should have cut your hands and feet off, sold you to a poacher." The insult was childish but steeped in the poison of their personal history, she made it stick like tar.

319

"It took him ten years to have a real affair. The coward," she said. "Martin, the great lover, turning his black light on waitresses and understudies," she said accusingly. "Sure, he stopped, when he couldn't get it up anymore. What young woman wants an impotent old man, running a failing business, with his crippled wife's money?"

She was pushing all the buttons available to the long-suffering wife, without evoking, or desiring pity. Catherine wasn't holding her wounds up to evidence her husband's crimes, she was inserting them under his skin, opening old scars, and hoping to leave fresh ones. I wondered how much her husband was going to take. It occurred to me this was an old fight. He'd heard it all before – but I hadn't, and I didn't know how long he would suffer that. He had yet to say a word or move a muscle.

I broke the silence with the news Catherine had twice ignored. "The police have your daughter's killer in custody."

Catherine jumped in front of the statement like a speeding bus. "This is Eddie, we're lovers. He's half your age, and twice the man."

We weren't, and I wasn't.

"That's not true," I said. I could feel Catherine's roiling glare. "I'm a private investigator." I opened my wallet to show Durand my photostat. He wasn't interested. "I'm came to Paris to investigate a case of blackmail," I lied. "A case in which your daughter was the culprit. My investigation led me to a private club that traded in illicit sex. Your daughter was blackmailing the members of this club, using your name as a kind of implied threat.

"But she didn't act alone. She had help from someone on the inside, someone who fed her names of club members – men with wives and jobs, who would be easily embarrassed, easily leveraged. He helped her squeeze these men – until one of them went over his head. The club's Concierge set a trap for the blackmailer. Ricard Moreau knew that if Adrienne were caught collecting the payoff, he would take the fall for them both. He had to do something. He killed her and told the Concierge that she'd confessed to the blackmail. Your daughter didn't have to die and you didn't have to sign her death warrant."

Neither Adrienne's mother nor her father spoke. Neither expressed anguish nor grief. There was no feeling of relief, of inching toward closure. What hung in that room was a curtain of blind rage. Martin Durand returned his wife's dead-eyed stare – her teeth bared, preparing to eat him alive.

"He doesn't own any club!" Catherine growled. "He doesn't own the clothes on his back. It's all mine. The casino, the playhouse, everything. And his men," she scoffed, "they moonlight because he doesn't have the balls to reign them in. When my parents found him, he was just another grease-ball working in the kitchen. My mother thought he was handsome, told my father to put him out front. She was right, you would have thought he was born in that tux."

Martin Durand looked as if he hadn't heard a word of his biography.

"Say something!" Catherine screamed at him. The tracks in the powder on her cheeks had long since dried. She lunged against the tether of her powerless legs. Concealed in her satin robe was a .32 caliber pistol. She held it in both hands, like a dead bird, showing her husband what he'd done. She wrapped both hands around the pearl handle and leveled the shiny nickel barrel at her husband.

Martin Durand took the coat that hung over his arm and placed it on top of his suitcase. He walked to the fireplace and pulled the poker from the rack. Durand stalked Catherine. His wife's hatred crawling through his veins quickened him, like a hunter entering the jungle, euphoric over the closeness of death.

I threw myself between them. Martin swung the poker like a baseball bat. I covered my head. The iron shaft cracked against my elbow. The pain dropped me to my knees. Hacking blows fell across my back, the heavy wrought iron divining my unprotected spine. Martin Durand kicked me in the ribs until he was sure I would stay down. My arm was full of needles. The pain in my back and ribs made it hard to breathe and impossible to move.

Martin stood in front of Catherine, the poker at his side.

"I never loved you," she said. "You were a dark, exotic thing that other women wanted, and that I could possess. And you never loved me. Whenever someone praised you for your loyalty or made some pitying remark about how much you must love me, it made me sick. Feigning devotion with your hand up a waitress's skirt. You made me look like a fool. As if I cared what you did.

"You didn't stay out of love, or duty, or because I was pregnant. You stayed because I handed you the reigns. I couldn't run the business – not from this chair! I needed your strength. You were strong enough to do the work, and dumb enough to control."

I pulled myself to my knees with the help of one of the divans. Catherine was reading my mind. She wore a smirk on her face like her boyfriend had pushed me in the mud for asking her to dance. "We used to throw the best parties, Mr. Hammond," she said. I think she expected Martin to turn around and finish me but I was no threat to him. She was the one with the gun in her hands. "The house was always filled with interesting people." There was a movie playing behind her eyes again. "And at the end of the night, we would pair off." She laughed. "I know what you're thinking but we were all adults.

"Martin was so obvious. I knew who he would spend the night sniffing around as soon as they walked through the door. Sloppy, easy women, falling out of cheap sequin dresses. Never anyone with class. The little fools were so flattered that a gentleman like monsieur Durand paid them such attention," she said mockingly. "If they only knew how recently removed he was from hairnets and aprons, that he was no different than the busboys they were used to fucking.

"Please don't think me jealous, Eddie," she laughed. "I played too. There were rich men, young men, artists, actors. They were not deterred by my condition," she said stroking the tops of her legs. "They liked the submissiveness more than they would admit. Especially the rich ones," she hissed as if coiling herself around a suitor in front of us. "Some took more advantage than others.

"It wasn't a traditional marriage but it worked," she continued. "Until *Her*. After *Her*, the parties stopped. The house was no longer full of interesting people. Not once he had *Her*." The words crawled out of Catherine's mouth like an insect and required an effort for her to expel. I thought she was referring to Adrienne. Key-parties had to go by the wayside when the kids were old enough to know how many aunts and uncles they have. But another woman had come between them, she stared at them now from the posters on the wall.

"You stopped our parties so you could be faithful to your mistress," she screamed. "That wasn't the deal. Say you never loved her and I won't kill you where you stand."

The ultimatum brought her husband's attention back to the little nickel automatic.

"Say it," she snarled.

Martin Durand shook his black head.

"You say it!" she screamed.

Durand gripped the iron poker tighter.

Catherine turned to me and said: "After I had his whore killed, I caught him crying."

I got to my feet but I was too late.

Durand leapt at his wife with a single ferocious swing of the poker. He roared – every unspoken word of the last twenty years smashed into one unintelligible syllable. A clap of thunder seemed to come from the high ceiling as if the roof had been torn in half above our heads. Catherine's head was thrown over the back of her chair, hanging as limply as a wet towel. A pool of blood formed behind the wheels.

Martin dropped the poker and clutched his back. When he pulled his hand away, it was wet with black blood. He fingered a small hole in the front of his shirt. Blood, dark and thick as molasses, poured lugubriously into his hands. Durand steadied himself on the arm of the divan before sinking onto it, leaving a bloody hand-print on the dusty rose upholstery like a doily.

There was no need to call an ambulance, she was dead and he was dying. Martin Durand sat in his living room with his hand over his belly. He sat with his back to the wife who had pursued him their entire married life. I sat on the coffee table in front of him. If he was going to break his silence in these final moments, I'd be there as his confessor. He might say he regretted it all, or insist he'd do it all again. He might try to convince me that he and Catherine had truly cared for one another, or swear that he'd never loved her.

Durand lifted his black eyes from the hole in his belly.

"If you knew it was your daughter behind the blackmail, would you have let them kill her?" I asked.

He said nothing. Durand sat in the bright white room, bleeding into the furniture like ink. He would outlive his wife by minutes. In her recounting of their life together, Catherine Durand had made no mention of their only child, their murdered daughter, their most unloved Adrienne.

*

I took the metro to Montparnasse. The boulevard didn't seem as long this time. I cut through the courtyard between apartment buildings. Just as before, the door to the lobby was unlocked. At that time of day, the maudlin music of French soap-operas swooned behind more than one apartment door. When I reached the foot of the stairs to the fifth floor, the girl from the metro, who collected a blackmail payment as Adrienne Durand, was locking the door of the apartment opposite the dead girl's.

She turned to start down the stairs and froze. She didn't look happy to see me. She was less beautiful today than the day we met. Regardless, I patted my pockets, searching for my resolve like mislaid car keys. She'd reinvented herself, the current iteration looked very uptown. She wore dark brown cigarette pants with her boyfriend's blue button-up, sleeves rolled above a collection of bangle bracelets. Her hair was slicked back, folded like an omelet, and captured in a tortoiseshell bear trap. I watched a forced smile dissolve into the stark realization that I was there for her.

"You found me," she said, scanning the landing and the stairs. She was waiting to see how I would play it. Maybe I was still under the impression that she was Adrienne Durand. Maybe I didn't know about her and Moreau. I wasn't a cop – I wasn't even French. I couldn't arrest her. And I had come alone.

"Who are you?" I asked her.

This time, the smile was real. It was long and sick, dripping with pride and amusement. "I'm Adrienne," she said brightly. I thought there may be a chance she didn't know that Adrienne was dead. But her smiled sealed it.

"It's over," I said. "The police have Moreau."

She covered her heart with her hands. It looked as if she were about to cry – then her eyes rolled and her face hardened to stone again.

"What was she to you?" I asked.

"You mean, were we friends? Adrienne didn't have friends," she said, looking at the door to dead girl's apartment. "She was the girl across the hall. The one with all the money."

She watched as I started up the stairs. "Moreau was the inside man," I said. "He chose the marks. Adrienne had the leverage of her father's name to blackmail the members. How did you figure in?"

"Stop," she demanded when I was mid-flight. I'd treed her like a cat at the top of the landing. "I didn't come in until the end. I followed Adrienne until I discovered what her game was. I watched Moreau leave her apartment at hours that meant they were friends – so I made him my friend."

"Did he tell you he was going to kill her?"

Her laughter echoed in the stairwell. "He never wanted to kill Adrienne," she said. "He was in love with her." The girl from the metro said that Moreau told her about the plan, how my client had offered me to the mob as a staked lamb, and how the Concierge's men were going to pounce on whomever showed up to collect the payoff. "He didn't have a clue. I had to explain it to him," she said. "He didn't understand that if he and Adrienne were discovered, he'd be the one to go down. As long as Daddy's little girl could implicate someone else, she'd get off scot-free. It was a good thing he told me instead of her."

"You told Moreau to kill her?" I asked, as I started up the stairs again. She was playing it cool, but her eyes widened as I drew closer. I paused to watch her breathe.

"It was the only way to put it all on her," she said.

"If he was in love with her, why did he tell you?"

"Because he didn't trust her," she smiled. "I don't think she trusted him either. I know I didn't."

"But you were more than happy to step into her shoes," I said.

"I have a couple of pickups today," she said as she pushed past me on the stairs. "I expect they'll be the last. News of Adrienne's death is bound to hit the papers."

"Her father's death too," I said. "You've lost everything, the marks, your leverage, and your protection."

She shrugged. "It was too good to last."

"You used Adrienne," I said.

She stopped on the landing below like she was stuck in mud. She turned around and looked up the stairs at me. "You're right. I did."

"You sacrificed her."

"I did."

"It was as good as pulling the trigger."

"She wasn't shot," she said. "You're being dramatic." She moved quickly down the remaining flights with me on her heels. By the time we made it to lobby floor, I felt a tension in my hands like I had strangled Adrienne myself. The girl from the metro took one final glance at the fifth floor, as if her fallen meal-ticket was still alive somewhere behind the police-tape on the apartment door. She reached into her over-sized bag and produced a pair of sunglasses that matched the contraption in her hair. The large, dark glasses were too wide for her face and gave her the alert, predatory look of a praying mantis. She pushed open the lobby doors and skipped down the front stoop. I followed her through the park. I didn't think she could give me the slip in flats.

"I want to know why," I said. "Why the accent, why the put on? Why pretend to be Adrienne when collecting the money? Did you hate her that much?"

"Is that what this is about," she asked, "justice for Adrienne?"

If there was justice for anyone, it was too late. But justice would always be late. It was only ever a consolation, was never restorative where death was concerned, and justice had never prevented anything. There was no one left to seek justice for. The girl's parents, aside from their complicity in her murder, lay dead by each other's hands.

"Adrienne Durand was a horrible person," she said. "If you ask me, she got what was coming to her."

"If being an asshole were a death sentence, we'd all be in trouble."

"I know you would," she said. "If you saw her closet, you'd know the money she was taking off those men wasn't paying for the kind of clothes in it. Don't you get it? She didn't need the money. She was doing it for kicks. It was a prank to her."

"What was it to you?" I asked.

"For me it *was* the money," she admitted.

"After Moreau killed Adrienne, he went looking for something. He tossed her apartment. He had to break the lock to do it. But you didn't – you just had to bat your eyes at the super, say you were retrieving a scarf. Adrienne kept the money in the apartment, didn't she? You beat Moreau to it and didn't tell him that you found it."

She stopped and looked at me over the dark glasses. She stuck an angry finger in my face. I waited for her to threaten me, or to tell me to stop following her, but after a second, we were walking again. She tried to quicken the pace, but the thwack of her flats on the paved walk sounded like a tire with a nail in it.

"You know what occurred to me this morning?" I asked.

"I'm sure I don't care," she snapped, scanning park benches, mindful of who might be listening.

"Of all the things thrown around Adrienne's apartment, there were these big hatboxes on the floor of her bedroom." I exaggerated the size of the boxes with my hands. "Hatboxes, I thought to myself, but no hats."

"She wore an eight, I'm a two," she growled. "I took the hats. What's your point?"

"Point is, Doll, are those hats the only evidence in your apartment?"

We hit the boulevard and she began searching the other side of the street for a Samaritan with broad enough shoulders to rearrange my face if she screamed. But my face was swollen and gruesome and the pilling black felt of my pea coat may as well have been gorilla fur. We were in the wrong part of town for heroics. No one noshing in a café in this neighborhood would dream of laying a glove on me.

"I couldn't give the police a name," I said, "but I sure as hell told them where to look for those damn hats."

"She lent them to me. Adrienne and I were friends," she testified.

"With only her killer to back it up, and without a single picture of the two of you together, the cops will punch holes in that like a train ticket."

We'd reached the entrance to the metro and I followed her down the unlit stairwell into a world of flickering light, fetid air, and the mechanical roar of the subway platform. A train pulling out of the station left the tracks empty.

You could see for fifty yards in either direction before the dark horizon turned the tunnels black. It couldn't have ended any other way. Lambs were eaten as they were destined to be eaten and wolves were trapped as they were destined to be trapped. We were the only two left and I wanted to know just how much of a wolf she really was.

"What do you want?" she asked. "Money? You look like you could use it. You're a drifter – or at least adrift. It's written all over you."

"Was Adrienne aware of you? Did she suspect for a minute? Did she even know you were there?" I asked. "No," I shook my head. "You were nothing to her. You're an American. Her mother said she wouldn't have given you the time of day. But she underestimated you, didn't she?"

"People have underestimated me my whole life," she snapped. A sneer ruined her face. "Adrienne was beautiful and fearless. I watched her stop a mark on the street. He was looking all around like he wanted to hit her. She balled up his fist in her hands, daring him to do it. He paid her off right then and there. She walked straight into Chanel and bought a pale blue clutch. In her mind, there was no one on her level. When the whole world is beneath you, you might want to watch your step."

The arriving train slowed to a stop behind her. We waited out the hiss of the air-brake and the shrill, metallic proclamation of the stop.

"If you run, you'll spend the rest of your life looking over your shoulder," I said. The bodies rushing off the train divided us like flood waters. We stood in the deluge of strangers until I cleaved my way back to her. "They already have Moreau for her murder. I think if you explain to the police – "

She dragged her fingernails down the side of my face. "Explain that to the police." She boarded the train with the flood of passengers, disappeared behind the closing doors, and left me alone on the platform with blood on my cheek.

ABOUT THE AUTHORS

James Whelpley is a detective noir writer from central Texas. The short story, The Boss's Daughter, was adapted for Starlite Pulp from his full-length debut novel, *Dancing in the Trap*. The second book in this series, *Tenerife,* was released in March 2022. Whelpley cites Raymond Chandler, Dashielle Hammett, and Ross MacDonald as his biggest influences, but also John Updike and Kurt Vonnegut Jr. Whelpley is a graduate of the University of Texas at San Antonio, where he studied Early Western American Literature as well as Greek and Roman classics. He likes hot jazz and cold drinks. But who doesn't?

Michael Bracken (www.CrimeFictionWriter.com) is the Edgar- and Shamus-nominated, Derringer-winning author of about 1,200 short stories, including stories published in *The Best American Mystery Stories* and *The Best Mystery Stories of the Year.* Additionally, he is an Anthony-nominated anthology editor and the editor of *Black Cat Mystery Magazine.* He lives and writes in Texas.

Jim Towns is an award-winning filmmaker, writer and artist. His feature films include *Prometheus Triumphant, House of Bad, State of Desolation* and the upcoming *The Beast Inside,* as well as the streaming series *Immortal Hands.* He also co-hosts the popular "Borgo Pass Horror Podcast" His short fiction has been published in print and online by Burial Day, *Switchblade Magazine,* Dead Fern Press, *Castle of Horror,* Hellbound

Books, and many more. His first nonfiction book *American Cryptic* was released in 2020 by Anubis Press, and his debut novella *Bloodsucker City* is available through Castle Bridge Media. 2023 will see the publication of his follow up to *American Cryptic*, *American Boogeywoman*. He lives in San Pedro, CA, with his wife and several mysterious cats.

P Moss is an author of twisted fiction whose short stories have appeared in several magazines and anthologies, and his latest novel *Dead Ringer* was published in October 2022. Learn more at pMoss.com

Brian Townsley is a graduate of the Master of Professional Writing (MPW) program at USC, and is also an alum of the mighty California Golden Bears. He is the author of three books of poetry, as well as the novel *A Trunk Full of Zeroes*, and a collection of Sonny Haynes short stories, *Outlaw Ballads*, out now. He was the recipient of the Intro Award by the AWP, and had 'Wicked, Wicked Rain' from *Outlaw Ballads* make the Distinguished List in *Best American Mystery Stories 2019*. He often wonders what his characters are up to when he is not writing them. He lives with his wife Ilana in Southern California.

Charlie Jones lives in and writes about Philadelphia. His short story Netherworld Express, which takes the reader on a ride on the Broad Street subway to their final destination, appeared in the anthology The Devil You Know Better published by Critical Blast Publishing in Spring, 2022. Another short story, December Twelfth, won second prize in the state-wide competition held by Pennwriters, also in 2022. His Mike Maxwell stories take place in the late twentieth century and highlight the human cost of the greed, corruption, and racism rampant in Philadelphia. He owes a debt of gratitude to the giants of the genre, Chandler and Hammett, and a deep bow to the high priest himself, Hemingway.

Eric O'Neal is a labor and delivery nurse who loves writing, video games, movies, playing music, his wife, his infant son, their three cats, and lists. In addition to being a first-time dad, a writer, and a nurse, he is also going to school to become a Women's Health Nurse Practitioner, as well as running a very lengthy Dungeons and Dragons campaign for his wife and friends. He would like someone to explain to him why he thought so many responsibilities would be a good idea with a newborn in the house. Eric writes about what fascinates him: Americana, science fiction, fantasy Westerns, his crippling fears of death and cosmic horror, and his Jewish heritage. He is currently flipping the pages of the complete works of H.P. Lovecraft, but do not let that scare you off; it's just high time he read some classic works. He cannot stand the taste of coffee, and he is quite tall.

Eirik Gumeny is the [insert superlatives here] author of the cult-favorite Exponential Apocalypse series. He's written for WIRED, Cracked, Nerdist, SYFY, a couple of medical textbooks, and even The New York Times once. Born with cystic fibrosis, Eirik still has cystic fibrosis, because that's how genetic diseases work. In 2014, he received a double lung transplant and technically died a little. He got better.

Chris Jones is a young up-and-coming writer who's blasting into the fiction scene with his Blitzkrieg style of flash pulp storytelling. His lightning-fast tales of action and adventure will hit you like a haymaker and send you spinning... But you'll keep coming back for more. Check out his wild rock n' roll style at chrisjonespulp.com and follow him on Instagram @chrisjonespulp to see what's coming next.

Timothy J. Spadoni is a new author, who recently retired from a career in the IT industry and now resides in the small town of Pingree Grove in the Elgin, Illinois area. In 2021, He realized a long-time dream of completing his non-fiction book on writing songs with a ukulele. It is appropriately titled Write a Song Now! With Your Ukulele, and is available on Amazon Kindle.

Tim is working on a series of short stories and novellas centered around the fictional town of Sandy Shore. These stories fit into the science fiction, supernatural, and magical reality genres and involve various interrelated characters who experience one or more of the strange goings on in the idyllic lakeside town. He is looking to publish his first collection of Sandy Shore stories in the first quarter of 2023.

Michael Ritt is an award-winning Western author. He was born in Chicago, grew up in Wisconsin, but is currently living in a 600-square-foot cabin in the mountains of Western Montana. He has been married to his redheaded sweetheart, Tami, since 1989. He is a Western Fictioneers Peacemaker Award Finalist three years in a row. His debut novel is the winner of the Will Rogers Gold Medallion Award for Western fiction and was a Finalist for two separate Peacemaker Awards. His short stories have been published in numerous anthologies and are available through Amazon, Barnes and Noble, and other online retailers as well as brick-and-mortar bookstores. His first Western novel, *The Sons of Philo Gaines*, was released in November 2020. It is available everywhere books are sold. Mike is a member of Western Writers of America and Western Fictioneers. He enjoys reading history, theology, and natural science. You can read more about him and his writing by visiting his website at michaelrritt.com.

Andrew Miller has previously published short stories in the Jacked Anthology from Run Amok Crime, Apocalypse Confidential, Close to The Bone, Pulp Modern, Switchblade, and Broadswords and Blasters. His first novella LADY TOMAHAWK was released in L.A. STORIES in January of 2022 from Uncle B. Publications. His first novel, *Namaste Mart Confidential*, will be available on Run Amok Crime books in 2024.

337